I0701434

IN RUINS

A BLACK FALLS HIGH NOVEL

A DARK BULLY ROMANCE

K.G. REUSS

BOOKS FROM BEYOND

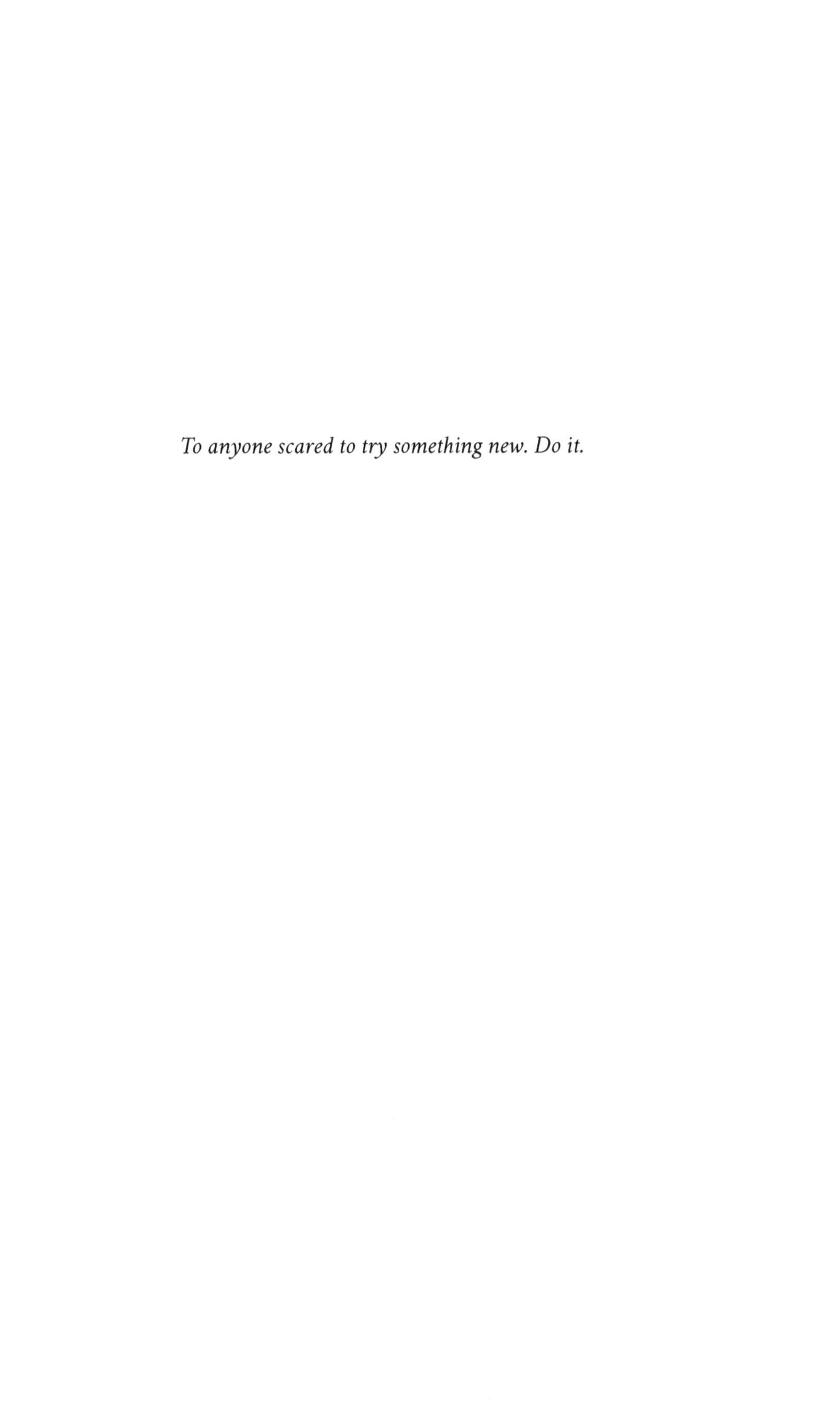

To anyone scared to try something new. Do it.

Speak softly and carry a big stick.

— THEODORE ROOSEVELT

WARNING

This is a reverse harem bully romance. There are multiple male love interests. Do not proceed if you don't like four men and one woman together. Please check author's note on kgreuss.com

Due to dark content, reader discretion advised.

PROLOGUE

"Fox! Wait!" I squealed as I panted, trying to keep up with my best friend.

He stopped in the thick foliage and turned to me, a giant smile on his boyish face, his blue eyes sparkling. Tiny beads of sweat dotted his forehead. My heart trembled in my chest at the sight of him. It had been doing that a lot lately whenever I was near him.

I swallowed down those butterflies and caught up to him. With an easy smile, he took my hand in his and pulled me through the thick forest. He didn't release me until we stood beneath the old oak tree where our treehouse was suspended in the mighty branches.

"Dad said he's going to add onto it for us," Fox said as he stared up at the treehouse. It wasn't small by any means, but it wasn't large. Kurt, Fox's dad, had a thing for building things. He'd built the treehouse for us on Fox's sixth birthday. He'd added windows, a slide, and ropes for climbing. Fox could bring anyone he wanted out there, but my best friend and neighbor only ever chose me.

It was our spot. He promised it always would be.

Mom said Fox would outgrow me as we got older. I glanced at him as he stared up at the treehouse, throwing out new ideas for adding an upstairs to it complete with a rope ladder. We were going to be thirteen soon. Girls had taken notice of Fox since school started a few months ago. I'd watch from the background as he laughed and started making new friends. He'd started playing more sports, particularly football, and had recently started hanging out with the cool kids—Cole, Enzo, and Ethan. They didn't even know I existed.

Fox wouldn't leave me behind, though. He promised.

"Maybe your dad can put one of those windows on the ceiling," I offered as Fox grabbed hold of the rope hanging from the small balcony and began hoisting himself up with ease.

"That'd be cool!" Fox called out as he climbed to the top and looked down at me. "Come on, Rosie! Take the rope up."

I looked to the swinging rope and frowned. There was no way I'd be able to climb it.

"You can do it," Fox shouted from above, waving me up with a smile on his face.

Dang the butterflies in my tummy as their wings beat wildly. I grabbed that rope, desperately wanting to make him happy.

"Wrap your foot around the rope and use it as a step," Fox instructed, his brows crinkled as I slid down the rope with a whimper. "Try again, Rosie! Come on! I know you can do it!"

I nodded and swallowed hard before grabbing the thick rope again, vowing I'd make it to the top. With every ounce of energy I had, I pulled and fought my way up, sometimes sliding down, my hands burning.

"Almost! You almost have it!"

With a final pull, I reached to the edge of the balcony. Fox's warm hands greeted me as he helped me the rest of the way, a massive smile on his handsome face.

I let out a squeak of air as he wrapped me in a tight embrace.

"You did it. I knew you could," he whispered, his breath sending goosebumps through my body as it tickled the shell of my ear. "I didn't doubt you for a minute."

He released me, that smile I loved so much still on his face, and took my hand, tugging me into the treehouse. Amy, his mom, had brought up bean bags and a thick carpet for us before the start of summer since we'd been spending more time there. Kurt had left a cooler in a corner and had mentioned filling it for us before we left.

Fox went to the cooler and pulled out two cold sodas and handed me one.

"Your dad is so cool," I said, taking the soda from him.

"He left some snacks too," Fox replied, nodding at the small table behind me. He was right. Bags of chips and cookies sat there. "Mom said not to ruin dinner, but I think she forgot we're staying out here tonight. I don't know how though. She had Dad bring out clean sleeping bags for us."

I giggled and snatched a cookie from a package. "Your mom is cool too. I love her." I bit into my chocolate chip cookie and sighed. Glancing back to Fox, I caught him staring at me, a strange look on his face.

"What?" I asked awkwardly, covering my mouth before I blew crumbs out.

He shook his head and went to the lantern and lit it. "Nothing."

"It's something," I prodded, settling down on an oversized bean bag and watching him as he moved to claim his spot beside me, not bothering with his own bean bag.

"Bean bag hog," I grumbled as he wiggled next to me.

"This one is mine. Mine is black, yours is pink. Remember?"

I scoffed. "Pink clashes with my hair."

Fox chuckled and picked up one of my long, red braids, a tiny smile playing up the corner of his lips. "I love your hair. It's so cool."

I blushed beneath his compliment.

"I, um, like yours too."

Fox snorted and rolled his eyes as he snagged a cookie from me. "My hair's black. There's nothing fancy about it."

"There is to me." I shrugged, my heart beating fast. Fox smiled again. He always smiled when we were together. Even I smiled more.

"Then I guess we're even, Rosie. We both have cool hair." He bit into his cookie and chewed in silence for a moment. "Want to tell ghost stories?"

I looked out the window. Darkness had settled. I always cringed whenever Fox wanted to tell stories. He was a pretty good storyteller and had some of the spookiest stories I'd ever heard.

"OK," I agreed, cringing.

He reached over and turned down the lantern, so it was only a dim orange glow in the treehouse. Then he grabbed one of the sleeping bags and draped it over us before he pulled the other bean bag beneath our legs, so we had a makeshift bed.

I snuggled against his chest, listening to the even beating of his heart. The soft whoosh of air as he breathed in and out added extra comfort. He rested his arm over my shoulders before launching into his story about a monster from the lake who could only come on land once every twenty-five years.

"What does he do when he comes on land?" I asked, my voice shaking as Fox paused his story.

"He takes virgins to the murky depths and feasts on their bones. His watery home is made from the bones of his victims. Sometimes when you sit on the beach at night, you can hear them cry out for mercy over the sound of the waves."

"Why would he do that to someone?" I ventured, both scared and curious about the monster Fox claimed existed in our lake.

"Because he can, Rosie. Does he need more reason than that?"

I shook my head as Fox gave me a squeeze.

"Your turn. Tell me a story now."

I bit my lip. I didn't have a story. Mine always sucked and made him laugh instead of being afraid.

"So, um, once there was this guy with a hook for a hand—"

"Rosie," Fox groaned. "Come on! That's so cliché! Everyone knows that story!"

"I don't have one. Scary stories freak me out, Fox. I get scared to go to sleep."

"Why?"

I shrugged against him. "I don't know. I don't want to get eaten by a monster. And I always believe you when you tell me stuff."

Fox lifted my chin up with his finger, his dark brows crinkled. "Always?"

I nodded. "Always."

His blue eyes raked over my face for a moment before he spoke. "Then believe this. I'd never let the monsters get you, Rosie. I'll always chase them away. I'd hunt each and every one of them down before I let them near you."

"Promise?" I whispered, my voice trembling as he leaned in.

"Promise." His warm lips met mine in a gentle, curious kiss, his fingers trailing along my jaw.

"You kissed me," I breathed out when he pulled away.

He smiled down at me. "You kissed me back."

"T-that was my first kiss." I touched my fingers to my lips, the tingle from his still buzzing through them.

"Mine too," he whispered, his cheeks flushing pink. "But I wanted it to be with you. I kinda had this thought all our firsts would be together. We're best friends forever, Rosie."

"I wanted it to be with you too," I admitted before going quiet. When I spoke, my voice cracked, "Do you promise forever, Fox?"

"Yes," he murmured. "I promise. Nothing will ever come between us. Best friends are forever, right? Me and you, always, Rosie. Do *you* promise?"

"I promise, Fox." I snuggled against him, my heart fluttering like mad in my chest.

Fox had kissed me. He kissed me!

And he promised forever.

I only wished I'd known forever would only last a week until everything fell apart.

"Get on your knees and lick my shoes, freak," Juliet Croft hissed at me, her dark eyes filled with malice.

"Juliet, I'm sorry—"

She let out a cackle, drawing more attention to us in the school cafeteria. Juliet was the school's mean queen. She had it all and still thrived to make my life a living hell. Being cheer captain and Miss Popularity wasn't enough apparently because there I was standing in the middle of the cafeteria with her demanding I lick her shoes like I was some kind of animal.

"Bitch, did you not hear what I said?" Juliet's ugly glare hardened, her red lips twisted into a deep sneer that made me shake where I stood. Her girl group of scavenging pigs all looked at me with smug expressions on their faces.

Lick her shoes or lick the ground. I knew they'd put me to the floor. Either way, I'd be licking something other than my wounds by the time this encounter was over. They'd made it their life's missions to screw with me.

My only ally was my best friend Jamie. Mr. Bates held her after chemistry class because of a low test score. We traveled everywhere together, knowing full well what being alone in our high school meant, at least for me. This, however, was a fight I'd have to battle on my own.

The snickers and quiet laughter from everyone watching the scene unfold had my stomach twisted in painful knots. My palms were sweating. Each breath ripped harshly from my chest.

I had to get out of this nightmare.

"I-I didn't mean to bump into you," I started, swallowing the lump in my throat. "It was an accident."

"Accidents aren't free, honey." Juliet took a step closer to me, flipping her nest of blonde hair over her slender shoulder. I held my ground despite my quaking body. "They're mistakes, and you have to pay for your mistakes. That's how this works. Now get on your knees and lick the food off my shoes like a good little bitch."

"Get on the floor like she told you or get put there," Melissa Thompson, one of her goons, threatened me as she mimicked the same hair flip Juliet had done. Her dark curls fell back across her shoulder.

Juliet's lips curled up into a wicked grin. She had backup. She knew it. I knew it. Fighting the inevitable was impossible. I was a nobody at Black Falls High.

I dropped to my knees, my face burning with humiliation. The silence in the cafeteria was deafening. My pulse thundered in my ears. Everyone was waiting for my next move.

I let out a whimper of pain as Juliet fisted my ponytail, pulling it so hard I thought she'd pull it straight out of my head. Loose red curls escaped from my hair tie, cascading over my shoulders. She tugged my head back, so I was staring up at her.

"Say you're sorry for getting food on my shoes."

"I'm sorry for getting food on your shoes," I croaked, a tear slipping down my cheek as she yanked my hair harder.

"Now clean up the mess you made." She released my hair, shoving me aside.

I tumbled over, righting myself before I hit my head. On my hands and knees before her, I silently cursed my existence as a nobody.

Letting go of my dignity because I knew a beating would come if I didn't, I leaned forward, ready to lick the salad dressing off her perfectly pink pump.

"Enough," a deep voice boomed out, freezing me in my spot. I knew that voice.

Fox Evans.

Football quarterback. One of the most popular guys in school. Hot as fire. And my former best friend. I'd grown up with Fox. We'd been so close as kids that I thought nothing could tear us apart. Hell, he even promised me nothing would.

He was a liar, and I hated him with every ounce of my being.

We'd grown apart after Fox's mom died in a car accident when we'd hit middle school. We went from promising forever to one another to him withdrawing from me. He became popular and left me behind. Now I was just a nerd on her knees, ready to the lick the shoes of her tormentor.

"Hey, baby," Juliet cooed.

Fox's expensive trainers came into my line of sight as I stared at the floor. In my moment of despair, I'd forgotten Fox was dating Juliet. It was a great way to twist the knife.

"What the hell are you doing?" Fox's voice was a low growl.

"Having this bitch clean up the mess she made."

"Have some class, Juliet. This is bullshit and over-the-top, even for you."

"Baby—"

"Get up," Fox snapped at me, completely ignoring Juliet.

I wasted no time getting to my feet, hanging my head in shame. Again, the cafeteria was silent. Had any of the teachers been there, I may have been safe for a moment, but no. It was just us students left to our own devices. Evil devices.

"What the hell is the matter with you?"

I thought he was talking to Juliet, so I didn't answer as I silently prayed for an escape.

"Freakshow, he's talking to you." Juliet reached out and gave me a shove.

I stumbled back, catching myself before I tumbled onto the lap of the person sitting behind me.

"I-I said I was sorry," I started, my voice cracking. I hadn't intended on looking at Fox, but I locked my gaze on his, my heart banging painfully in my chest. He was so handsome it hurt. Muscular, full lips, dark hair, blue eyes that were so bright they looked like they were peering through my soul. I'd always loved his eyes. I hadn't looked into them in a long time. Not since we were twelve, and he gave me my first kiss in our tree fort in the woods on his parents' property. Not since he'd stared me down in his driveway and told me we couldn't be friends anymore.

Both times had left scars on my heart. This time would be another one I'd learn to move on from.

"You should be," he snapped, his eyes flashing in anger. I flinched away from him like he'd struck me. "Get the fuck out of here, Rosalie."

I stared at him dumbfounded. I wasn't sure if I was surprised over him remembering my name or the fact he was letting me go. Whatever it was, I knew even though our friendship had ended years ago, he was the answer to my prayers in that moment. I wasn't about to look fate in the eyes and spit.

I ran out of the cafeteria, my tail between my legs, mortified beyond anything I'd ever been before, the deep boom of Fox's voice as he told everyone to get back to lunch echoing around me.

"I heard about what happened in the cafeteria," Jamie called out in a soft voice as she sat on my bed.

I was curled up into a tight ball, vowing to remain there until forced out. After I'd left the cafeteria, I'd gone home. I couldn't face being in classes after that. I'd been hiding out beneath my covers ever since.

I grunted an answer, clutching my blankets around me tighter.

"Rosalie, come on. Talk to me," Jamie pleaded.

"What's there to talk about? Juliet humiliated me today."

"I heard Fox Evans came to your rescue though. That had to have been the silver lining."

I knew she was trying to make the situation better considering everyone loved Fox, but it wasn't helping. I hadn't loved him since we were kids and he'd broken my heart.

"It's just fuel on an already burning building," I groaned, finally sitting up. "He stuck up for me. Or at least got me out from beneath Juliet's high heel. But that only means she'll gun for me more now since Prince Charming just made her look bad in front of everyone."

"Oh." Jamie grimaced, her nose wrinkling as she realized the implications.

"Yeah, *oh.*"

"We're almost done with high school, Rosalie—"

I snorted. "We're a month into our senior year, Jamie. It's a long time until graduation. *If* we even make it out alive. At this rate, the mean team is looking to grill us alive."

"But think of how awesome it'll be once we're out," she pressed, her dark eyes hopeful. "You got your full ride to Pendleton. You've wanted to go Ivy League since I met you back during freshman year. It's your first-choice college. You made it in, and you've already received a full ride. You're graduating at the top of our class. Forget about what those assholes say or do. They won't make it half as far in life as you will."

I gave her a watery smile. Ivy League wasn't my dream. It was my dad's. I only pretended it was mine to make it easier. I wanted to have a career in music. I loved singing. When I'd mentioned I might be interested in pursuing it past high school, an ugly, bulging vein surfaced on my dad's forehead, causing me to back away with a weak laugh, citing I was only kidding. It didn't stop the lecture about how music and the arts were a complete waste of time and effort. He even told me if I kept it up with wanting to do it, he wouldn't help me pay for it. I'd have to figure out how to fund my education on my own. It was go big or stay home and live in my parents' basement. So, I studied my ass off to get into his dream school. Letting my dad down wasn't an option. I never told anyone about my love of music. Except Jamie. I told Jamie everything. But it always hurt too much to admit my love of music wouldn't be a part of my future.

Pushing those feelings down, I pulled her in for a quick hug.

"Thanks, Jamie." I wiped at my eyes as we broke apart. "I think I needed to hear that."

"Don't worry, sis. I got you." She grinned at me. "Now, let's forget about those jerks, order in some pizza, and watch a movie. We can be bums for tonight."

"Don't you need to study for chemistry?" I gave her a quizzical look.

Her lips tilted down, the scowl overshadowing any joy she had. "Girl, I'm already doomed. Save yourself and don't worry about me. I'll be lucky if I can pull a D out of that class."

"A D is passing," I offered, my voice squeaking.

Jamie let out a laugh. "You'd freak out if you ever got a D. *Or the D.*" Her eyes sparkled with laughter as she waggled her brows at me.

I cringed at her mention of sex. Jamie was as bad as I was. Neither of us had gotten any. She said she was holding out for the perfect guy and that it'd be special. She was so adamant about her desire for perfection, she'd been a revolving door with dates, hoping to find *the one.*

"I'll get *no* D, grades or other, as long as I'm at this school. Studying is the only thing that keeps me from going nuts. Plus, everyone knows what a loser I am." I frowned down at a piece of lint I'd been picking at.

"You're not a loser, Rosalie. You're beautiful. That's probably why Juliet hates you—"

"If I were beautiful, I'd be in Juliet's spot, not her doormat."

"Would you *want* Juliet's spot?"

I shook my head. "Good point. I hate Fox. I hate all the people she hangs out with. I'd be the worst Juliet ever."

Jamie chuckled. "To be fair, I think you *could* enjoy it if you let yourself go. I mean, not only is there Fox, but there's also Ethan Masters, Cole Scott, and Enzo De Luca." She ticked off the names of Fox's best friends and crew. There were more guys in their group, but those four were known as the Four Horsemen. A name they took to heart whenever it was mentioned.

They were gods in the school, each on the football team. They were the most popular guys. Every one of them was panty-dropping gorgeous. Juliet had already laid claim to Fox, but the others were still up for grabs if a girl was fast enough to nab one. Everyone knew the guys liked to mess around with lots of girls. Fox was the only one tied down by one.

"I don't stand a snowball's chance in hell with any of them," I scoffed. I'd only been kissed once in my life and that had been by Fox. Now that I'd been on my knees for Juliet, there was no way in hell anyone would want me. They'd get attacked just for being with me. I could appreciate no one wanting that for themselves.

"I think you could. I think if you stood up for yourself, you'd be a force to be reckoned with."

"You're nuts. Did you get high in chemistry or something?" I raised a brow at her.

She shrugged. "I just think you don't give yourself enough credit, Rosalie. You're pretty. You always keep yourself under wraps, hiding in your oversized hoodies. Let them *see* what they're screwing with. Start your own posse. Or take over Juliet's. Maybe even get revenge on her so she knows not to mess with you."

"OK, you're crazy." I laughed, chucking my pillow at her. She caught it and grinned at me. "You need to stay away from the coffee."

We both laughed, but something about Jamie's words struck a chord with me. All my life, I'd wanted to be more. Maybe I had something to prove to Fox. He'd left me, saying we were growing apart. That I wasn't cool enough. That he needed space.

I could be cool.

Or maybe I could continue to daydream about it.

I woke with a groan the following morning. The sunlight streamed in through my open curtains. Instead of tugging my blankets back over my head, I trudged to my feet and went to my bedroom window to close the curtains. I froze as my hands reached their destination.

Fox lived next door to me. Our bedroom windows faced one another. When we were kids, we'd sit at our windows and wave goodnight to each other. Since the day he walked away from me, his curtains had been closed.

Today, they were wide open, giving me a view of his shirtless torso as he moved around his room. He looked like he'd been carved by the gods, all tight lines and hard planes of muscle hugging his body. His dark hair was a mess, his mouth turned down into the brooding look I remembered from when we were kids. He often wore it when something was troubling him.

A pang of worry for him set over me, but I pushed it away. I wanted to thank him for helping me out. Maybe he'd be useful if Juliet came back for revenge. It was worth a shot, even if I was feeling tongue-tied just thinking about approaching him.

I was so intent on thinking of ways to approach him and thank him for his help that I didn't realize I was still staring out my window at him.

His blue eyes met mine. The embarrassment of being caught staring at him raced over my skin, blanketing me in warmth.

His eyes narrowed at me for a moment before he moved to his window. I held my breath, wondering if he'd slide it open and shout over at me like he'd done when we were kids.

Instead, he stopped at the glass, his eyes boring into mine, before he snapped his curtains closed.

"*Shit,*" I whispered, clutching at my chest. That had been intense. Feeling weird from being caught staring, I made my way to my bathroom and showered. Despite my current situation, I sang while scrubbing my hair. I let the warm water pelt me. The words to a new song I was working on came pouring out of me.

Once done, I went to my closet and rifled through my clothes. Jamie was right. I *did* wear a lot of hoodies and oversized clothes. I rummaged around in the depths before unearthing a pair of skinny jeans and a black turtleneck my mom had gotten me for Christmas. I'd stuffed them into the back of my closet because the turtleneck hinted at my abdomen, the slight sliver of skin making me panic. Since the jeans were low rise, that made the sliver of skin even worse.

But today was a new day. I wanted to look confident, like none of the shit that had gone on bothered me. I'd never let them break me. I'd vowed it when I was twelve and Fox had left me, and I was vowing it still.

I put the outfit on and pulled my long red curls back into a high ponytail then surveyed myself in the mirror. If I didn't know better,

I'd think I was one of the pretty, popular girls. I forced a smile onto my face. The smile was a damn lie, but Mom always taught me to keep smiling regardless of the storms tormenting me.

I dabbed on pink lip gloss and some mascara before slipping my feet into leopard print ballet flats. They seemed like a safe bet. At least I wouldn't break my ass in them. Well, with any luck.

I snatched up my backpack and bounded downstairs. Mom had breakfast going. Dad was already shoveling eggs into his mouth while trying to read the morning paper. It was the usual breakfast routine.

"Morning, honey." Mom glanced at me as she placed a piece of toast next to my scrambled eggs and handed me the plate. My stomach rumbled at the smell of Mom's pancakes.

"Morning." I took the plate from her and sat in my spot at the table.

"How was school yesterday?" Dad looked at me over the top of his paper. It was times like these that I wished I had a sibling they could focus on. My parents were great, but they were also always pushing me to be better.

"Fine," I mumbled around a mouthful of fluffy eggs, my eyes on my plate.

"Then why did we get a call from school saying you missed afternoon classes?" Dad folded his paper and placed it on the table, his gaze leveled on me.

I fidgeted in my seat, chewing slowly. I didn't want to tell them about the trouble I had with Juliet. I never told them. They'd be at the school in a heartbeat, making everything a million times worse. That potential kept me painfully silent.

"Rosalie, is something going on we should worry about?" Mom sat at the other end of the table with her breakfast, worry in her eyes.

"You know you need to maintain your grades to keep your scholarship to Pendleton. I won't have you screwing up your future by skipping classes," Dad ground out, his eyes narrowed at me. "This better not be related to music, either. I already told you—"

"It's not that. I-I started my period," I blurted out, wincing. It seemed like a good safety net, so I took the leap. "I-I had nothing on me to help, so I came home. The cramps were killing me."

Dad wrinkled his nose. "I see. Well, that's fine. I, uh, need to go."

I breathed out a sigh of relief. Dad hated girl talk. If I ever wanted to get rid of him, I just had to mention my period, bras, or anything related to the two, and he'd vacate a room.

"Do you have enough tampons?" Mom asked. "I'm going to the store today. I can pick you up some."

"Thanks, Mom. That'd be great." I gave her a quick smile that she returned. I wasn't sure what was worse, the guilt eating at me over lying to my parents or going to school and facing my tormentors. Both were stressing me out.

"Done so soon?" Mom's stare followed me as I walked to the counter and put my plate up.

"Yeah, my stomach is upset. I think I just need to get to school."

"OK, hon. I'll see you tonight. Have a great day!"

I gave her a hug, grabbed my bag, and walked out to my car. *Why couldn't my dad just be proud of me and my love of music?* He treated it like it was a disease. Hell, he'd never even heard or seen me perform. He'd never given me a chance. When I'd been cast as the lead in the musical freshman year, he made me drop out.

Sighing, I slid behind the wheel of my new car. My parents had gotten it for me as an early graduation and eighteenth birthday gift. They wanted me to have something nice for when I left for college. Something reliable. I loved it. It was my small piece of freedom. Like anything else, it came at a price. Good grades. Pendleton. My love for it only extended to my hatred of all the things I had to do to keep it.

I climbed behind the steering wheel and started the engine. A glance across the lawn had me watching Fox as he came outside wearing a tight, black t-shirt, low-slung jeans and aviator sunglasses. His hair was a perfect mess. I swallowed, wondering if now would be a good time to thank him. I was just about to open my door when he got into his blacked-out Jeep and reversed out of the driveway.

Sighing and cursing myself for being a wuss, I backed out of my driveway and followed a few cars behind him to school. He wheeled his Jeep into the spot deemed his and hopped out. Ethan was already standing on the sidewalk, waiting for him. I watched from my car at the back of the lot as they gave each other some weird guy handshake. Enzo joined them a few moments later. His jet-black hair was styled in his signature faux hawk. Enzo was Italian. The girls in school liked to joke and call him an Italian stallion, a phrase he apparently lived up to.

The guys gathered in a small circle, laughing and talking. Soon, Cole, the blond hair, blue-eyed heartthrob, joined them. Cole always looked like he just stepped off the beach with his hair a windswept mess. I'd never interacted with any of them except for Fox.

Steeling myself, I got out of my car. I'd thank Fox. The mean queen wasn't around, so I should be good. At least that's what I told myself as I strode across the parking lot, my focus on the guys. Before I realized it, I was standing next to them.

Enzo was the first to notice. His dark eyes roamed over me. Butterflies banged to life in my belly. He probably didn't have a clue who I even was unless he kept up with who Juliet and her squad of plastic tormented. Since her list of victims was long, I doubted I stood out.

"Check it out. Cafeteria girl," Enzo said, putting to bed any idea he didn't know who I was.

Fox frowned at me while Ethan and Cole surveyed me with something that looked like both disgust and intrigue.

"Um, Fox?" My voice was stronger than I expected, which helped to calm me. "Can I talk to you for a second?"

Fox's blue-eyed gaze roved over me before he snickered. "Not a chance, freak."

The heat rose in my cheeks as I stared back at him. I wasn't sure what to do. I hadn't expected he'd be such a jerk. I shifted my backpack on my shoulder, feeling awkward.

"You can talk to me," Cole called out as I backed away. "I love a girl who's willing to get on her knees to lick my shoes."

"Perhaps some other time," I choked out, trying to keep some of my dignity.

The backs of my eyes burned. There was no winning with these people. While I'd never had an encounter with the male population of the elite, I hadn't figured they'd be such assholes. Guess silence didn't make someone a good person. It just made them a bystander.

Don't let them see you cry.

I turned on my heel and fled, not stopping until I made it to the second-floor girls' bathroom. Once locked inside my stall, I let the waterworks flow.

At least no one but them was around to see my humiliation in the parking lot.

It was the only assurance I had. I took the small victory and clung to it.

It took me twenty minutes to get myself together. I'd only missed homeroom. With my head down, I made my way to my locker and gathered my books for calculus.

When I turned around, I came face to face with Fox.

"Fox?" I gasped, backing up and hitting my locker. He leveled his icy blue stare on me. I swallowed hard, wondering if this was a cruel joke.

"What the hell did you want this morning?"

Surprised, I floundered for words. "I-I,"

"C'mon, Rosie. Out with it." The use of the nickname he'd given me when we were six years old playing in his backyard came rushing back like the force of a hurricane.

"Rosie! You can't catch me!" six-year-old Fox shouted, his eyes bright with amusement.

I ran faster, trying to catch him during the game of tag. His mom cheered me on in the background. Fox swerved to the left, using his peewee football moves on me. But I knew his moves. I followed and knocked him to the ground, both of us breathless as I landed on top of him, pining his arms. "Looks like you lost," I taunted.

He sighed, his chest heaving from the run. "There's always next time."

The sound of his heavy exhale snapped me out of my trip down memory lane. My breath caught in my throat as I stared up at his towering form.

"I only wanted to thank you for helping me in the cafeteria."

His expression softened as he gazed down at me. "You disappointed me."

"What?" I wasn't sure if I'd heard him right.

"I never thought I'd see you let someone break you like that. It was sickening. You looked pathetic on your knees."

I bristled at his words. "And I never thought you'd turn into such an asshole. I guess we're both disappointed, huh?"

"I did you a favor, Rosie. You owe me for it." His gaze darkened.

"I don't owe you shit," I hissed up at him, feeling brave. "You put me through hell. If anyone owes anyone, it's *you* who owes *me*." I jabbed my finger in his chest for emphasis, not sure where my courage was coming from, but not wanting to back down.

He reached out and grabbed my hand, closing his large one around it. I winced beneath his tight grip.

"You should've stayed a nobody, Rosie." He tugged me so close our bodies pressed against one another.

"I'm still a nobody," I rasped, my heart hammering in my chest at his nearness.

He let out a soft chuckle, his warm breath tickling my face. "You were until you got my attention again. Such a bad girl."

I shivered against him. He had my back pressed against the lockers once more.

"I like this look on you," he continued, brushing a stray piece of hair away from my face. "And your hair." His eyes swept over my red mane in its high ponytail. "It was always my favorite."

I swallowed down a whimper, my breath hitching as he leaned down to murmur in my ear, "Do you know what happens to bad girls, Rosie?"

"No," I choked out.

"They get ruined." His lips brushed against the shell of my ear. "The next time you're on your knees, it'll be for me." He pulled away from me, releasing my hand. His gaze hardened, his eyes sweeping over my trembling body. Something flashed in the blue depths, but it was so fast I wasn't even sure if I saw it. "You owe me, Rosalie. I'll be back to collect."

He didn't wait for my answer. He turned and walked away, leaving me shaking against my locker, wondering what the hell had just happened.

CHAPTER 2

fter my encounter with Fox, I had a hard time concentrating. He wasn't the sweet boy I'd once known. In his place was a fierce, dominant man. While it terrified me, it also turned me on. I'd never reacted to a guy that way before. Something was *very* wrong with that picture.

"Rosalie. Hey!" Jamie called out to me as I walked down the hall later that afternoon at lunchtime. I was starving but didn't want to risk another cafeteria scene. Ian Hall, one of our part-time friends, walked next to her. Ian was the guy who imagined himself a ladies' man. I'd seen him with a handful of girls over the years, but nothing that stuck long-term. He wasn't bad looking with his sandy brown hair and dark, twinkling eyes. He was the editor for *The Wildcat Roar*, our school's newspaper. While Jamie never admitted her crush on him, it was there. And it was huge.

"Hey." I smiled at them.

"I can't do lunch today. I have a yearbook committee meeting with Ian." Her eyes were wide as she jerked her thumb at Ian, who was smiling at me. "I'm so sorry. I know you don't want to eat alone after everything—"

"It's fine. I wasn't planning on eating anyway, at least in the cafeteria."

"Rosalie," she groaned. "Please tell me you won't eat in the bathroom. That's *so* gross."

I gave a non-committal shrug that had her rolling her eyes.

"You could eat in the library," Ian offered. "Or I'll skip the meeting, and we can go to my car—"

"Uh, no thanks." I gave a rushed laugh, glancing at Jamie, who was frowning. "I'll be fine."

"I don't mind," Ian continued. "We don't hang out enough anyway, and this yearbook stuff isn't such a big deal. Jamie can hold it down for one meeting."

I cringed, noting the crestfallen look on Jamie's face.

"It's cool. Thanks for the offer." I plastered a fake smile on my face, wanting to get out of there before Jamie became upset. "I'm trying to lie low anyway, what with Juliet and all. The stall in the bathroom is a good place to do that."

"You need to take back your life." The look on Jamie's face had morphed into something angrier at my mention of Juliet. "Punch that bitch in the face. Have your revenge and break her nose."

"When did you become so violent?" I glanced over at her as we all walked down the middle of the hallway.

"Since that bitch hurt my best friend. I don't enjoy seeing you this way. You're so strong, beautiful, and smart. You're losing yourself because of this shit. I hate it. We're only a month into the new school year. You need to stand up for yourself. Take no prisoners. Show that bitch and her posse who's running this campus."

"Damn, you're fired up today," I joked weakly as we stopped at my locker.

"Well, you would be too if you saw your best friend suffering." She folded her arms over her chest and gave me a pointed look. "Or at least your ass better be."

Ian's phone buzzed then. He cast me a wink before answering it. I was grateful he'd moved away from us so I could talk to Jamie for a minute without him listening in. The last thing I needed was him hearing me and printing some outrageous story in the paper. Not that I thought he would, but my track record with good things happening was on the low side. I'd rather be safe than sorry.

"I talked to Fox this morning," I mumbled.

She dropped her arms away from her chest, her eyes widening.

"What did he say? What happened? Spill."

"Don't you guys have a yearbook meeting?" I glanced at Ian who was still on his phone, not seeming like he was paying us the least bit of attention.

"Screw the meeting. I want details."

I didn't waste time. I told her everything that had happened earlier at my locker with Fox. Her eyes grew wider as I spoke, her lips parting until her mouth was wide open.

"It sounds like he wants you to suck his dic—"

"Jamie," I hissed, darting my gaze around to make sure no one was listening to our conversation, Ian included. The halls were almost empty, and Ian was still on the phone.

"You should do it. It's perfect. Take that bitch's man. *Yahtzee, Rosalie.*"

I shook my head, my face flushing. "No. It's not like that. He was just tormenting me in the only way he knows how."

"By getting your panties wet?"

"God, Jamie. Do you need to be so vile?"

"Uh, yes? We're talking about Fox Evans here. He's every girls' wet dream in this place, yours included. Hell, you've even kissed him before—"

"We were twelve," I shot back. "It didn't count."

"It sure as hell does. One day when someone asks the sex god who his first kiss was, it's your name that'll be on those succulent lips. *Do it.* March your cute ass into that cafeteria right now and plant your mouth on his. I guarantee he'll kiss you back."

"There's something wrong with you."

"Maybe." She shrugged. "You could be getting laid right now by Fox, but instead you're standing here telling me all the dirty things he said to you instead of taking him up on his offer. *I'd* say there's something wrong with *you*." She gave me a pointed look.

"Go to your meeting. We'll talk later." Ian was off the phone. He smiled at me as he stopped next to Jamie.

"Sorry about that."

"No worries," I answered. "We were just having girl talk."

Ian chuckled. "Aw, I missed it."

"I promise it was nothing worth hearing." I glanced at Jamie who had her eyebrows raised at me. "You guys need to go. I'll talk to you later."

She grinned, backing away.

"I'm wearing you down, Rosalie Elizabeth Bishop."

Ian shot a look between us, interest on his face.

"You're really not."

"Yes, I am. We both know it."

"I can't hear you," I called out, turning away from her. She let out a boisterous laugh before the sound of hers and Ian's footsteps disappeared.

With a sigh, I grabbed the sack lunch I'd made last night and walked outside. The bleachers seemed like a good place to sit, so I wandered out to the football field and sat down, staring out to the empty field. I never attended games. What was the point when everyone hated me? That was like rooting for the bad guy.

I was lost deep in my thoughts, nibbling my sandwich, when a warm hand rested on my shoulder.

"Rosalie, fancy meeting you out here."

I looked up to see who the deep voice belonged to. My heart thrashed violently in my chest as my eyes met the green ones of Ethan Masters. Beside him was Cole Scott, looking like a windswept god with a smile on his face.

"I-I was just leaving." I rose to my feet and gathered my lunch, ready to get the hell out of there, but he snatched my lunch away and Cole pushed me onto my butt. I choked down my whimper as he stepped around me and sat on the bleacher next to me. Ethan took up residence on my other side.

I stared down at my hands, my leg bouncing.

"You're a nervous little thing, aren't you?" Cole asked, his large hand coming to rest on my thigh. He applied pressure to stop my bouncing leg. "Relax, Rosebud. No one is here to hurt you."

"Scared to eat in the cafeteria?" Ethan cocked his head at me, green eyes narrowed.

"I-I just wanted some fresh air—"

Cole tightened his hand on my thigh, making me wince. "Don't lie to us, Rosebud. You could get into trouble for doing that."

I nodded, swallowing down the bile which had risen in my throat.

"Look, could we just get this over with?" I asked, glancing between the two of them. I had to sound brave or risk being eaten alive out there alone. "Just do your worst and be done with it. I don't want to be late for my next class."

They both laughed, but it wasn't a laugh of mirth. It was almost cold.

"What do you think we came out here to do?" Ethan's hand rested on my other thigh. I stared down at both hands on me and let out a shaky breath.

"Whatever everyone does to me to make themselves feel better," my words were soft but strong. It was the truth.

Cole chuckled. "Mmm, you want me to do to you what makes *me* feel good? I'm game." His hand moved higher on my thigh. I grabbed it to stop its trek.

"Don't."

"Or what?" Cole challenged, his eyes locked on mine.

"You'll be sorry."

With his other hand, he cradled my face. "We both know that's not true, Rosebud. There isn't much fight in you." He thumbed my bottom lip, his own lips parting. My pulse raced as he leaned in. "I don't even think you realize what you started."

"I didn't start anything—"

"You got our attention." It was Ethan's turn to talk. Cole's hand fell away from my face. "That probably wasn't the best idea."

"I don't want your attention. In fact, I want you to leave me the hell alone. Aren't there other girls you can damage out there?"

They both chuckled like I'd told a joke.

"It's not the other girls we want though, sweetheart." Cole captured my face again and gave it a hard squeeze as he got to his feet, towering over me. His leg came up between mine and shoved them apart as he pushed me back, leaning over me.

"Do you know what we do to little girls like you?" Cole's breath was hot on my face. I stared up at him unmoving. "Scared girls?"

I shook my head slightly as he gripped my face tighter.

"We own them."

I swallowed and let out the softest whimper. A slow, dark smile curved Cole's lips up as he pressed his knee harder between my legs. A tear squeezed out of the corner of my eye as a heat swept through my core. It was a conflicting feeling. I was both afraid and turned on. My brain couldn't process it all.

"Yes, sweetheart, cry for me." Cole leaned into me more and pressed his lips to the corner of my eye where the tear had slipped out. He didn't move away. A soft sigh escaped his lips before he whispered in my ear, *"You've been chosen."*

With that, he released me. Cole straightened up, and Ethan got to his feet. Both of them walked away from me, but not before Ethan called to me from over his shoulder, "We'll be seeing you, Rosalie."

CHAPTER 3

I didn't tell Jamie what had happened to me on the bleachers. I wasn't sure if it would provoke the guys more, and since Ian was hanging around, I didn't want him to overhear. With all the confusion going through me, I didn't even know if I *wanted* to provoke the guys. But I did want to know what they'd chosen me for. However, given our combined histories, I imagined it was for something I wouldn't want. Maybe more torment. Being owned by them made my pulse race and not necessarily in a bad way.

The rest of the day zipped by with no further incidents. By the next day, I'd grown used to telling myself the guys were just trying to scare me and I had nothing to worry about. I'd glimpsed Fox around midnight outside, going into his house after arriving home. His curtains were still closed.

When I woke up, I did my normal routine. I slipped on a green sundress my mom had gotten me on one of her many shopping adventures. Then I hefted my mess of red curls back into a ponytail and made my way downstairs for breakfast. By the time I got to school, Fox was already there, talking to the guys on the sidewalk.

I had to pass by them to get into the school. Hauling in a nervous breath, I grabbed my bookbag and made my way to the front doors, keeping my head down. I didn't want to catch their attention.

That all went to hell when Enzo called out to me, "Cafeteria girl! Come over here!"

"*Shit*," I hissed. I kept walking, pretending like I hadn't heard them.

"Cafeteria girl!" Enzo shouted again.

Go away. Go away. Go away!

I was almost to the front steps of the school when a warm hand grabbed my elbow and pulled me to a halt.

"When you're called, you answer," Cole growled in my ear, his blue eyes dark. Knots of anticipation corded through my guts. He pulled me to the group of guys, pushing me into the center.

"There she is. *Sunshine*." Enzo reached out and gave my ponytail a tug. "Where were you going so fast?"

"Well, it's time for school, so I was, uh, going," I answered, hoping I sounded stronger than I felt at that moment.

"Smart ass." Ethan grinned. I returned his grin with a wobbly one of my own.

"Have you had any trouble lately?" It was Fox. I spun and looked at him. His jeans and blue polo clung to his hard muscles. His dark hair was still messy, like he'd been running his fingers through it all morning.

"Just with you guys," I answered, holding my head up and locking eyes with him.

A small smirk spread across his face as the guys laughed. He hadn't smiled at me in ages. My heart ached at the sight. He'd been so different since his mom passed away. All I'd wanted to do was help him through it, but he'd pushed me away and became my enemy.

"Look at our girl, having us pegged," Enzo said.

Our girl?

I couldn't have heard him right. It made my heart jump in my chest for reasons I didn't have time to explore.

"We're having a party at Cole's Saturday night," Ethan broke in. "You should come."

I glanced at Fox, wondering what he thought about it. He stared back at me. I figured he'd have told me to get lost.

"I don't go to parties." It was the truth. I'd never been invited to one before, not that a lot of invitations went out for these events. However, to hang out at an elite party meant you probably should at least have your name known or you'd risk getting shoved into the pool. At least that's what happened to Jason McCormick, a guy from my calculus class. They'd pushed him into the pool. There were even videos online of him breaking down in tears after being pulled out when people realized he couldn't swim.

"I think you need to correct yourself." Cole grasped my hand and gave it a squeeze. "You *didn't* go to parties. You will now."

"No, I won't." I tugged my hand free of his.

"I assure you, you will," Cole growled back. "I'm picking you up at eight. Be ready."

I stared wide-eyed at him before glancing to Fox for confirmation. He stepped forward and tucked a loose piece of hair behind my ear.

"Be ready at eight, Rosie. If you don't go with Cole, you'll go with me, and I promise you'll have a lot less fun with me in the car."

He backed away and gave the guys a nod. They moved so I could step through their circle. I spotted Jamie in the distance, worry painted over her delicate features. I was sure she'd witnessed the whole thing along with probably a hundred other students as they passed by us.

I stepped through the guys, my heart racing. My mind was reeling.

"Hey, Sunshine," Enzo called out to me. I paused and looked at him over my shoulder. "You look beautiful today."

My cheeks heated as I rushed away. I thought I'd hear laughter from them behind me, like Enzo's compliment was a joke. But no, there was silence.

"What the hell was that?" Jamie yelped when I reached her.

"I don't know."

"Are you OK?" Her eyes swept over me. "Were they mean?"

I shook my head. "No. Not so much." That stumped me. They

hadn't been mean. They'd been dominant and bossy, but not *mean*. Even Fox hadn't really been.

"They're staring at us. I mean you." Jamie averted her gaze from the guys. "They look hungry."

"What?"

"Like, they're staring at you like you're an all-you-can-eat buffet. What in the hell is going on?"

"I wish I knew," I muttered, pushing past her. I could still feel their stares on me. I launched into telling her what had happened on the bleachers and then with Fox as we walked to my locker. I couldn't process it all and holding it in wasn't helping. I had to tell someone. She gave a low whistle as the floodgates opened, and I spilled everything to her.

"I heard they do it together."

"What?" I stopped, shoving my books into my locker and turned to look at her. "What are you talking about?"

She glanced around before leaning in to whisper to me. "I heard they do it together," she repeated.

"Do *what* together?"

"*It.* Sex. I heard they share girls. Mona from my PE class was talking about getting it on with Cole and Ethan. I overheard her say it was amazing."

I wrinkled my nose at the information, pushing down the butterflies that were churning a storm in my belly. Mona wasn't popular by any means. She was a band geek with mousy brown hair and big, luminous eyes. I'd never spoken to her, but I assumed she was a nice girl.

"They said they chose you. What if *that's* what they meant?" Jamie stared at me with wide, unblinking eyes. "I mean, come on, Rosalie. Ethan was seeing Chloe Morris last year before Enzo was. And wasn't Fox dating Mandy Peters right around the same time Cole was? What about Fiona Wells? She was seen with all the guys. They're hot, babe, but they do tend to be seen with girls like us from time to time."

I opened and closed my mouth several times before I shook my head. Jamie was right. All of the guys had been seen at one point or another with a girl far below their league. "No. Not possible. You forget Fox is in that group, and he *hates* me. I think it's something else. They'll probably shove me into the pool on Saturday."

"Fox stuck up for you. He wants some too. Even if it's good old hate sex."

I rolled my eyes at her. There was no way. I was a nobody.

But Fox said I'd gotten his attention.

No. No way. It was another cruel intention.

"So you're going on Saturday?"

I shook my head. "No. My parents are going out of town this week for my dad's work. Dad is taking my mom to some opera in the city after. I'll be home alone. That means lounging in my pajamas and ordering takeout while streaming movies I've seen a hundred times."

"I wish I could join you," Jamie groaned, leaning against the locker next to mine. "My parents are dragging me to a fiftieth wedding anniversary party for my Uncle Artie and Aunt LouAnn."

"Bummer." I wrinkled my nose at her.

She nodded her agreement. "Ian said he was going to the party though. At least he'll keep you company if you go."

"I guess," I mumbled, catching the quick grimace on her face. "What's going on with you two?"

"Nothing." She shook her head and pulled her bottom lip between her teeth. "I mean, I *wish* something, but you know how Ian is. He likes not being attached."

"You should just tell him how much you like him."

She shrugged. "I'd rather not lose him as a friend or make things weird. I'll suffer in silence."

The fact she wasn't denying she liked him meant she was feeling it. I gave her a sympathetic nod.

The bell rang, so we had to break up our conversation. When we reached a T in the hall, we said our goodbyes, her shuffling away with her head down. I didn't get time to contemplate it because I caught sight of Fox and Juliet down the hall. She was pawing all over him.

The other guys were leaning against the lockers. They must have come in using the east entrance because I hadn't seen them pass by my locker. Juliet pressed her mouth to Fox's, but his eyes were open and locked on me as she kissed him.

I flushed and looked away from him only to lock eyes with Cole. A shiver crawled through my body as I passed by.

I thought I was in the clear, but an arm snaked around my waist, startling me. I peeked up to see who was touching me.

"Enzo's right," Cole said, keeping pace with me. People cast us funny looks and rightly so. He was clutching my waist like we were an item. "You look beautiful in that dress."

"Thanks," I murmured, praying I'd get to my class soon.

"You're so fucking shy. I love it," he continued. "And sexy as hell. Watching your tight little ass sway in this short dress is doing something to my head."

Goosebumps swept through me. "Then don't look at me."

He let out a soft laugh, giving my waist a squeeze. "It's hard not to. You're perfection."

The pitter-patter of my heart was making me breathless. It was nice having someone talk to me like I was a walking sex goddess, but considering the source, I found myself more concerned with the motive behind his words. When we reached my classroom, he tugged me to a stop and stared down at me.

"Come to the party. You'll have fun."

"Why? Why are you guys suddenly interested in me? I've been suffering here at this school for years and no one gave a damn—"

"That was before we saw you on your knees." He licked his lips, his blue eyes flashing. I flushed beneath his stare. "Besides, I told you you're doing something to my head."

"Then get it looked at."

He pressed me against the lockers, a mischievous sparkle in his eyes. He grabbed my hand and pressed it to the front of his jeans where he was sporting a hard-on. My pulse roared in my ears, a sweeping heat rushing through my body.

"*This* head. And I'll see about having it looked at." He released my hand and backed away. "I'll see you around."

He sauntered away like nothing had happened, leaving me frozen where I stood, my breath coming in gasps.

CHAPTER 4

"**B**e good, hon." Mom wrapped me in a quick hug outside their SUV later that night.

Dad ruffled my hair like he did when I was a kid. "Call us if you need anything."

"I will. Love you, guys." I watched as they got into their SUV and fastened their seatbelts. Mom waved to me as they backed out of the driveway. They were leaving for a week. I watched them until they disappeared down the street before moving to go into the house. I stopped when I realized Fox was standing by his car, staring at me.

Ducking my head, I made for the front door. I'd almost reached it when he caught my elbow.

"Where are your parents going?"

I looked up and pulled away from him. "None of your damn business."

He grabbed my hand as I reached for the door, halting its journey to freedom.

"I asked you a question."

"And I gave you an answer," I snapped, tugging my hand from his grip. "Go home, Fox."

He pushed me against the brick of the house, making me wince.

My heart thrashed in my chest as he stared down at me, his chest heaving.

"Don't forget who you're talking to, Rosie."

"Likewise, asshole."

He widened his eyes at me. "I always knew there was a bit of fire in you. Maybe we can bring it out."

"Since we're on the subject of *we*." I scowled as I peered up into his blue eyes. "Tell your band of goons to leave me alone."

"No."

"*No?*" I snorted at him. "I'm serious, Fox. I don't want any part of whatever you're planning. I'm hurt enough by people in school. Don't add to it. At the rate I'm going, it'll cost me thousands of dollars in therapy to get rid of my anxiety and self-loathing."

His gaze softened as he looked down at me, his demeanor changing. The ice melted away, and for a moment, I was staring up at my old best friend.

"I don't want you to hurt, Rosie." He brushed his knuckles against my cheek. "I've never wanted you to hurt."

His confession had my heart clenching in my chest.

"Then why did you leave me?"

It was the wrong thing to say. His eyes hardened, his lip turning up into a sneer.

"I have to go." But he didn't move. He continued to stare down at me, the sneer falling away, leaving parted lips behind.

"Then why are you still here?" I whispered.

"I don't know." His eyes swept over my face. He reached out and tucked a loose strand of hair behind my ear.

"I used to dream of you," his words were a soft whisper.

"What?" I furrowed my brows at his admission.

He licked his lips. "I imagined what it would be like to run my fingers through your hair. I always wanted to. The color. The curls. They always fascinated me."

I didn't understand what I was doing or why I was doing it. I reached behind me with a shaking hand and pulled the rubber band out of my hair, letting the wild, red curls cascade around me. His breath hitched as he took in how I looked.

"I don't think I've ever seen your hair down."

I nodded. It was true. If my hair wasn't in pigtails, ponytails, or a long braid, then it was in a tight bun. I never let it down. It went to my waist in a tangle of thick, red waves.

He reached out with a shaky hand and ran his fingers through my hair, a look of awe taking over his features. I closed my eyes, breathing slowly as he raked his fingers through my hair.

I kept my eyes closed after his touch disappeared. I wanted to log away the memory of how his fingers felt running through my hair. In that moment, he was the boy I once knew. I opened my eyes, expecting to see him peering down at me. Instead, all I saw was his back as he walked with his head down across his lawn, his hands stuffed deep into his jean pockets.

He didn't look back.

Some things never changed.

CHAPTER 5

I wrapped my arms around my body pillow as I settled in bed Saturday night, eager to watch the latest episode of my favorite series. I'd been waiting all week for it to release and had no intentions of moving from my spot even if my house burst into flames. I'd finished the song I'd been working on, making sure to tuck it away deep into my folder labeled for a science class I no longer took. I didn't know why I kept writing songs. They'd never see the light of day once they reached that folder at the bottom of my desk drawer.

The opening credits had just ended when my doorbell went off.

"Nooo," I groaned, squeezing my eyes closed in frustration. Sighing, I sat up, waiting to see if whoever it was would go away. A moment later, the bell rang again, followed by a loud knocking. Jamie was away at the anniversary party for her aunt and uncle, so I knew it wasn't her.

Dread filled my belly when I glanced at my alarm clock and saw that it was 8 P.M..

Another ring from the doorbell and another loud pound on the door. *Cole.* He said he'd be here. Judging by how loud he was getting with my front door, I'd have to explain the dents in it to my parents if I didn't get off my ass and answer it.

I wasn't ready to go to an elite crew party in more ways than one. My hair was in a messy ponytail, and I was in my pajamas—shorty-shorts and a white tank top. Knowing better than to keep him waiting any longer for fear of further damage to our front door, I made my way downstairs and tugged the door open.

"What the hell do you want?" I snapped at him.

He cocked his head at me, his eyes narrowed.

"Why the hell aren't you dressed? I said I'd be here at eight."

"If memory serves me, and I'm sure it does, I said I wasn't going."

"And if memory serves *me*, I told you that you were."

I folded my arms over my chest and stared him down. He was on *my* turf now.

"Despite whatever clever little plan you guys have, I'm not your property. I'm not going. Now get the hell out of here."

Instead of backing away and going to his car, Cole took a menacing step forward.

"You forget your place. I don't mind reminding you, though."

I let out a squeak of surprise as he charged forward and lifted me over his shoulder like I weighed nothing, slamming my front door closed behind him.

"Put me down, asshole!" I shouted, struggling against his firm hold. I pounded my fists into his back, but it was like smashing against a brick wall for all the good it did me. He responded by clapping my ass cheek, causing me to howl and writhe.

"If you think that hurt, wait until we get to your room," he growled, taking the stairs two at a time.

His words twisted my tummy into knots of anticipation.

"Which room?" he demanded when we reached the top of the stairs. When I didn't answer, he clapped my ass again. "You answer me when I ask you a question."

"Second door on the left," I hissed through gritted teeth.

He moved toward my room with ease. Once inside, he tossed me onto my bed. I bounced twice, my ass sore from his hand. He hadn't stopped. He went to my bedroom window and tugged the curtains open before coming back to me and sinking to the mattress. I scooted away from him, scared of what was happening.

"Come here."

I shook my head.

"Rosalie," his deep voice was a dangerous snarl. "I'll tell you once more. *Come. Here.* If you don't, you'll be one very sorry girl."

Fear coursed through me at the way he was staring at me, so I scooted over to him.

"Stand up in front of me."

I hesitated for a moment before the dark look in his eyes had me stumbling to my feet. He reached out and moved me, so I was in front of him. His hands were on my waist, holding me in place, so if I wanted to bolt, I couldn't.

"Do you know how fucking beautiful you are?"

"What?" My voice shook as I frowned down at him, confused at the turn of events.

His fingers threatened the edge of my waistband, sending tingles rocketing through me.

"You heard me." He chuckled softly. "Why are you so surprised?"

My breath hitched in my chest as his warm lips pressed to the bare slit on my abdomen between my tank top and shorts. A tingle raced through my belly before settling in the warm spot between my legs.

"I want you to get ready and come out."

"Cole, I—"

He was on his feet, looming over me before I could finish my sentence, both hands cradling my face.

"You don't know me well yet, but what I want, I get."

"You don't know me well either," I answered in a throaty whisper, trying to get my wits about me. "But I don't take orders from you."

"That's where you're wrong, Rosebud. You know why?" he murmured, thumbing my bottom lip. My breath caught in my throat as I stared up at the impossibly beautiful creature before me.

"Why?" I rasped, curiosity flooding every fiber of my being.

"Because. Falling in line and doing what I tell you excites you. I can see it in your eyes. You need someone to take charge and pull you out of your comfort zone."

I scoffed at him, my heart slamming against my chest.

Was he wrong?

"I'm not like the other girls you mess around with," I answered in a shaky voice. "I know what you're about, Cole. And I'm not so hard up that I need you to try to fix the things you think are wrong with me."

"What gave you the idea I think there's anything wrong with you?" He cocked his head at me.

Damn. He was a smooth talker. No wonder women fell at his feet. I couldn't be one of them, though.

"You know how everyone feels about me—"

"No offense, Rosebud, but I don't give a shit how everyone feels about you. I only care about how *I* feel." He moved away from me and went to my closet. I watched in silence as he rummaged around inside it before pulling out a jean skirt and tank top.

"Put these on. I want you to wear them tonight."

I started to protest, but he pressed his finger against my lips before leaning down, his warm breath on my face.

"Do what you're told, Rosebud. Enjoy being mine." I stiffened as he brushed his lips against mine. He didn't close his eyes. He watched my every movement like a hungry predator before pulling away and pushing the garments into my arms.

"Get dressed. We're going to have some fun,"

I nodded, my heart jumping in my chest.

This was absolutely insane. The last thing I'd expected was to be doing what Cole told me to do. I turned, noting his soft chuckle, my face heating to a million degrees.

I said a silent prayer that this wasn't some screwed up joke. As I turned to go to my bathroom, I saw Fox staring at me through his window.

Please don't let him have seen Cole kiss me!

The look on his face though told me all I needed to know.

He'd seen everything.

CHAPTER 6

"**S**tick close to me tonight," Cole instructed from the front seat of his sports car.

"I thought you said everything would be OK?" Panic rose in my chest. The video of Jason being shoved into the pool lit up my mind.

"Everything *will* be OK. But in case it isn't and all that."

I stared at him wide-eyed. "This is your house. *Your* party, right?"

"It *is* my house, but the party is everyone's."

Sighing, I folded my arms over the black tank top he'd picked out for me. When I'd walked out of my bathroom wearing the outfit, my hair pulled into a high ponytail that cascaded down my back, Cole had gotten to his feet, stuffing his phone away, his eyes sweeping over me. A hunger burned in his gaze that made me ache in so many confusing ways.

We fell silent, my mind going back to Fox standing in the window. He'd looked impassive, his eyes darting from me to Cole before he'd turned his back and left the room. Something told me Cole finishing what he'd started wouldn't happen until Fox gave the OK. Knowing I'd never be one of the cool kids, I'd have to make do with the hot memory.

"Cole?"

"What?" He glanced over at me.

"What's really going on?"

"We're going to my place—"

"You know what I mean. Why are you interested in me?"

The laugh that erupted from Cole had me frowning. That hadn't been the response I thought he'd have.

"What makes you think I'm *interested* in you?"

"You're kidding me, right?" I demanded angrily. "You just made that speech in my bedroom about me enjoying being yours and how no one else's feelings matter but yours. Y-You kissed me."

Cole narrowed his eyes at me as he pulled the car into his driveway and put it in park. My heart banged painfully against my chest as he undid his seatbelt and leaned over to me, unlatching mine in the process. His eyes locked on mine with his slow, deliberate movements.

The shock rattled around inside me as his warm lips met mine in a deep kiss, his tongue dipping into my mouth, tasting me. I let go for a moment, relishing in how normal, *how good*, it felt to let go and experience him, despite the smarter part of my brain screaming for me to abort mission and run and hide from him and his friends.

Our tongues danced against one another's, my breathing coming in sharp, small gasps as his hand cupped my breast before moving south. Nerves made my eyes flutter open. I let out a soft whimper at his touch, my inner voice screaming at me to tell him to stop. The proverbial devil on my shoulder was yelling at me to just let it happen. In that moment, I wanted whatever he'd give me. His fingers trailed along the edge of my skirt before finding their way beneath.

I'd never been touched like that and never anywhere close to there. Having only ever kissed Fox when we were kids, I was running on zero experience. I was just doing what felt good and hoping he liked it because the alternative was soul-crushing. Cole could ruin anything he wanted with a single word. That's the pull he and the guys had.

The groan of approval from him had me wanting him to ruin all the parts of me just so I could feel what it was like to be with someone like him.

My breath caught as his fingers skimmed my center against my panties, anticipation threading through me. I never let anyone touch me like that. Everything was screaming internally again to push his hand away, but that one tiny voice in the background whispering, pleading, with me to let it happen, won out.

"Just because I want *this* doesn't mean I want *you*." His breath tickled my ear as he whispered in it.

I jerked away from him. The ecstasy fizzled before being snuffed out like a candle with his words.

"You're an asshole." I shoved his hands away from me, feeling humiliated and angry at myself for letting go, thinking this could be different. Or better. Or *anything*.

"Rosebud, wait—"

I opened the door and got out, slamming it behind me before he could finish his sentence. When I turned, I was face to face with Ethan.

"Going somewhere?" He raised a brow at me.

"Yeah. Home." I stormed past him down the driveway, not giving a damn if anyone saw me and my attempt at freedom. Ethan's firm grip on my elbow had me stopping in my tracks though.

"Calm down. Come on. Don't let Cole ruin your night. He ruins everyone's nights. Come back and have fun."

I looked up at Ethan, frowning. It was a bit of a walk back to my place from Cole's. He lived in the rich section of town. His mom was a surgeon. His dad was some big shot attorney. His house alone could probably fit both mine and Fox's houses inside it.

"I want to go home."

"Well, that won't happen, so best make do with a shitty situation." Ethan surveyed me with a no-nonsense look. "We'll make sure you get home later. For now, you're coming inside, and we'll have some fun with you."

The way he said that made me scowl even as a tiny smattering of curiosity twisted in my guts.

"Like pushing me into the pool and getting me wet so you can record it and make fun of me?" I challenged.

Ethan chuckled softly. "Oh, you'll be getting wet, but it won't be from the pool."

I shook my head at him, the heat from his words creeping up my body to my face.

Deciding maybe there was at least one decent human at the party who'd give me a ride home, I marched past Ethan to the house, a new resolve settling in.

"You need to loosen up."

"Walk a day in my shoes, pal." I reached for the door, but he stopped me.

"Rosalie, you may never get another chance like this. Consider this a tryout tonight. If you want to live free of bullshit, let go. Whatever happens tonight, let it. I promise it'll be worth it. We're making memories."

I snorted at him. "What are you? A motivational speaker?"

"Maybe." He cast me a quick smile that made me relax. "Did it work?"

I shrugged. "You don't know me, Ethan, but my life sucks—"

"Only because you focus on that. Let it go. One night. Kiss. Touch. Drink. Tonight, you aren't Rosalie, the girl who gets *picked on*. Tonight, be Rosalie, the girl who gets *picked up*."

"Are you talking about..."

He smiled and cast me a wink before pushing open the front door. "Your call."

I swallowed, breathing out. *Could this be the answer to my torment? A night of fun and letting go?* I bit my bottom lip.

It was worth a shot.

CHAPTER 7

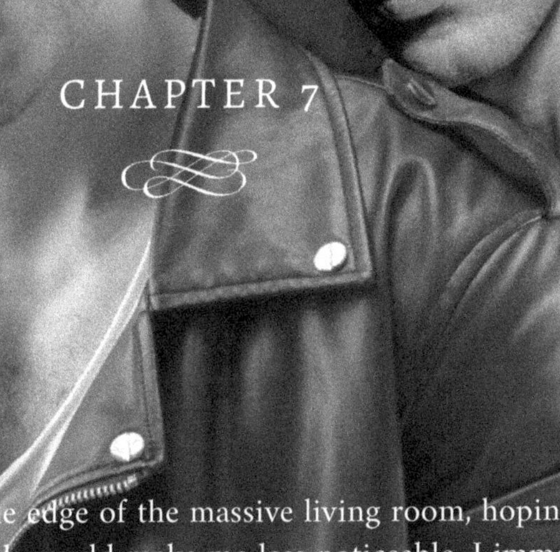

$\mathcal{I}$ kept to the edge of the massive living room, hoping being in the dark would make me less noticeable. I immediately had second thoughts the moment I entered the room. People were dancing to the music while passing drinks, cigarettes, joints. It definitely wasn't my scene. I craned my neck, hoping to find someone I knew so I could ask for a ride home.

Andy Warren, my lab partner from last year, was leaning against the fireplace mantle, looking extremely uncomfortable. Deciding he was probably my best bet, I made my way over to him.

"Hey, Andy."

"Rosalie?" His eyes widened as he took me in. "Wow. I didn't expect to see you here."

"Likewise." I offered him my best smile. He grinned back at me, the tension leaving his shoulders.

"It's not really my scene, but Carrie wanted to come." He shrugged helplessly as he trained his eyes on Carrie Winston, a junior from school. Carrie was probably next to take over Juliet's spot after we graduated. Only difference was, Carrie was nicer.

"You two are seeing each other?"

"No," he laughed, shaking his head. His mess of dark curls bounced on his head. "I wish, I mean. We're just friends."

I gave him a sympathetic look.

He shrugged helplessly. "I was actually thinking about taking off."

"Really?" I asked, excitement coursing through me. "I could use a ride. I'll give you some money—"

"You don't have to pay me, Rosalie," he scoffed. "You got me through biology. The least I can do is give you a ride back to your place."

"Thanks."

We grinned at one another.

"There you are, beautiful." Cole's arm wound around my waist, cinching me to his side. He planted a kiss on my temple.

Andy's gaze darted between us, confusion and surprise both warring it out on his face.

"I'm actually leaving." I attempted to untangle myself from Cole. "I'm going with Andy—"

"No, I don't think you are, right, Andy?" Cole's icy gaze landed on Andy who backed away despite being close to the wall.

"Uh." Andy's eyes volleyed between us again. "Sorry, Rosalie, I, uh, I have to use the bathroom."

He didn't wait for my plea. He rushed away, leaving me with Cole.

"You asshole," I hissed at him. "What the hell is the matter with you? Why are you tormenting me?"

"I haven't even begun to torment you, Rosalie," he growled in my ear. "That business in the car was just a warm-up to what I have planned for you. We have business to discuss."

I shoved him away. "We don't have shit to discuss."

He was quick to grab me, his eyes moving around the room to make sure no one was watching. "You need to relax. Come on. Let's get you a drink."

He grabbed my hand and pulled me through the room. I ducked my head as people openly gawked at us. When we reached the kitchen, he reached in the fridge and grabbed a can of soda for me.

I arched my brow at him. Ignoring the can, I grabbed a cup of beer from the counter.

"You normally drink?" he asked me.

"Not really." I started to lift the cup to my mouth, but Cole grabbed it from my hand.

"Then you can only have one. Don't want you unable to keep your wits about you. And don't *ever* accept a cup that you didn't watch someone pour. Don't you know how to take care of yourself?" He filled a cup with alcohol for me. "Try it."

"You poison it?" I raised a brow at him, half-serious.

He rolled his eyes and sucked down some of his drink. "You saw me pour it for you."

I knew I wasn't getting out of trying it, even though I'd originally had no intentions of drinking it, so I tipped the glass back and chugged down a moutful before sputtering.

"Gross," I coughed out, wiping my mouth.

"It gets better." He nodded to my cup. "Enjoy it while we make our rounds."

"Cole, I seriously just want to go home. I don't fit in here." I looked around with unease at all the people I either didn't like or didn't know.

"You're here with me. You fit in."

"You've already pissed me off. You're only looking to get laid."

He shrugged. "Maybe. But so are you. You wanted it in the car. I felt how wet you got when I touched you." He moved in close to me, his lips near my ear. "You ever had someone get you off, Rosalie?"

A violent heat swept through me, pooling in more than just my cheeks at his words. He let out a soft chuckle.

"That's what I thought. Come on."

I didn't know what was happening or why I was doing what I was doing. Maybe it was the fear of being chucked in the pool. Maybe it was the excitement of being accepted, even for a night. But I tipped that plastic cup against my lips and swallowed down the liquid courage, my eyes locked on Cole's knowing gaze.

One night couldn't hurt.

CHAPTER 8

"Wow, Cole Scott, huh?" Ian's voice pulled me away from watching Cole at the keg as he filled his glass and talked to one of the guys on the football team.

"No," I snorted. I let out a giggle.

Ian raised an eyebrow at me. "How much have you had to drink? And I thought you weren't coming."

"I don't know on all accounts." I crinkled my forehead, trying to keep the room from rotating.

"You look really good tonight."

It was my turn to raise my brows. I giggled again as I swept my gaze over him in his dark jeans and t-shirt.

"You're not too bad yourself." The words were out of my mouth before I could stop them. I hadn't intended them to sound like I was hitting on him, but he seemed to interpret them that way because his lips tilted up into a smile.

"I didn't mean that," I backtracked, wincing. "I meant you look nice. Not like I want you or something." I was rambling, breathless.

He stepped closer to me, the smile still on his lips. "I wouldn't be upset if you did."

Jamie's face flashed through my mind, and I shook my head.

"I-I..."

Ian laughed. "No worries. Looks like your boy is coming back. But if it's not working out with him, come find me." He leaned in to whisper in my ear. "I won't tell anyone. Our secret."

He pulled away and winked at me before sauntering off, leaving me speechless.

"Tell me you weren't chatting up Ian Hall," Cole grumbled at my side, handing a drink to me.

I pulled in a deep, calming breath and plastered a smile on my face. "You're not blind, Cole. Of course, I was." I took a sip of the soda he'd gotten for me. I guessed he meant it when he said he'd cut me off. But he wasn't the boss of me.

"I really want you to rethink that and answer again. Ian Hall is off limits to you. Fox hates him. I hate him. Even Ethan's bleeding heart hates him, and Ethan likes everyone."

I narrowed my eyes at him. "Sounds like a good reason why I *should* like him."

"Not if you know what's good for you, Rosebud."

"Seriously, Cole. My friend Jamie is practically in love with him. If I did anything out of line with him, it would ruin my friendship with her. So chill."

"I'll chill when I know he's not sniffing around you, looking for a piece."

"You're not my boss, Cole," I sighed, setting my soda down on the counter. "Ian is a friend. I can talk to whoever the hell I want—"

"Not him, Rosalie," he hissed through gritted teeth, his blue eyes darkening. "I don't give a shit if your friend has a hard-on for him. That doesn't make him safe. Stay away from him. Got it? He's not one of us."

I rolled my eyes, trying to play off how frightening Cole was in that moment.

"Whatever. I'm not one of you."

"You are tonight. Be a good girl and fall in line like you're told."

"Maybe I don't want to be a good girl," I shot back, snatching his still full cup of beer and gulping it down like I was in the desert, dying of thirst.

It was Cole's turn to roll his eyes. "This is your one warning. Ian is off the table. He's not your friend from here on out. If you don't listen to what I'm telling you, you'll be very sorry. I'll show you how bad things can get when you disobey what you've been told."

"What are you? The Godfather?" I slurped down the last few swallows of his drink and handed him back the empty cup, daring him to keep pushing me.

A muscle ticked along his jaw, but he remained silent, his eyes locked on mine. The look he gave me sent shivers through my body and not necessarily bad ones. I pushed the feelings away, citing inebriation and temporary insanity as the cause for my sudden lack of judgement.

After an intense staredown, he approached me, his arm winding around my waist again.

"I love your defiance, Rosebud. Keep it up. It's going to be so much sweeter for me when you're broken. You can come willingly or you can fight it. Either way, we win."

I choked down a whimper as he gave me a quick squeeze.

The spinning intensified as Cole led me away from where we'd been standing and over to the guys, much to my displeasure.

"Hey, Sunshine." Enzo grinned at me as Cole stopped us next to his friends.

I didn't even care that Juliet, Melissa, and Tara, another of their crew, were glaring daggers at me. I was still hung up on Cole saying he was going to break me.

"Hi," I slurred out on autopilot.

Fox's eyes swept over me, his lips set in a straight line.

"Are you having fun?" Ethan asked, taking a drink from his own plastic cup.

I glanced at Cole. "Not really."

Cole rolled his eyes at me.

"At least you don't actually have to look at you." Juliet did her hair flip, a sneer on her lips. "Poor Cole."

"Poor Cole? Poor us," Tara added, glowering in my direction.

"Juliet. Tara," Fox growled. "Enough."

Juliet rolled her eyes, and Tara fell silent.

"Whatever," Juliet scoffed. "Take the trash out when you're done, Cole."

She flounced away with her clones before anyone could say anything.

"She's a bitch. Why are you with her, Fox?" I popped an eyebrow at him, wanting to know what the hell he saw in her. I figured he'd get upset at the question. Instead, he only shrugged, his eyes focused on her across the room as she laughed with her friends.

"Here, Sunshine. Try this." Enzo pushed a small shot glass into my hand. "We'll cele-brate."

"What are we celebrating?"

"You being here tonight. It's about to get lit." His dark eyes focused on Cole, who frowned at him. Probably telling him I wasn't allowed to have more alcohol. But if I was going to have to stay here with them, I was going to need it. They didn't get to decide for me.

I volleyed my gaze between them, not caring what the hell they were talking about. Throwing my drink back, I finished it and was quickly handed another. I finished it only to down one more.

"That's enough," Fox growled as Enzo moved to hand me another. I swayed on my feet, my head spinning worse than before. "She'll end up throwing up."

Enzo shrugged and drank it down himself.

"Who the hell are you to tell me what I can and can't do?" I demanded with a slur, jabbing my finger in Fox's chest. He stared down at me, an eyebrow quirked. "I'm in charge of me!"

"Easy, champ." He rolled his eyes. "Just don't want you getting blackout wasted or sucking some random guy off in the bathroom."

I wrinkled my nose at him. "If I want to do that, I can. You're not the boss of me."

"Like you even know how. Aren't you a virgin?" He cocked his head at me.

I ground my teeth and stumbled back. Anger coursed through me.

"Is that what would make me cool? Losing my virginity?" I raised my voice.

Enzo pulled his phone out and recorded me. I shoved him away as he tried to get closer.

"Maybe. But we all know you're holier than thou and would never do it. Uptight freakshow, can't even get laid when she offers it up. No one even wants that shit for free."

"Fox, man, come on," Ethan butted in, glancing between us.

I shook my head, my curls bouncing. With a snarl, I pulled my hair out of its rubber band, letting the red ringlets cascade around me like a firestorm.

"I could get laid, Fox. Imagine what it'll feel like for me when he runs his fingers through my hair. Imagine what he'll feel like, getting to pull it while you're down here with your bitch of a girlfriend catching some mediocre missionary-style sex." I narrowed my eyes at him as he stared back at me, a muscle popping along his jaw. "It'll be his name on my lips. Not yours. Never yours."

I backed away from him and gave a satisfied smirk at the anger on his face.

"I'm out of here."

"Rosebud, wait—" Cole called out to me as I stumbled away.

"Let her be someone else's problem," Fox interrupted. "She's a waste anyway. There are more in the book."

I ground my teeth, rubbing my eyes with my fists as I staggered through the writhing bodies on the makeshift dance floor. I didn't know why I was fighting off tears over his words.

Fox had a way of ruining anything I was involved in. Why he cared that I was a virgin and then had to poke fun at me over it made the tears burn hotter.

"Shit. Sorry," I hissed, stumbling back as I ran into someone.

"Rosalie, you OK?" Ian's concerned voice sounded out as warm hands took me by the shoulders to steady me.

"No. I mean, yes. Great. I love parties," my voice cracked as I locked eyes with him. He frowned at me.

"Come on." He pulled me through the crowd and out the patio door.

The cool night air woke me as he led me to a railing off to the side. The sound of the party hammered loudly behind us. "What's wrong?"

"Nothing." I shook my head.

"Liar."

I cast him a half-smile. "Same shit. Different day."

"Ah, yes. The elite." He leaned against the railing beside me and looked up at the moon. "They hate me too."

"So I've heard." We both grew quiet before I spoke a moment later, "Why do you come here if they hate you?"

"Free beer. Weed. The opportunity to talk to pretty girls." He winked at me, making my face heat. "They've yet to kick me out of one of their parties, but they don't hide the fact I'm not welcome."

"I wouldn't bother coming," I muttered.

"I do it because it pisses them off."

I let out a sigh. "Well, you're a doing a great job."

Ian nodded, his eyes narrowed as he looked around. "Getting under Cole's skin is a hobby of mine. The guy's a douche. Rich, pretty boy who gets whatever he wants."

It seemed there may be a story behind his words, one that was probably too heavy for my current inebriated state.

Ian let out a sigh and glanced over at me. "How about a drink?"

I shook my head. "I've already had way too much."

"No such thing, Rosalie. Besides, you and I should have a little fun tonight."

I scoffed. "You mean hanging outside an elite party being pissed off isn't fun?"

Ian moved closer and brushed his thumb against my bottom lip. "That's not the kind of fun I'm talking about."

I swallowed hard and let out a nervous laugh. He switched gears so fast my head spun. "I-I can't. I've never … and Jamie."

"Are you telling me *no*?" He leaned in, his eyes locked on mine. When I didn't move away from him, he closed the distance and brushed his lips against mine. My breath hitched in my chest.

"Prove them wrong, Rosalie."

"I-I can't. Jamie. She-she'd be upset. And-and you and I are friends. I don't feel that way…"

Ian let out a sigh and pulled away from me. I thought he was angry by how stiff he'd gotten.

"I'm sorry if I gave you the wrong impression, Ian—"

"No. You didn't." He cast me a quick smile. "How about that drink instead?"

I nodded, giving in. One drink wouldn't hurt.

"I'll go grab us some. Wait for me?"

I nodded again. He turned and left me standing there. My head still spun. Hopefully, one more drink wouldn't end up with me puking in Cole's mom's begonias.

"Here," Ian said, returning with two cups of beer. "Drink up. Let's forget about all the shit and just relax. What do you say?"

"Sounds good." I breathed out a sigh of relief at his lack of irritation. I took a sip of the beer, Ian's eyes locked on me.

"It tastes better if you drink it faster. Nothing worse than piss warm beer." He tipped his cup back and downed half of it.

I chuckled and did the same, nearly draining the cup.

A smile turned his lips up. "See? Much better. You'll start feeling good in a minute."

"I doubt it. I'm already dizzy as hell."

"No worries, Rosalie. I'll be here to catch you when you fall."

I let out a chuckle and rubbed my head. When I shifted my weight, I wobbled. I must have drunk that last beer too fast. It had gone straight to my head.

"You OK?" he asked softly.

I let out a shaky breath as the world lurched. My hands clutched the railing. Ian's warm hand on my back was like sparks being pounded into my flesh. My body felt hyper-aware, yet sluggish and foreign.

"I-I feel weird," I breathed out. I blinked my eyes, my vision tilted and blurry.

"Come here," Ian murmured.

It felt like I should protest, but my brain no longer felt connected to my mouth. His warm embrace had me nuzzling against his chest.

"Wha—?" I slurred, a strange buzzing tearing through my body as he tried to steer me away from the railing.

"Come upstairs with me, Rosalie," Ian whispered in my ear.

"I feel weird. Ian. Some-something's wrong."

"Come upstairs," he called out again, sounding far away even though he was beside me. "You can lie down. I'll take care of you."

Lie down. Yes. I needed to lie down.

I went wordlessly with him, the sounds and lights from the party strobing slowly around me.

I stumbled at the stairs, sounds roaring in my ears. When I glanced behind me, Fox stood in the middle of the crowded dance floor with Enzo, both staring up at me as I ascended the steps. I wanted to call out to them, but for what I wasn't sure. I feared if I let go of Ian, I'd crash down the stairs to my death, so I turned my head and continued to follow Ian to the hallway.

We stopped outside a door. Ian rapped on it twice before pushing it open and bringing me inside.

"Can you take me home?" I mumbled, swaying where I stood.

Ian let out a soft chuckle as he closed the door.

"In a few minutes. Let's just relax in here."

I didn't pull away as he led me to the bed. I sank down onto it and put my head in my hands.

"How much did you have to drink?"

"Too much," I muttered. "Plus what you gave me."

"Come here." Ian pulled me onto my back beside him.

"My head's spinning," I whimpered. "I feel strange."

"You're really drunk. That happens. It'll go away in a few hours." He shifted beside me, so he was propped up on his elbow staring down at me.

"What?" I whispered, wiping at my eyes again, hoping to fix my blurry vision. It looked like there were two of him looming over me.

"What about earlier? You never told me why you were so upset,. What made you cry?" He pushed a wild curl away from my face.

I shook my head, wincing as the spinning reached a new level of intensity. "The horsemen. Fox made fun of me because I'm a virgin. Called me *freakshow*."

Ian paused for a moment. "You're a virgin?"

"Damnit," I groaned. "I can't drink anymore. I say stupid shit."

"It's not stupid. I knew you didn't date, but I figured you opted to get it on the side."

I shook my head morosely. "No. I definitely don't."

"We could fix that."

I blinked rapidly as I stared up at his two faces. He reached out and tilted my chin up. My head was so heavy.

"We-I-I can't. Jamie—"

"Rosalie, it's just us in here. No one has to know. And Jamie has nothing to do with this."

"She likes you. A lot." I swallowed thickly as I stared up at his blurry face.

He crinkled his eyebrows. "Well, I like *you* a lot. And we're alone in here together. We should take advantage of that." His lips met mine is a soft, warm kiss. His warm hand caressed my upper thigh.

My brain commanded me to move, but my body wasn't responding. Something was seriously wrong. Being drunk wasn't supposed to feel like this. I didn't kiss him back. I lay beneath him stiff, my mind racing with wild thoughts.

"Don't be like this, Rosalie. We could have fun. Me and you. One wild night together. Our secret. We'll both get what we want."

"What do you want?" I whispered. My tongue was thick in my mouth, making the words sound funny.

"You for a night. I've wanted you for a long time." He thumbed my bottom lip, his eyes dark. "I won't tell anyone."

"But Jamie—"

"Shh," he hushed me, pressing his lips against mine once more before kissing along my jawline. "Jamie isn't here. Just me and you. Let's help each other."

"You'd keep it a secret and won't tell her?" I asked, barely able to keep my eyes open. I wasn't even sure what I was saying. I didn't like Ian that way. I needed to get up. *Why won't my feet move?*

"Hell no," Ian murmured. "But it doesn't matter anyway. I'm not with her."

"Mmm. I don't think so. I don't want to." I breathed out, forgetting why I was there or what I was doing. My eyes flickered close. Behind my lids, I imagined Fox. But instead of him sneering at me, he was smiling at me. I wished he wanted to kiss me. My body felt heavy. Numb.

A mouth on mine pushed any grasping of coherent thought out of my mind. My wish was coming true. Maybe he changed his mind. Maybe he wanted me. If he did, I could show the guys I wasn't a waste of time.

I kissed him back, threading my fingers through his hair. The only thing I could focus on was proving Fox wrong. Showing him I was worth something. A soft moan escaped my mouth as kisses were peppered along my collarbone, taking the straps of my tank top down in the process.

"You're so amazing," a voice murmured, his mouth on mine again.

My sluggish hands seemingly acting on their own, tugged at his shirt, effectively removing it from him. I wished I wasn't so drunk so I could see him better. But he was just a flesh colored blob of muscles. They were nice muscles. I fumbled with the button on his jeans as he removed my top. My fingers weren't cooperating. But he helped me out. We managed to get beneath the blankets, him grinding himself against my center, my hips rising to meet his movements through our clothes.

"Fo—" I choked out as his hands moved beneath my panties and ran along my slit. What I was able to actually feel, felt so good.

"Rosalie," he grunted, rubbing my clit in slow, deliberate movements.

I writhed against his seeking touch, breathing hard as a bout of tingles formed. Reaching out, I rubbed my hand against his hard length as he moaned into my mouth through our fevered kiss. I wanted to make him feel good. Maybe then he'd want me.

"Well, well, well," Cole called out. "Looks like you two are having a good time."

"What the hell, Rosalie?" Fox roared behind Cole.

I blinked rapidly. *How did Fox get behind Cole when he was on top of me?* That must have been some potent beer if I was seeing Fox in two different places. With clumsy hands, I touched the head buried in my neck. My vision cleared for a split second. *Oh no.*

"Ian, what are you doing?" I gasped, clutching the sheet to my body.

He toppled off me onto the bed, letting out a groan of frustration. The hot tingles in my body were doused in cold dread. It hadn't been Fox kissing and touching me. *How didn't I know it was Ian?*

"Get the hell out of here before I tear every fucking appendage from your body," Fox snarled.

I squinted through blurry eyes to see Enzo, Ethan, Cole, and Fox glowering at me and Ian, who was now buttoning his pants and putting his shirt back on. Fox's attention focused on me more intensely, like he was trying to figure something out.

"What the hell are you guys trying to do?" Ian demanded. "The door was closed. Don't you pricks knock?"

"My house. My rules," Cole shot back. "And Rosalie isn't allowed to get fucked in my house without my permission."

"You're an asshole. Come on, Rose—"

"Rosalie is staying here. You're leaving," Fox declared. He moved over to the side of the bed I was on.

"You're crazy if you think I'm leaving her with you guys—"

"Listen, pal," Enzo broke in. "You have two choices. Do what we just told you or get your ass kicked. It's four on one. You be the judge of how that would turn out."

"Leave him alone," I slurred, my eyes shuttering closed before I forced them open. I had double—no, triple—vision. "It was a mistake. I didn't know it was him."

In the corner, Enzo was pointing his phone at us. *Wait.* It was Fox's phone. I recognized the blue case. I'd seen him with it countless times. I didn't know why the phone was aimed at me, but something told me I wasn't going to like what it was when I became lucid again.

Fox tilted my face up toward his. A frown turned his lips down. "Rosalie, what did you take?" he whispered.

"N-nothing," I stammered, swiping my hair off my face. "I was just drinking beer."

Fox's expression turned murderous, and he strode over to where Ian still hovered in the room. Fox gripped Ian's shirt. "Did you fucking drug her?" he growled.

Drugs? What did Fox mean? Ian gave me something? Was that why I was so confused and couldn't get my body to cooperate? Tears gathered in my eyes and started trickling down my cheeks. Groaning, I clutched at my head as the room spun. I didn't even notice Ian leaving.

"Rosalie?" Ethan pushed my mess of hair over my shoulder as he knelt in front of me.

"Mm?"

"Let's get you out of here, OK?" He dragged my tank top over my head, making sure I was covered.

"Home?" I looked at him hopefully, swallowing the vomit threatening to erupt from me.

"Take her to Cole's room. He has a bathroom in there in case she gets sick." It was Fox's voice. "I'll make sure that prick left."

Warm, strong arms were around my waist, guiding me through the door. The loud music from the party hammered at my ears, my head spinning worse than ever. I squeezed my eyes closed to ward off the onslaught of lights as I tried to stumble down the hall.

"Easy," Ethan murmured in my ear. "It's hard to walk with your eyes closed."

I mumbled out a reply that didn't sound remotely close to words. The click of a door opening met my ears. Ethan led me inside as I leaned heavily against him.

"Come on, sweetheart," he coaxed as he led me deeper into the room. "There you go. Have a seat."

My butt met the softness of a mattress. I swayed in my spot, moaning.

"Do you need the bathroom?" Ethan knelt in front of me and tilted my head up to look at him before I gave it a slight shake. I was met with a vision of three of his handsome faces. I gave him a wobbly smile.

"You're so handsome."

His lips quirked up into a smile, his green eyes sparkling.

"You're really drunk."

"I'm mad too." I blinked my eyes, trying to regain normal vision. "Fox ruins everything."

"He does have a tendency to show up at the worst times, huh?" He pushed my tangles away from my face.

"I don't get it. He doesn't like me. He doesn't want me to be a virgin because it makes me a loser or something. But when someone was showing me attention he was right there to ruin it." I started weeping. "Besides, I thought it was Fox. Thought he'd changed his mind. And I was about to lose my virginity to the boy I loved long ago. Not be a loser anymore, but then real Fox stopped imaginary Fox from taking me," I blubbered, barely coherent.

Ethan let out a soft chuckle. "You really are out of it. And to be fair, Rosalie, I think real Fox did you a favor. Losing your virginity isn't something you want to happen under the influence of anything, especially drugs when you aren't in complete control of yourself. And Ian probably isn't the best guy to lose it to even sober."

"I know," I muttered. "He's not one of you guys."

"Right. He's not one of us." He reached out and gave my hand a squeeze.

"Why are you the nice one?"

He laughed again, this time louder, his hand still squeezing mine. "Is that what I am?"

"Well, you're less dickish than the other three."

"I'll take that as a compliment."

We were silent for a moment, the music from the party wafting around us.

"Are you going to take me home?"

"No. Fox wants you to sleep it off here. I think that's best too. We can look out for you if you're here. Make sure there are no bad side effects. We'll keep you safe."

"I don't need you to look out for me. You're the bad guys—"

"Shh," he instructed, placing a finger to my lips. "You need to rest. I'll be right back, OK?"

I attempted a nod but it only made my head spin more. Instead, I just sat on the bed with my head hanging down as Ethan got to his feet and left. A moment later, he was back, tilting my face up and holding out two glasses of water.

"I can't drink two glasses."

"It's one glass, sweetheart." He laughed, offering me the drink. "You need to drink it. It'll help."

I took it without further questioning and swallowed down a mouthful, grateful for the coolness as it blanketed my insides. A contented sigh left my lips as I handed the glass back. Ethan placed it on the table and turned back to me, gently pushing me down onto the bed.

"Are you going to touch me?" I whispered as he lay beside me. I was surprised when a warm blanket was placed over me.

"No, sweetheart. I don't make a habit of screwing drunk women. I prefer my ladies lucid and wanting."

"I knew you were the nice one." I closed my eyes, letting out a breath as the spins took over.

He chuckled softly again, pulling me to him. "Sleep. I'll make sure you're OK."

I think I mumbled out another reply, but I couldn't be sure. My world went dark, Ethan's arms wrapped tightly around me.

CHAPTER 9

I woke up with a groan, a heaviness draped over me. I peered through dry, squinted eyes to find myself face-to-face with a sleeping Cole. His face was inches from my own, his arm resting over my midsection. While that was a problem, my concern increased when I realized there was another arm around my waist and behind me another warm body pressed against me.

The pounding in my chest overshadowed the one in my head as I fumbled beneath the blankets to make sure I was fully clothed. A breath of air left me when I realized my clothes were still in place.

I needed to get out of there. I wasn't sure how though. One of them would surely wake, ruining my getaway. I tried to inch away from Ethan but found myself closer to Cole. I shifted slightly, holding my breath, hoping maybe I could slide out from beneath them and escape at the foot of the bed.

"Going somewhere, Rosebud?" Cole's muffled voice met my ears as I attempted another shift.

I froze in my spot as he peered at me through slitted eyes. My heart nearly stopped. He was gorgeous with his messy hair and pouty lips as he locked eyes with me.

"I-I need a drink," I stammered.

"I'll get it," Ethan said from behind me, giving my waist a slight squeeze. His warmth disappeared a moment later, leaving just me and Cole in bed together.

"You're a bed hog," Cole commented, adjusting his head on the pillow to get a better look at me.

I didn't say anything. I looked away from him, struggling to remember what I'd done the night before. It was then that I realized Fox was sleeping in a chair by the window, and Enzo was curled up on the floor in a sleeping bag.

They'd all stayed in the room with me.

"We have a lot to talk about."

I jerked my attention back to him, wincing.

"I just want to go home, Cole. Please."

He scooted closer to me and tugged my body up against his. My breath hitched in my chest at his nearness.

"Say that again."

"Say what again?" I exhaled out a shaky breath.

"The part where you begged me."

I swallowed down the whimper as I stared back at him.

"Please, can I go home?" My words came out in a choked, shaky whisper.

"I don't think so." He brushed his lips against mine so gently, he barely skimmed them. "Not until we talk."

I didn't get a chance to ask what we'd possibly need to talk about because Ethan came back and handed me a glass of water. I sat up, much to Cole's annoyance, and slurped down the cool drink.

"Thank you."

"You're welcome, sweetheart." Ethan placed the glass on the nightstand and got back into bed, surprising me. It must have shown on my face because he gave me a wink, his sweet smile making my heart flutter.

"Isn't she nice to wake up next to?" Cole commented, trailing his warm touch against my jaw.

"Yes," Ethan agreed, shifting closer to me.

I couldn't believe I was in bed between two of the hottest guys at Black Falls High. And they weren't being mean. I had to be dreaming.

"She's so nervous." Cole chuckled softly, his warm breath tickling my skin. Goosebumps popped up all over my body as he moved to rest his hand on my abdomen now that I was on my back.

"We won't hurt you, Rosebud. Unless you like that." Cole nuzzled against my neck, peppering kisses along it. I couldn't stop myself from arching my neck to give him better access.

Ethan and I stared at one another, a tiny smile on his lips. It felt odd and strangely hot to have Cole kissing my skin with Ethan watching.

I jumped when Fox called out, "Knock it off."

Cole rolled away with a groan, putting distance between us. Even Ethan moved away, casting me a quick, reassuring smile in the process.

"You're a fucking buzzkill, Evans," Cole grumbled as he lay on his back and stared at the ceiling. "What's the rule? If you aren't getting any, none of us can? That's messed up. You know that's not how this works."

"Piss off," Fox grumbled.

"Would you guys shut the hell up?" Enzo muttered from his sleeping bag. "I'm trying to sleep here."

"Get up," Fox grunted, getting to his feet. His gaze locked on mine. The heat from the situation crowded my skin, making me feel like I was on fire. There I was, lying between two of the sexiest guys I knew, and there Fox was, looming over me with a strange look on his face. A look that made my tummy twist with excitement.

He blinked, and it all disappeared, a scowl replacing everything that had almost been on his face.

"Rosalie, do you know what the hell happened last night?"

I sat up, trying to untangle myself from Cole, who'd wrapped his arm around my waist again. He cast me a smirk, clearly enjoying the discomfort he had me in.

"I drank too much and wound up in here with you jerks."

"Easy," Cole grunted, giving me a squeeze.

"Before you ended up in here with us jerks, you were shirtless and getting fingered by that dweeb from the school paper," Fox continued.

"After he drugged you," Ethan added.

"I-I didn't know it was him. When he asked me earlier, I told him no. In the room, when he was kissing me... and touching me..." I shuddered as I thought about *his* hands on me. Cole tugged me against his chest with a growl. "I didn't think it was him. I thought it was..." I glanced over at Fox.

The vein in Fox's neck throbbed as he glared at me.

Cole ran a hand down my spine. "Rosebud, I told you not to drink so much. And I told you to never drink something you didn't watch get poured. This is why."

I pushed back from him, jabbing my finger into the center of his chest. "Remember what you said? I should let whatever happen, happen? Well now look at the mess! This is your fault because I listened to you!"

Cole snorted. "If you'd have listened, you'd have been naked in my bed, not incoherent with someone else."

Fox snarled at Cole's words. But I didn't dare look at him. *Oh, god. I'd been imagining Fox's hands were on me when it had been Ian's.* Nausea made me lightheaded.

"Do you have any idea what could've happened to you if we hadn't come in when we did?" Ethan asked.

I stiffened in my spot, images flashing through my mind. Bad images. I scrambled to get out of bed, nearly knocking Ethan off the edge in the process. I stumbled around, looking for my shoes.

"What the hell are you doing?" Enzo asked, sitting up. His hair was a dark mess, his eyes tired as he watched me with interest.

"I-I need to go. I have to talk to Ian—"

"That's the last thing you're going to do," Fox hissed, tugging my shoes out of my hands. I opened my mouth to protest, but he shoved me back onto the bed. Cole was quick to wrap his arms around my waist so I couldn't get up.

"You don't have any right—" I started, but Fox shook his head at me, his blue eyes flashing.

"I have every fucking right, Rosalie. You were about to screw some loser at a party. What the hell is the matter with you?"

"Why do you care? And I thought I told you that you're not the boss of me!" I ground my teeth, wanting to tear into him. Cole's hold on me tightened, like he knew exactly what was going through my mind.

"I *am* the boss of you." Fox breathed heavy, his chest rising and falling as his anger grew. I'd never seen him so mad before. If I wasn't so angry, I would've been afraid of him in that moment.

"Like hell you are!"

"Easy, Rosebud. Hear Fox out," Cole admonished.

I ground my teeth and glared at Fox.

"I guess you need your memory prodded."

I held my breath as Fox dug around in his pocket and pulled out his phone. He approached and knelt in front of me. Bile rose in my throat as I watched the image play on the screen. It was me and Ian, tangled up in one another on a bed. I winced as we started removing each other's clothes. It grew even worse when we began touching one another, our lips never breaking apart. In my mind, it had been Fox, not Ian. I didn't want Ian. I never wanted Ian. But it didn't look that way on the screen.

"Why do you have that?" I whispered hoarsely, tearing my eyes from the train wreck on the screen and looking at Fox. Something told me I wasn't going to like the answer.

"Insurance." The word was loaded, cocked back and ready to ruin my life. I knew it.

"For what?" I asked, shaking.

Ethan reached over and squeezed my hand.

"To make sure you fall in line and do as you're told." Fox moved away from me and paced the room. I twisted my fingers nervously, waiting for the nail in my coffin.

"We own you, Rosie. If this video gets out, everything will be ruined for you. You'll be ruined. As much as I'd love to watch you crash and burn, I feel like I have a better use for you. That *we* have a better use for you."

"What are you talking about? You said yourself that Ian drugged me. I didn't have any idea what I was doing. I didn't *choose* to do that with him." My voice grew hoarse as I stared at Fox.

"It doesn't look like you were an unwilling participant. No one can tell you were drugged in this part. So, in order for us to not send the video to everyone in school or upload it to the best porn sites in the country..." Enzo started, glancing around at the guys.

Ethan shifted next to me. Fox continued to glare.

"Yeah?" I prompted.

"You become ours," Ethan finished, his voice low.

I frowned over at him. "What?"

"Ours." Cole rolled his eyes as he released me and moved to sit beside me. "Like we own you. You do what we tell you to do, when we tell you to do it, including sucking my dick if I tell you to."

"You'd really upload a video of me almost getting raped?" I screeched, tears prickling my eyes. "Screw you!" I snarled, jumping to my feet.

"That's the point." Cole chuckled.

"I'm not your whore. You can have anyone you want. Why me? Why this?"

"Why not?" Cole challenged.

"You didn't mind being a whore for Ian last night," Fox said at the same time, his glare hardening.

I snapped my attention to him. "I told you, I didn't think it was him. This is all your fault. *You* did this!" I hissed at him, my hands balled into fists.

"I didn't do shit," he scoffed, shaking his head at me. "That was all you, Rosie."

"You were mean to me—"

"Everyone is mean to you. You'd think you'd be used to it by now."

"What the hell is the matter with you, Fox? We used to be best friends. You promised we always would be! What the hell is this? You decide to blackmail me to be your bitch instead? You have a *girlfriend*! What are you going to do? Have me suck you off while you're on the phone with her, telling her that you love her charming viper personality?" I shouted, my throat tight from anger. I let out a yelp as Fox pushed me down onto the bed, his hand over my mouth.

"I cannot emphasize this enough, Rosie, but shut your damn mouth before something really bad happens." His blue eyes were hard as he glared down at me.

I shook beneath his hold, anger bubbling to a boiling point within me. I'd made a mistake. But I wasn't about to be blackmailed because of it.

He removed his hand from over my mouth.

"What if I say no?" I lifted my chin in a challenge at him.

He shook his head at me, his eyes wide. "Then you'd be an idiot. We have a video of you and Ian screwing around, which conveniently looks like you actually did screw him. Willingly. You don't want that to get out, do you? You don't want your parents to hear about it, right? What about if it got sent to Pendleton? I heard they don't like scandals. Having an amateur porn star on campus probably isn't good for their image. You could lose your full-ride to the college of your dreams, your way out of this town. Face it, Rosie, you belong to us until we say otherwise. The only answer you'll give any of us is yes."

My breath hitched in my chest. They had video of me and Ian. If Jamie found out, it would end our friendship. She'd never believe I didn't *choose* to betray her. Tears welled in my eyes at the thought of losing my best friend.

And my dad. He'd hate me.

As if reading my mind, Fox nodded at me. "We have everything."

"Why are you doing this, Fox?" I choked out through the silence. "We were best friends—"

"I'm doing it because you *owe* me," he hissed through his teeth. "We're going to ruin you. This is just the jumping off point." He released his hold on me and moved away.

I sat up, staring back at the guys who had my future in their hands, all of them waiting for my answer. I couldn't belong to them. They'd make my life hell. There had to be another way.

"No," I whispered in a strangled voice.

"No?" Enzo cocked his head at me, before looking around at the guys.

"No," my voice grew stronger, louder. "I'm not doing it. Do your worst to me."

"Sunshine, I don't think you understand what could happen to you if we let this video out into the world—"

I got to my feet and backed away from them. "I-I don't care. I won't let you control me."

"You'll change your mind soon, Rosie." Fox eyed me, his lips tipped up in a sneer.

"Then I guess we'll see about that." I turned and fled the room, not looking back. If running away worked for Fox, maybe it would work for me.

CHAPTER 10

hen Monday hit, I promised myself to pretend like nothing had ever happened and prayed Fox wouldn't release the video. I hoped our former friendship *might* mean something to him. Him wanting to ruin me for reasons I couldn't comprehend had me on edge. I'd never done anything to him but care for him. He was my everything growing up.

"You look like crap," Jamie commented as I shouldered my bag. I'd barely slept. Dark circles rimmed my puffy eyes. "Are you sick?"

"Sick of this place," I muttered. Jamie's eyes widened as someone tugged my hair. I glanced over my shoulder to see Enzo smiling at me. My heart plummeted at his presence.

"How was your weekend, Sunshine?"

"Shut the hell up," I snapped at him. His grin widened as Jamie glanced uneasily between us. "I'm sure you know how my weekend went."

"You're right. I do. That's why I think we should talk before things start happening."

My stomach clenched. Trepidation coursed like a raging river. "What things?"

His dark-eyed gaze moved from me to Jamie who had the sense to back away slowly before hightailing it out of there right before she offered me an apologetic smile.

"The sort of things a girl like you wouldn't want to get out into the world."

My body vibrated with barely contained anger.

"Did Fox tell anyone?" I demanded through gritted teeth.

"I think you already know none of us has said a word *yet*." He reached out and wrapped one of my curls around his finger from my ponytail, a smile on his face. "It's in your best interest to accommodate our demands."

"What?" I took a step toward him, my anger barely contained. "What demands? What do you jackasses want from me?"

Enzo stared back at me, the humor leaving his face. "We told you that we want *you*. You've been chosen, baby girl. You really should consider our offer. Things could get ugly if you don't."

I glance around fearfully. Some students cast us odd looks, no doubt confused about why Enzo was talking to me.

"Imagine things going from bad to worse, Sunshine." He leaned in and whispered in my ear, his words cold. I shivered from the weight of them. "It begins today in case you need a little prompting."

"Enzo, wait!" I called out as he turned to go. He paused, his dark eyes locked on mine. "Please—"

His lips curled up into a smile. "Meet us on the bleachers at lunch. Oh, and Sunshine? Save the begging for later. You'll need it."

I stared after him, my heart racing.

Things really were going from bad to worse.

I SPENT the morning with my stomach aching. A million scenarios raced through my mind at what the guys wanted from me. Do their homework for the rest of the year, clean their lockers, wash their gym clothes, and basically be their beck and call bitch. Cole's colorful words from his bedroom raced through my mind, making me blush. I hadn't had the guts to talk to Ian yet. I needed to do that. If he told Jamie... My stomach clenched harder.

"Earth to Rosalie!" Jamie called out.

I shook my head and glanced over at her as I stuffed my bag into my locker. "Sorry," I mumbled.

Jamie rolled her eyes at me. "Where we having lunch today?"

"I-I have to meet the guys at the bleachers," I muttered.

She frowned at me. "What the hell is going on with you and them? I mean, they've been paying a lot of attention to you lately. What happened?"

I shrugged. "Probably want me to do their homework for them."

"*Ugh*. What a bunch of dick bags. Fine. Find me when you're done, OK? We can plot out how to fail them slowly over time. I'm going to see if Ian wants to have lunch."

I gave her a weak smile and a nod before she disappeared down the hall to the cafeteria. The moment she was out of sight, I raced in the opposite direction, knowing Ian was in the library since I'd seen him go in there right after the bell rang.

He sat at a table, flipping through a textbook when I approached him.

"Hey," I breathed out in a shaky voice.

He looked up at me, a smile playing on his lips. "Hey."

I twisted my hands nervously in front of me as I stared at him.

He put his pencil down and sighed. "Are you OK? I was worried about you on Saturday. The guys didn't hurt you, did they?"

"No," I answered, sitting down in the chair beside him.

He turned to face me, his brows furrowed. "I had fun, Rosalie—"

"It shouldn't have happened. I didn't want it. You drugged me. I'm sure it was just a mistake. You're a nice guy."

Our sentences came out at the same time. He nodded and gave me a tight smile.

"Maybe for you it was a mistake, but I meant what I said. I *did* have fun. I'd like to finish what we started. It seemed like you were into it."

"Ian, no. Jamie really likes you. She's my best friend. I don't want to hurt her, so I'm not going to tell her what you did. I-I was drunk and upset, so that didn't help things. If she finds out about what happened—"

"So what if she finds out? It's not like you're the first girl I've ever fucked, Rosalie."

I widened my eyes at him. "We did *not* have sex, Ian. You know we didn't."

He shrugged. "Prove we didn't. Prove you didn't want it. I can tell Jamie what happened. I can tell her how I was knuckle deep in that tight pussy while you stroked my dick. Then I can tell her how quick you were to spread your legs for me after I fingered you." He gave me an innocent smile before continuing. "We can finish what we started, and I'll keep quiet. If we don't, I'll have to tell her. It's what a friend would do."

I stared at him open-mouthed and in disbelief.

"Are you serious? You know half that shit didn't happen, and the half that did, certainly didn't happen the way you're saying—"

Ian shrugged again. "If I tell her it did, then it did. Who's she going to believe? Me, coming to her in honesty, or you, hiding it? I want you. It's that simple. Give me what I want, and it all goes away. Tell me no and watch your world fall apart." He surveyed me with a confident smirk on his lips. "Seems like an easy choice to me."

I got up from my chair so fast it toppled over behind me.

"You're a fucking pig, Ian."

"I'm your dirty little secret." He reached out and took my trembling hand in his, his thumb rubbing a circle on the top of it. "If you want to keep it that way, best pay up."

Disgust washed over me, and I tugged my hand from his grip before backing away.

"That's fine. I'll give you some time to think it over. I'd hate for the story to get out and all that considering what you could lose. Don't wait too long. I'm not the patient sort."

I couldn't bother to reply to him. The disgust had turned to a sickness which twisted my guts. I thought we were friends, but hell, I'd also thought that about me and Fox and look how that turned out. I stumbled out of the library, my heart in my throat. Not only did I have the horsemen on me, but now Ian was gunning to ruin my life. All for something that happened that I didn't even want.

My day kept getting worse. As much as I wanted to avoid the horsemen, I had to go out and meet them at the bleachers. Drawing in a deep breath, I steeled myself and made the trek to the football field. I could see the guys milling around the bleachers—Cole and Ethan sitting on them with Enzo and Fox standing. They were all talking like they didn't have a care in the world.

"Hey, she made it," Enzo called out, smiling at me.

Fox cast me a look over his shoulder while Ethan's eyes raked over me. Cole didn't bother looking at me, the jerk.

I folded my arms awkwardly over my chest and stood in front of the guys.

"Welcome to our inner circle," Enzo continued with a grin.

"Can we please get this over with? I'm already having a bad day, and you assholes probably aren't going to make any improvement on it."

"Watch your mouth," Fox growled as he moved behind me.

I shivered but kept my head held high.

"Your boy Ian?" Cole lifted a brow at me, his signature smirk on his lips.

I ground my teeth as I stared past him, noting that Fox moved so I could see him.

"It's going to get worse. You were warned." Fox folded his arms over his chest and leveled his gaze on me. "You just don't fucking listen."

"Tell me what you want me to do. Homework? Laundry? Write your papers?" I sighed in exasperation, throwing my hands up in the air.

"That could be nice." Cole nodded. "But I don't need homework help. I'm second in our class rankings right behind your sexy ass."

I widened my eyes at him. I hadn't known he was ranked second in our class.

He gave me a nod. "Surprised?"

"Yeah, you don't strike me as the scholarly type."

He laughed. "Ah, how little you know about me, Rosebud. We're going to fix that. Hell, maybe I'll even take over your spot. Or maybe you'll let your grades slip for me."

Dread filled my body at his words, a strange buzzing coursing through me. I couldn't lose my ranking. I'd worked so hard for it the past four years. It might even cause me to lose my scholarship to Pendleton. My dad would kill me.

Cole nodded knowingly at me. "Be a real shame, huh?"

"Stop teasing her," Ethan broke in. "She's already upset."

"She should be," Fox snapped. "After all the shit she's been pulling, she deserves to squirm a little."

"I haven't done anything!" I shouted at him. "It's your girlfriend who teases and bullies me. I've never provoked her. I've never provoked anyone. I only try to survive here. Why can't you let me? Why torment me?"

"I told you why." Fox took a step closer to me. I stepped back until I found myself against the bleachers. "You owe me—"

"For what? Because you came to my rescue after your abusive bitch of a girlfriend accosted me in the cafeteria for an accident?" My voice became shrill as I stared up at his intimidating figure. "If that's the case, punish me now, but don't *keep* punishing me."

Fox reached out and fisted my hair, angling my head painfully. I let out a hiss, my eyes watering, as he glared down at me, his grip tightening on my curls. "Oh, Rosie, I do plan on punishing you. The thought of putting you on your knees satisfies me more than you know. So keep it up. You have no fucking idea how much I want to punish your ass."

"*We* only want to get to know you," Ethan interrupted Fox's onslaught. Fox released me, sending me shifting into a bleacher. I winced as one caught my ribs. "It won't be as bad as you think, Rosalie. We picked you out of the hundreds of other girls here."

"For what?" I whimpered, looking at all the guys in turn. My eye caught Cole tucking a black notebook into his bag before looking back at me, no trace of emotion on his face. "*Why* me?"

"Because you're beautiful. Smart. Fragile. And honestly, we just want to break someone." Cole shrugged, giving me a big smile and a wink. "You're chosen. And since Fox has to exact some revenge on you, it seems perfect. We all get something out of it."

"You're nuts."

"Maybe." Enzo shrugged. "But by the time we're all done here, you'll be just as crazy. You'll be one of us."

"I don't *want* to be one of you—"

"Well, you can definitely choose to deny us." Fox pulled his phone out. My heart raced as I stared fearfully at him. "But this video can either stay hidden or it can be made public. Judging by how close you are to your friend Jamie and how much she likes Ian, I bet it would really hurt that friendship of yours. Imagine how that'll be. Quiet Rosalie Bishop fucks the guy her best friend's in love with. It'll break her heart."

I swallowed down my tears and glared at him.

"What'll you do once you're all alone?" Fox murmured, moving closer and thumbing my bottom lip. I flinched away, but he took my face roughly in his hand and squeezed, forcing me to look up at him. "No friends. Everyone thinking horrible things about you. You knowing those thoughts are true. What will you do, Rosie?"

My bottom lip trembled as I stared up at him.

"I used to love you, Fox," my words were choked as I said them. His eyes widened, his lips parting. "You were my everything. Now you're my nothing. Forcing me to do your bidding only makes me hate you."

Fox froze, staring down at me. The silence around us was deafening. It took him a moment, but he came out of whatever daze he was in to lean in and whisper in my ear words that made my heart break as he gripped my face

"I never loved you, Rosie. I only ever pitied you." He released my face, but not before giving me a quick, patronizing pat on the cheek.

I pushed past him, not bothering to stop as Ethan called out to me. Even when Cole joined in calling my name, I kept moving.

I had to get away and breathe. To hell with finishing the meeting.

CHAPTER 11

Maybe I hadn't really voiced my choice, but Fox must have taken it upon himself to prove to me how very serious he was. I realized that the next day as Juliet shoved me in the locker room after gym class.

"Hey, skank," she simpered. "Heard you and Jack Gildner were screwing in the crow's nest on the football field at lunch yesterday."

Melissa and Tara snickered as I stared back stupidly at them.

"That's a lie."

"That's not what I heard," Melissa piped up. "I heard you sucked off both him and his weirdo friend, Aaron."

I ground my teeth at them. "Where did you hear that?"

"I made it up." Juliet flipped her hair. "But after I tell everyone, it'll be a truth, and I doubt Jack or Aaron will deny it."

"It's a lie because I was with *your* boyfriend on the football field," I hurled back at her.

Her eyes widened for a moment before she struck me in the face, sending me tumbling back against my locker.

"Listen here, bitch," she snarled, fisting my ponytail and yanking so hard my eyes watered. "We're going to end you. Fox has given us the green light. He was the only thing stopping us before. But now?" She cackled wickedly in my ear, tightening her grip. "You're fair game."

She released me, shoving me back. I slid down the lockers onto the bench, my face aching where she'd struck me, and my head hurting from the grip she'd had on my ponytail.

"Do yourself a favor and fall in line," Tara spat at me. "Or this is only going to get worse."

"What do I have to do?" I rasped, afraid the guys had told them everything.

"I don't know what you did to piss the guys off, but I suggest trying to make it right be-cause at the moment, it's not looking good for you." Juliet looked at her friends. "Ladies."

She flounced away. Melissa spilled my gym bag all over the floor before leaving.

If this was just the beginning of what the guys had planned, I was in for a rough time.

"What happened to your eye?" Jamie demanded as we sat down at a table in the back of the cafeteria.

I stared at the guys as they laughed and acted like nothing was going on in their world. Like they hadn't just set the hounds of hell snapping at me.

"Huh?" I muttered, tearing my glare from the table of nightmares.

"Your eye. It's red." She touched her own eye for emphasis.

"Oh." I waved her off, lying, "Juliet hit me in the face with a volley-ball during gym."

"What a bitch." Jamie shook her head, shooting a scowl over to where Juliet was kissing on Fox. "I wish her herpes would just kick in already."

I poked listlessly at my salad. The air around us shifted. I didn't need to look up to know who'd joined us.

"Ladies," Ian said.

"Hey," Jamie answered, her voice breathy.

I opted to continue stabbing at my salad.

"Rosalie, anything new and interesting going on with you?" Ian's voice carried a note of sarcasm.

I chanced a look at him and frowned. "No."

"I heard you were screwing around at Cole's party over the weekend—"

"Shut up, Ian," I snarled at him, slamming my fork down. Jamie looked between us as Ian settled in his seat, her eyes round.

"Did you mess around with someone at Cole's and not tell me?" Jamie asked, leaning forward after the shock of Ian's words melted away.

"Yeah, Rosalie. Didn't you tell Jamie?" Ian stared back at me with mock innocence.

"Ian, please," I whispered. "Not now."

"Then when?"

"What the hell is going on?" Jamie called out, her gaze volleying between me and Ian.

"Nothing. I drank too much and kissed Cole. That's it."

Ian let out a derisive, cold laugh as he shook his head. He leaned back in his chair, putting it on two legs.

"You made out with Cole Scott on Saturday?" Jamie squeaked. "Are you kidding me? Why didn't you tell me? Is that why they've been lurking?"

"It's not important."

"The hell it isn't! I can't believe you didn't tell me! What was it like?" She sat forward, staring at me. I glanced at Ian who shook his head in disbelief at me.

"It was... fine."

"You're fucking ridiculous," Ian snarled, slamming his chair down and glaring at me. I swallowed hard as he got to his feet.

"Ian, please," I choked out.

He nodded at me. "Soon, Rosalie."

He backed away, still glowering at me, before turning on his heel and storming away.

"What's his problem?" Jamie looked back at me, frowning.

"I don't know. He caught me with Cole. He was upset." The lies kept coming. I hated myself for them.

"Ian is really protective." Jamie nodded thoughtfully. "He means well."

Yeah, right.

I chose not to respond out loud, opting to going back to my salad once more.

"Don't look, but Fox is staring at you right now."

I kept my eyes down.

"Oh no. He's coming over. Ethan is with him."

Shit.

Awful scenarios raced through my mind. He was going to dump my lunch on me. At least it was just a plain salad. That might not be so bad. *Oh god.* What if he dumped Jamie's lunch on me. She'd gotten spaghetti. I had to get out of there.

Without so much as a goodbye, I was on my feet and hauling ass out of the cafeteria, not bothering to look back. With the crash of the cafeteria door banging open again as I raced down the hall, I picked up my pace, my heart slamming against my chest. I hung a right then a left, finding myself at the door to the guys' locker room.

"Shit," I whimpered, glancing over my shoulder behind me. Heavy footsteps thudded toward me. Knowing I didn't have another choice, I darted inside the dark room, swiveling my head left to right as I sought a hiding place. Deciding a dark corner with football equipment was my best option, I lunged forward and buried myself inside, praying I wouldn't be seen.

The squealing of the door opening had me holding my breath. I watched through a space in the equipment as Fox and Ethan came into the room.

"She had to have come in here." Fox looked around.

My breath came in soft, short huffs, my body as still as stone as I watched them move around the room like predators.

"Rosalie?" Ethan called out. "Come on, sweetheart. We aren't going to hurt you. We only want to talk."

Bullshit.

"Rosie, you don't need to hide. We heard about what happened in the locker room after gym this morning. I want to make sure you're OK." Fox paused in the center of the room, looking around again.

Liar.

"I'll check the back." Fox moved toward the back of the locker room out of my line of sight. The showers had to be back there. Ethan prowled close by, stopping right in front of me.

"Rosalie," he hissed, not looking at me. I stiffened.

"I know you're behind the equipment. Your foot is sticking out." He paused, glancing over his shoulder. "You're going to have to come out."

I stilled, knowing the jig was up. I let out a squeak as warm hands circled around my arms and tugged me out of my hiding spot. I came face to face with Ethan.

"There you are." He smiled down at me. "Why are you running?"

"You know why," I whimpered back. Ethan didn't get to answer me because Fox came back into the area.

"I knew you were in here."

The door banged open. Cole and Enzo entered. I stared in horror as Enzo grabbed a metal chair and propped it beneath the door handle, effectively trapping me inside with them.

"Please, let me go." I struggled against Ethan's hold. His grip tightened on my arms until I winced. Noting that, he immediately loosened his hold.

Ethan was definitely the nice one.

Cole took his spot, seeing Ethan's moment of weakness.

"Keep fighting, Rosebud. It only excites me," Cole grunted in my ear as I struggled against him. I stilled, knowing he wasn't lying. He chuckled victoriously in my ear. "Good girl."

"We've given you ample time to decide your fate, Rosie. Now we need an answer." Fox lifted a dark brow at me.

"My answer is fuck you," I snapped back. Fox rolled his eyes at my dramatics.

"You seemed pretty cozy out there with Ian," Enzo added, stepping up to me. "That wasn't good. Flaunting your fuck boy is a bad idea, Sunshine."

"I'm not cozy with Ian! He makes me sick!" I shouted back at him. "He's threatening me like you guys are." I sagged back against Cole, feeling defeated.

"Ian is threatening you?" Fox asked, his voice a low, dangerous rumble.

I nodded miserably.

"What's he saying, Rosebud?" Cole demanded, his voice matching Fox's.

"That he wants to finish what we started. If I don't, he's going to tell Jamie."

"I told you he was a piece of shit," Enzo spat. "Didn't I say that?"

"It'll be taken care of," Fox ground out, silencing Enzo.

"How?" I demanded.

"Don't worry about it. I said it'll be taken care of," Fox snapped, his eyes darkening.

I shrank away from him, deeper into Cole's hold.

It felt like I was in some of sort of high school mafia snuff film with Fox being the kingpin.

"Why do you guys even care? Is it because it's a competition to out me?" My voice wavered as I tried to compose myself.

"That's exactly what it is, Rosebud," Cole growled in my ear. "You belong to us. Our little whore. We call the shots."

"I'm not your whore," I snarled back.

Cole chuckled softly in my ear as his hold on me tightened. "You're whatever the fuck I say you are. We run this place."

I ground my teeth, itching to plant my foot in his groin as his hard-on brushed against my backside. Despite being angry, I couldn't ignore the rush of tingles which shot through my body at his nearness.

As if knowing that, he whispered in my ear again, sending a flurry of goosebumps through me. "I fucking love that *you* love it. We're going to have so much fun with you."

"Agree to our demands, Sunshine. We'll make sure everything else is taken care of." Enzo leveled his dark gaze on me, pulling me away from Cole's madness.

"I'm scared," I choked, admitting out loud what I was sure they already knew. Maybe they'd find an ounce of compassion in their hearts to let me be.

That hope tumbled to the ground and shattered at my feet when Fox spoke. "Then you're already halfway there."

"Fear is an excellent motivator," Cole added, giving me a squeeze.

Fox pulled his phone out and thumbed through it for a moment before glancing up at me.

"What do you want with me? What do I have to do?" My voice shook again. "What makes you go away?"

"Depends on our mood. Maybe some homework. Maybe a blowjob." Cole's lips brushed the shell of my ear with his words. "Or maybe I bend you over a chair and fuck your tight little ass. It varies depending on what sort of day I'm having."

"You're a pig. Are you trying to compete with Ian for the douchebag of the year award?" I tried to break away from him, the fear and lust warring inside me, both fighting for supremacy, but he tightened his hold.

"And you're turned on by the idea of it." Cole growled again.

I shook my head, hating that he was right.

"We can start off slow." Ethan cleared his throat, shooting a quick look at Fox who was glaring at me, phone in hand. "Since Fox isn't interested in being too close to you, maybe Cole could get you for a week—"

"I'm not a toy, Ethan! You can't just pass me around!" I snapped at him.

Ethan winced and looked down at his hands. "It's not like that, Rosalie. We can switch off so you don't feel so overwhelmed. I promise you I'm not going to make you screw me or suck me off, but I could use some help in calculus and chemistry."

Enzo and Cole snorted at Ethan's words. I scowled before leveling my gaze on Ethan.

"You want me to be your homework bitch?" I narrowed my eyes at him.

He flushed before muttering, "Among other things."

"What *other* things?" I demanded.

"Show her," Enzo said, a dark glint in his eyes. Before I could whip out a response, Cole knocked my legs out from beneath me, sending me careening painfully to the hard locker room floor. I let out a cry of agony as my knees connected with it. Tears filled my eyes.

"Keep that mouth open," Cole instructed darkly in my ear as he reached around to grip my face painfully.

Horror and disbelief flooded my body as Enzo stopped in front of me, his crotch inches from my face. I tried to turn my face away from his groin, but Cole forced me to continue looking at it.

"I want you to suck my dick, Sunshine."

Shivers inundated my body as my heart thudded uselessly in my chest. I clamped my mouth shut, despite the war inside that kept kicking up dust in my mind about wanting to taste him.

"Just open your mouth and put his cock inside, Rosebud." Cole let out a soft laugh.

I caught Fox's eyes as he stood only a few feet away, surveying the scene with narrowed eyes.

"Fox?" I whimpered. Whether I wanted a command, permission, or freedom, I didn't know. All I knew was that whatever his answer was, it would determine the outcome of the moment.

He moved forward and knelt beside me.

"Have you ever given a blowjob before?" he asked softly, his voice husky.

I shook my head as much as Cole would allow. Ethan stepped forward and looked down at me, a frown on his face.

"Well, to start, you'll need to unzip Enzo's pants."

He was serious. I looked up at Enzo, whose eyebrows were raised, clearly waiting for me to make my move. Cole released my arms. With shaking hands, I reached forward and fumbled with the buttons on Enzo's jeans. The lust inside me landed a right hook to fear's face, knocking it into a quivering mass of nerves on the floor of my mind.

My shallow breathing and the *zipppp* of Enzo's zipper coming down were the only sounds in the room. The massive, bulging outline of his hard-on could easily be seen through his dark boxers.

"Now, all you need to do is take his cock out and put it in your mouth," Fox instructed in a gruff voice.

"Fox," I whispered, looking over at him. My heart fluttered in my chest.

"Would you rather it be me?" he challenged softly, his eyes locked on mine.

I didn't even hesitate with my answer. "Yes."

A tiny, wicked smirk tugged the corner of his lip up. "Do you think I'd let your nasty mouth on my dick?"

The heat of embarrassment flooded my body before anger took over. I reached out to slap Fox, but Cole grabbed my arms and tugged me roughly to my feet. I barely registered Enzo zipping his jeans up.

"You're a prick," I ground out at Fox, my heartbeat roaring in my ears.

"And you're the little whore Cole said you were," he shot back. "*That's* how we prove our point. The next time, you *will* have a dick in your mouth. It's obvious you want one."

"No I don't," I hissed at him, the lie making me feel like I was sucking on a cotton ball.

"Liar." Cole laughed.

I ground my teeth and glared straight ahead.

"So, back to negotiations since my dick apparently isn't getting sucked," Enzo broke in. "In exchange for your servitude, we can keep Juliet and her girls off your case, or at least have her ease up."

The idea of being free of Juliet made me pause my anger. "You'd call off your dog?" I asked, narrowing my eyes at Fox. He shrugged.

"Sure. Until you screw up again."

I snorted bitterly. "What constitutes me screwing up?"

"Pretty much breathing, freakshow." Fox smirked at me.

I broke free from Cole and moved to Fox, jamming my finger into his chest. The smile slid off his face. "Call me freakshow again, and I'll rip your testicles off."

"Are you in?" he growled down at me, his blue eyes flashing.

I pulled my bottom lip between my teeth and stared up at him. Maybe I was screwed up in the head, but a tiny, niggling voice in the back of my mind hissed at me to scream yes and fall to my knees again. I pushed it away and stared defiantly up at him, my hands on my hips.

"Promise you'll tell Juliet to back off."

"I promise not to release your sex tape."

"Fox," I snarled. "Please. You just said—"

He rolled his eyes at me and unlocked his phone screen. I let out a gasp as he opened the share tab and starting adding people to an outgoing message with the video attached.

"Stop!" I squealed, reaching for the phone. He held his other hand out, stopping me from getting closer. "Fox, please! Please, don't! I'll do it. I'll do whatever you want. Just please. Please don't send that!"

The bigger part of me which wanted my freedom would have to suffer. I could lie to myself all night long, but I was at their mercy. I knew it the moment Cole forced me on my knees. Running, begging, crying, none of that would change what was happening to me. They owned me. I did the only thing I could do.

Willingly, I fell to my knees in front of him, clinging to his pant leg as I wept and pleaded with him not to send the video out. I could only imagine the horror and disgust on my parents' faces. The disappointment when Pendleton got it and revoked my scholarships and acceptance letter. The embarrassment of people seeing me almost be raped while not fighting Ian off. And Jamie. My guts twisted.

"What do I have to do?" I sobbed. "I'll do it. Whatever you want."

Fox put his phone away and stared down at me.

"Say it. Say you're mine."

"I'm... yours," I choked out, defeat ebbing from me in the form of tears. *Who the hell was I kidding?* I wasn't strong enough to fight them. Despite feeling a strange desire for the guys, I still knew I shouldn't. But I also knew I had to join them or risk losing everything.

Fox's warm fingers lifted my chin up so I stared up at him, tears free-falling down my cheeks.

"I told you the next time you were on your knees begging it would be for me."

He released me as I rocked forward, completely at his and his friends' mercy.

"We're going to have some fun, Rosie. Cole, take care of her." Fox moved away from me, only for Cole to take his place.

"Come on, Rosebud." Cole held his hand out to me. I placed my palm in his and let him pull me to my feet.

"What are we doing?" I whispered in a choked voice.

"I'm taking you home. Your parents aren't there. I'll decide what I want once we're in your bedroom."

Enzo removed the chair from against the door as Cole led me to it. I cast a backward look at the guys, my heart plummeting.

"Have fun," Fox murmured as Cole opened the door and pulled me out into the hallway.

CHAPTER 12

*M*uch to my surprise, Cole rummaged around in my closet before pulling out a black off-the-shoulder dress with little pink rosebuds printed on it. He grabbed a pair of tan suede boots out of my closet next and placed them on a chair next to the dress.

"I want you to wear that tomorrow."

"Does the king require anything else?" I muttered, watching him from my perch on the edge of my bed.

He nodded to my vanity. "Lip gloss. I love your lips. I find chicks who wear lip gloss sexy. Cherry if you have it."

I nodded dully. I had it. "Is that it?"

Cole moved to stand in front of me and tipped my chin up.

"This won't be so bad. Remember how good I made you feel that night?"

A rush of heat swept through my core as I remembered kissing him. Had I known it would result in me being their slave, I may have said no and fled like I'd planned.

You're not a slave to them if you want it.

I pushed the terrifying thought out of my head and focused on what Cole was saying to me.

"I can make it happen again. Would you like that?"

"No, because I don't need another video to deal with." My voice sounded strong through the lie as I glared up at him. He grinned and backed away.

"I'll pick you up tomorrow for school. Make sure you're wearing the outfit I've chosen. If you're going to be seen near or with us, you can't look like you crawled from a trash bin. Take the rest of the day to rest. You're going to need it."

"Like I'd dream of defying you." I rolled my eyes at him.

"Maybe you should. I could give you a spanking."

My breath hitched in my chest at his words. He winked at me.

"You're a dirty girl, Rosebud. I'll see you in the morning." And with those words, he left me alone in my bedroom, my mind in all sorts of dirty places despite my hatred of him and his friends.

I SHOWERED after Cole left and crawled into bed, worry setting in. When the sunlight streamed in through the slit in my curtains the next morning, I let out a groan. The phone ringing had me on my feet and shuffling to it. My parents put a landline in my room. I had no idea the purpose for it other than my dad's need for nostalgia.

"Hello?" I yawned.

"Rosalie, where have you been? We were worried sick!" My mother's voice wafted over the line, making me grimace.

I should've called them.

"Sorry, Mom. I didn't feel well last night. So I decided to turn in early."

"It's a good thing Fox lives next door! Dad had to call him to go check on you."

"Gee, thanks," I muttered, playing with a piece of lint on my pajama bottoms. I knew Fox had simply told them a lie since he knew I was home. I cast a quick peek at my curtains, my eyes narrowed. I imagined if they were open, I'd see Fox's curtains instead.

"Well, don't do that again. You had me nearly loading your dad onto a plane and heading home!"

"Sorry," I apologized again. That seemed good enough for her because we went through the pleasantries before her telling me to be good, despite the fact I was eighteen and could take care of myself.

When we hung up, I went to my chair and hurriedly put on the outfit Cole chose. It actually looked nice on me. Mom had picked it out a few months prior, citing a sale she couldn't resist. I did a quick twirl, braiding my hair and letting it rest over my shoulder. My green eyes didn't look so sleep deprived, thankfully. I dotted on the cherry lip gloss and some mascara before I went downstairs.

A knock on my door made me groan. Pulling it open, I found Cole on my front steps, looking like he'd just stepped off a cover of *Heart-throb Magazine*.

"You're early," I grumbled, not bothering to invite him in but not closing the door on him either. He stepped inside the house.

"I'm on time. I told you to be ready."

"Just getting my bag," I said, coming back with my book bag slung over my shoulder.

"You good?"

"The best I can be considering the circumstances."

"That works for me." He escorted me out to his car. I climbed in the front seat, impressed he'd opened the door for me. Cole still didn't seem like the chivalrous sort.

"Thanks," I murmured, pulling my seatbelt over myself and snapping it into place. He nodded and moved around to climb behind the wheel.

"I'm sorry about yesterday." He cleared his throat as we pulled out onto the street. "I know how scared you are."

I shrugged. "Not like that matters, right?"

He glanced at me, a rare non-cocky smile on his face that lit up his eyes. For a moment, he looked every bit the sweet, doting heartthrob girls dreamed about getting the attention of. "It matters, Rosebud. I promise it'll be worth it."

I nodded, not saying anything. Being blackmailed into becoming a puppet wasn't something I looked forward to.

He made a left turn onto the main road wordlessly.

"So what do I have to do today?" I shifted uncomfortably on his leather seats, wondering if I'd find myself on my knees again.

"Haven't decided." Cole shrugged. "Maybe we'll just have some fun. I don't need help with homework or anything like that."

"So you've mentioned."

His laughter wasn't the usual cold bark. Warmth seemed to radiate from him. He was in a rare mood. Usually, Cole was dark and scary. Today, he appeared the polar opposite.

"I still can't believe it."

"While you see the player and party guy, there's also a studious side to me. My parents would kill me if I didn't do well in school." He scowled at the mention of his parents. This conversation turned deeper than last time. I found myself interested.

"I heard they aren't around much."

He tightened his grip on the steering wheel. "Hardly ever. I was raised by a nanny until I turned fourteen. Then I was on my own. My older brother Colten left when he graduated four years ago."

I nodded, vaguely remembering he had an older brother.

"What does he do now?"

"He graduated with a degree in engineering. He works for a company in New York. He travels a lot."

"Do you get to talk to him often?"

"Not really. He calls me about once a week to see how things are and remind me to keep my grades up so I can get the hell out of here. I guess he's getting married next summer."

"Oh, that's cool."

Cole shrugged. "I haven't met her. Her name's Clarissa. He wanted to bring her home to meet our parents, but Mom and Dad were too busy doing whatever shit they do, so Colt decided to cancel. I'll probably meet her at their wedding, if he even bothers with one. Knowing Colt, he'll just jet off to Vegas and get it over with."

"I'm sorry."

Cole frowned at me as he parked the car.

"Why are you sorry? It's not your life."

I scoffed. "But this is, and I know how much things can suck."

For a brief moment, he looked sympathetic.

"I'll make sure you enjoy this then. A couple crazies together can only produce the best results, right?"

"I don't think that's how this works."

"It'll work. I know it will." He got out of the car and was at my door, pulling it open for me and offering me his hand. I took it hesitantly, waiting for him to let go so I'd topple to the ground. I was surprised when his grip tightened, and his arm wound around my waist.

"Look at everyone stare, Rosebud," Cole murmured as he led me through the parking lot to the sidewalk.

He was right. It was worse than the party. Cole Scott never stuck with a girl. And as far as I could remember, he'd never pranced around campus with one on his arm like he was doing with me. But he was guiding me like a show dog through the grounds, nodding and high-fiving people when appropriate.

"I don't like it."

"Why not? On my arm, you're untouchable. Eat it up, baby."

"Except by Juliet—"

Cole pulled me to a stop and angled my face up at him. "You're tough. You'll be fine. You've impressed me so far."

I blushed, looking away. He let out a soft chuckle before we started walking again.

"Aren't you going to stop and see the guys?" I asked as we veered to the front doors of the school, bypassing the guys who were watching us.

"Not this morning. I'm more focused on you. That dress is perfect on you."

I couldn't believe this was Cole Scott talking to me. I imagined me saying yes to the guys would have me on my knees again, scrubbing their football jerseys, doing their homework and sucking their dicks until my jaw wanted to fall off. *But this?* It was beyond my wildest expectations.

We stopped at my locker, and I stuffed the books from my bag inside. I was acutely aware of Cole's eyes locked on my every movement.

I spotted Jamie coming toward us, her movements slowing, apprehension on her face. I was about to point her out to Cole, hoping we could all get along since it would be a long year if I was stuck to the guys for however long, but he had other ideas in mind.

"Come here," he demanded softly, drawing me to him. "This is about to get really public, Rosebud." It was all the warning I got before he pressed his lips firmly to mine, his tongue sweeping inside. If there was one thing Cole Scott could do, it was kiss.

"What was that for?" I gasped when he broke the kiss off.

He only gave me that smirk of dark things to come which I was becoming familiar with.

"Um, Rosalie?"

I pulled away from Cole and peered at Jamie, whose gaze volleyed between me and Cole.

"Hey." I plastered a fake smile on my face.

Jamie raised an eyebrow at me, totally not buying it. "What's going on?"

"Uh, nothing." I winced, my voice an octave higher than normal. I sounded like an idiot. She gave me a pointed look.

"Baby, come on," Cole cooed. "You shouldn't keep secrets."

I shot him a glare to which he responded by smirking back at me, the devil in his eyes.

"Are you two seeing each other or something?" Jamie locked her stare on Cole. I had to hand it to her, she came off as tough, not backing down from him as he returned her gaze.

"Something like that," Cole answered. "Rosalie likes me so much that she just does whatever I tell her, huh, Rosebud?"

"You're an ass."

"You like it," he shot back, tightening his hold on me. His lips brushed against the shell of my ear as he whispered, "Play nice."

I forced a smile on my face.

"We're just having fun."

"Mm, bad girl." He chuckled softly. "Is that what we're calling it?"

Jamie blinked rapidly, clearly floored by our little display. "O-kay," she muttered. I could practically see the questions zipping around in her head.

"Give me your phone." Cole turned to me.

I shook my head at him. "No."

His stare hardened. He definitely didn't like to be told no. "It's not a request. Give it to me."

I nearly told him no again, but the look on his face had me digging into my bag and handing it over. He snatched it from me and typed something out before his own phone buzzed.

"Perfect. Now I can reach you whenever I want." He handed my phone back to me.

"Great," I muttered, trying to keep the brittle smile on my lips. "It'd be terrible if I were unreachable."

Cole winked at me before turning to Jamie. "So, Jamie, right?"

She nodded mutely.

"How about you and Rosebud do your morning ritual tomorrow instead? It's a bit crowded right now."

"Cole—" I started, anger coursing through me.

"It's fine, Rosalie. I only wanted to tell you the signups are posted for the fall musical. I figured I'd let you know since you said you were interested in trying out."

"Oh!" I let my excitement show. "When are tryouts?"

"Next month." Jamie glanced between me and Cole.

His expression darkened considerably. I knew he was close to letting his inner jerk out more, so I quickly bid Jamie goodbye, promising we'd talk later. She nodded slowly, confusion and hurt warring on her face.

"If I have to do this, could you at least be nice to my friends?"

We started our walk to my first class, Cole snagging my books out of my arms and carrying them in his, his other arm wrapped around my waist.

"You mean *friend*. Singular."

I shot him a glare. "Yes. She's the only one I have, and I'd like to keep her if you don't mind. I thought that was obvious considering I'm now your bitch."

He chuckled. "Sure, but you have us now. We're your new friends."

I snorted. "Bullshit. You guys aren't my friends. You don't care about me. You're my tormentors. That's not even close to the realm of friendship. And stop kissing me and touching me," I added as an afterthought.

Cole laughed, tightening his hold. "I'm claiming today as mine, so I do what I want."

"Is that what happens? You guys just call dibs?"

He shot me a smile and shook his head. "Not really. It's pretty up in the air. I'm sure you'll be hearing from everyone else soon enough. Maybe you should anticipate being bent over a desk with me buried inside that tight little pussy."

The heat raced across my skin at his words. He smiled knowingly at me as I tried to be tough. "Great. Can't wait for that," I said with an eye roll, but deep inside, butterflies flapped to life.

"You're so fucking sexy when you're turned on," he growled, stopping outside my classroom. "Just appreciate that we found this to be more enjoyable than releasing the video. I think if you open your mind, you'll find this could be a hell of a lot of fun."

I swallowed hard, looking away from him.

He was quick to bring my attention back. "We're only getting started. I'll be sure to let the guys know to go easy on you until you're more comfortable."

"Really? You'll go easy?"

He smiled down at me and thumbed my bottom lip, hunger burning in his baby blues. "I didn't say *I* would. If there's a hard truth about me, it's that I don't go easy on anyone."

"You're a jerk," I managed to say as he leaned in, his eyes locked on mine.

"From here on out, I'm your jerk, Rosebud. But I think you're going to enjoy how rough I am."

"You think so?" I rasped, leaning into him.

His lips tilted up into that dark smirk I'd become accustomed to. "If there's one thing I know, it's when a woman is interested in me. And you are most definitely interested. You think you shouldn't be, so you're playing hard to get. And baby, you definitely got me hard. I just need to make my move. It's coming."

"And let me guess," I said, feeling brave as I rested my hand on his chest. His heart beat fast beneath my fingers. "So will I."

"You can fucking bet on it." He brushed his lips gently against mine, heating me straight to my core. "I'll see you later."

I took my books from him, lost for words. His wink said it all as he backed away into the throng of students.

I was in so much trouble.

CHAPTER 13

"So what's going on with you and Cole?" Jamie tapped her foot at me, hand on her hip.

I knew this would happen. I couldn't avoid the subject for long.

"Nothing. We hung out at that party. I guess he's OK." The bland excuse did nothing for my cause.

Jamie gave me a look of disbelief. "I thought you hated those guys?"

I shrugged. "I do, but I'm trying to make this year better." I forced a half-assed smile onto my face. "It's our last year and all."

"Is something going on? You can tell me—"

I bit my tongue before the words tumbled out. Instead, I fixed the smile on my face better. "Everything's fine. Promise."

She gave me a skeptical look before finally nodding. We made our way into the cafeteria where we sat at our usual table in the back. Jamie brought a lunch. I had nothing and going to grab something didn't seem like the best idea since people had been whispering behind their hands about me and Cole all morning. I scanned the room, breathing out a sigh of relief when I didn't spot Ian. The last thing I needed was him.

119

Jamie was yammering away about yearbook committee when Cole's deep voice cut into my thoughts.

"Why are you over here?"

Jamie stopped mid-sentence and darted her eyes between me and Cole, apprehension on her face.

"Uh, because this is where I sit."

Cole glanced at Jamie before locking eyes with me. "I wanted you to sit with me today."

While his words seemed pleasant, his eyes gave away his irritation.

"What if we sat here?" I asked hopefully, glancing at the table where all the jerks sat. I'd seen Juliet come in with her evil wenches earlier. The last thing I felt like doing was breaking bread with the bitches.

"Not part of the plan, sweetheart. Come on. Jamie, I'm sorry, but I'm stealing Rosalie." Cole held his hand out to me.

"It's cool. I have some things I need to do anyway." She stuffed her half-eaten sandwich back in her bag, her lips turned down into a deep frown. "We still on for tonight?"

I nodded, taking Cole's hand. It was movie night at my place.

Jamie smiled and got to her feet.

"Sounds good. We can, uh, talk then. See ya."

I waved goodbye, watching as she left with her head down and allowed Cole to pull me to my feet.

"When I tell you to do something—"

"I didn't know the kings required my presence at their table," I snapped at him. "You never told me I had to sit with you."

"When you belong to us, you sit where we sit. You do what we say. It's not that fucking hard to grasp."

I rolled my eyes. "I forgot. The answer is always *yes, master*. I just didn't want my friend to eat alone."

Cole sighed and led me through the cafeteria. "Where's your lunch?"

"Don't have one."

We stopped at the table the crew occupied, and Cole pushed me down into the seat he usually sat in.

"I'll be right back."

"Wait, Cole—"

He didn't pause. He turned on his heel and left me sitting there feeling like a total loser. Sighing, I turned to face the crew, most of who stared at me like I was lost.

"You need to tell Cole to stop leaving his trash laying around." Juliet glowered at me from Fox's lap.

"I'll be sure he gets the memo," I muttered.

"How's your day been, Sunshine?" Enzo asked, scooting closer to me.

"I've had better."

"Are you and Cole dating?" Melissa butted in.

I stared at her in surprise as the table fell silent. "Uh, no."

"Jeff Gaston said you and Cole were kissing in the hallway by your locker this morning," she pressed.

Juliet and Tara both leaned forward. A few of the other cheerleaders stared avidly at me, waiting for a response. I glanced around at all the eyes on me. Terrence, James, Brent, Brandon, the others from the football team were looking at me like I'd sprouted a second head.

"It's nothing." I swallowed hard, my eye catching Fox's.

"That's what I thought. I told you." Juliet smirked at the girls. "Cole isn't that stupid. He likes the nasty girls. Maybe freakshow is just an easy lay—"

I was ready to pounce on her. Being called freakshow was getting old.

"Juliet," Fox scolded in his deep voice as I contemplated launching myself at her from my seat. "That's enough. Not here."

I raised my eyebrows in surprise. I hoped his stepping in didn't mean I'd owe him more. It certainly hadn't been my idea to sit there.

"She doesn't belong here, Fox." Juliet pouted, jutting her bottom lip out at him. "Make her leave."

I expected to see him give in to her, but he gave her a hardened glare, his body stiffening.

"She stays," he ground out, a muscle popping along his jaw.

Juliet's eyes widened in surprise at his declaration. "Either she goes or I do."

Fox's blue eyes traveled over to me. I was already on my feet, ready to get the hell out of there, but he shook his head at me.

"Rosalie, sit."

I sat awkwardly while the rest of the group looked like they were watching a tennis match, all eyes volleying back and forth between Fox and Juliet.

"Juliet, if you can't handle sitting at the same table as her, then maybe leaving isn't a bad idea."

The stunned silence from the table made my heart race. All because of me. No way. This would make her torment a million times worse.

"Um, it's really OK. I don't actually even want to be here, so I'll go." I stood up again, but Fox shifted his glare from Juliet and focused it on me.

"I *said* sit, Rosalie." The way he said it made shivers race through me.

I sat once more, deciding staring at my hands seemed like the best option.

"Are you kidding me, Fox?" Juliet's voice shook.

I chanced a glance at the two of them.

"Do I *look* like I'm fucking joking?" Fox lifted her and placed her on her feet. Her eyes darted around to everyone at the table. No one met her gaze.

"Her over me?" She balled her hands into fists.

"No, Juliet. You were given the option of dealing with it. You're the one throwing out ultimatums. I'm only answering. Cole brought her to sit with us. I have it on good authority this may turn into a regular thing, so either deal with it or leave. Pretty fucking simple." Fox sat back in his seat, not looking the least bit perturbed as Juliet loomed over him, her body trembling. She drew in a deep breath before settling into the seat next to Fox.

"I'm staying. But if she does anything—"

"She's never done anything. I think it'll be fine." Fox glanced over at me, a steely glint in his eyes. "You good, Rosalie?"

"Yeah," I muttered.

Enzo reached out and patted my hand while Ethan offered me a reassuring smile. No one else dared look in my direction. The moment I saw Cole approaching, I darted out of my seat, practically running to him.

"Didn't expect you to be so eager to see me," he greeted me as I stopped in front of him. He held a tray with two sandwiches on it along with apple slices and two cartons of milk.

"Cole, please. Please, can we leave here? Don't make me sit with those people."

Cole looked over my shoulder for a moment before his eyes darkened. "I know they don't like you, but you need to understand something, Rosebud."

"What?" I whispered, silently pleading with my eyes for him to have some sort of sympathy or understanding for my situation.

"I like the torment."

I choked down my cry of despair as he widened his dark smile at me and led me back to my own personal hell.

CHAPTER 14

*J*amie let out a gasp as Ian walked toward us in the hall a week and a half into my servitude. I'd just arrived at my locker with Jamie, grateful Cole had said I could drive myself for the day. It was the first day I'd been allowed to drive myself since this whole thing started. He'd also taken great pleasure in making me do his laundry. He sat on the dryer, annoying me and pointing out each time I wound up touching his underwear.

"What happened to him?" Jamie murmured, her face scrunched in worry.

"Looks like he tangled with some dudes he shouldn't have," Enzo said.

I hadn't heard him come up behind me.

He winked at me. My guts twisted at his words, my mind darting back to the day in the locker room when Fox said Ian would be taken care of.

Jamie looked at us for a moment before turning back to watch as Ian passed by, his head down, probably as both a means to hide from Enzo and hide the black eye, split lip, and purple cheek he sported.

"I have to see what happened. I'll talk to you later, Rosalie!" Jamie didn't wait for my answer. She shot off down the hall, calling out to Ian.

"Did you do it?" I whispered.

Enzo leaned against the locker next to mine, his dark eyes sweeping over me as I pulled my books out. "Do what?"

"You know what. Did you guys beat him up?"

Enzo shrugged and pushed off the locker. "A magician never reveals his secrets, Sunshine. Come on. We're wasting time talking about things that aren't important. I want to have some fun while I have you."

I swallowed thickly, looking up at him. "I'm with you today?"

"Do you not *want* to be?" He cocked a brow at me.

I shook my head, blowing out a breath. "Honestly? All of you are a pain in my ass that I wish I could be free from. Seeing as you all hate me and want my misery, I don't see my freedom coming up any time soon, so it's whatever at this point."

"Ah, Sunshine. You wound me." Enzo clutched at his heart in mock pain.

I studied him for a moment as he dropped his hands from his chest. "Did you guys really hurt Ian?"

Enzo stepped closer to me and leaned down. "My little ray of Sunshine. Why does it matter?"

"Because, you can't go around hurting people—"

"Who says we did? Maybe he just mouthed off to the wrong guy." There was a dark glint in his eye as he pulled away. "It's really not important. Come on. We need to get you off to class."

Sighing, I fell in step with him as we traversed the halls.

"I heard you want to try out for the school musical."

I shrugged. "Yeah. I was thinking about it."

"Can you sing?"

"I don't know," I mumbled, knowing damn well I could probably give anyone in the school a run for their money. Admitting it made me feel self-absorbed and egotistical, so I dodged the question.

"You don't *know* if you can sing but want to try out for a singing part?" Enzo gave me a look of confusion. "How does that work?"

"I figured I'd get into the chorus or something." I glanced at him. If I tried out for a chorus part, it would keep my dad off my back. Getting a lead part would make my home life difficult because Dad would accuse me of ignoring my academics for a pipe dream.

"You're too damn pretty to be singing in the background. Come over to my place tonight. We'll work on your audition." It was my turn to look confused.

"What? Why?"

"Why what?"

"Why do you want to help me?"

"Why would you think that I wouldn't?"

"Uh, I'd think the answer to that is pretty obvious." We stopped outside my classroom.

"You're a funny girl. We'll work on it tonight, OK?"

"I'm busy—"

"The only answer you have for me is *yes*, baby girl. You know that." He tweaked my nose, winking at me.

I scowled. "Of course, your highness."

He grinned. "I like your spunk, Rosalie. I'll see you after class."

And with that, he left me standing there, shaking my head. These guys were just plain confusing. They were all mean and bullies. But sometimes they did something that wasn't solely for their pleasure or to torture me. Something nice and considerate. Something for me. And it only made things worse when they slipped back to their group dynamic of being horrible to me.

"Ian said he was helping his dad clean out the attic, and the ladder came down from the ceiling and hit him in the face. Can you believe that?" Jamie stared at me with wide eyes as she tore her chocolate cupcake in half at lunch.

"No." I shook my head, knowing damn well it's wasn't an attic-related incident. If there was a ladder involved, it was probably handled by Fox and the guys as a weapon.

"I mean, that has to have sucked. He missed school because he said it was so bad his eye was swollen shut."

"That does suck," I murmured. I glanced around, wondering where Ian was. I spotted him sitting with some of his friends from the paper, his head down. He'd certainly lost his bit of swagger over the last week. Something about that gave me a sick sense of satisfaction. He'd been a real dick.

"Sunshine, where's your lunch?" Enzo flopped down in the seat next to me and brushed the stray hair which had escaped my ponytail away from my face.

"I don't know. I didn't get one."

Jamie frowned at us, no doubt confused about why it was Enzo up my ass and not Cole since everyone was talking about our recent hanging out. She'd been questioning me lately about what was going on, but I'd become an expert at smiling and dodging her questions.

I peeked over my shoulder at the crew table and saw the rest of the guys in their usual spots. They were bent over a notebook, Fox scowling and Cole smirking at him. Cole marked something in the book and closed it. Ethan met my gaze and gave me a smile before getting to his feet. Enzo noticed and grinned at me.

"Looks like we're getting company."

A moment later, Ethan slid into the seat on my other side. Jamie opened her mouth, her gaze volleying between the three of us. She swallowed down her bite of cupcake.

"Jamie, this is Ethan," I said awkwardly, nodding to Ethan.

Ethan grinned his boyish grin at her. "Hey. I heard you're on the yearbook committee. Any chance of getting a picture of us and putting it in the student life section?"

"Uh, yeah. Yeah. Sure." Jamie rooted around in her bag for a moment before unearthing her camera. She uncapped the lens and gestured for us to get closer for the photo.

The guys slid closer, Enzo wrapping his arm around my waist and Ethan resting his hand on mine.

"On the count of three," Jamie called out. "One. Two. Three!"

On three, both guys leaned in and planted a kiss on my cheeks. I scrunched my face up at the move, my heart racing. The flash went off, and the photo was captured.

"I'm going to want a copy of that." Ethan nodded to Jamie's camera. "I'll pay you for it."

"Same," Enzo echoed, nabbing a fry off Jamie's plate. She nodded her head vigorously.

"Yeah. Yeah, of course. I'll print copies off after school for you guys."

"Excellent." Enzo snatched another fry. "I'll be right back."

I watched him get up and go, leaving me with Jamie and Ethan. "Where's he going?"

"To get you something to eat." Ethan gave me a quick smile. I nodded. If nothing else, they all wanted to make sure I ate.

"So... Jamie, are you trying out for the musical?" Ethan's hand was still on mine. Jamie's eyes shot down to it quickly before she glanced at me.

"Uh, no. That's not really my thing. I might do some backstage stuff and grab the photos for the yearbook, though."

Ethan nodded. "Cool. I like photography."

I listened as Ethan engaged Jamie in conversation about her camera equipment. She visibly relaxed as the conversation moved to which lenses were best to use.

Knowing nothing about photography, I tuned them out, opting to look over at the crew table again. Cole was in a deep conversation with Fox. They looked mad about something. Cole's face reddened as he said something to Fox which ended with Fox snarling something back at him. A moment later, as if sensing me, they both peered in my direction. It wasn't a pleasant gaze that met me either. Instead, Cole got to his feet, shoving his tray at Fox and grabbing the notebook, before stalking away. Something was wrong. I glanced at Fox to find him still staring at me. Not sure what to do, I turned back to Ethan and Jamie, who were going on about which was better: digital or film.

"Both have their uses. I just like the old school feel to developing the film," Ethan said, squeezing my hand again. "In fact, I'd love if Rosalie would sit for me one of these days."

"Huh?"

He smiled. "I was saying I want to take photos of you. What do you think? Will you let me take your picture?"

Jamie sat back in her seat, curiosity on her face. I cleared my throat and let the wobbly smile spill onto my lips.

"The only answer I can give is yes."

Ethan let out a soft laugh and leaned in and spoke in a low voice only for my ears.

"You can choose to say no as well. I won't be upset. I'm not the others with their ridiculous notions. I want you to choose."

"You do?"

He nodded, a serious look on his face.

"They do too, but they won't admit it."

I rolled my eyes at that. "Yeah, right."

"Trust me. They do."

We didn't get to finish the conversation because Enzo showed up with a tray of food and sat down next to us again.

"What'd I miss?"

"Only the most confusing situation I've ever been in." Jamie shook her head.

I gave her the same brittle smile I'd been giving her for the past week.

Confusing didn't even begin to cut it.

CHAPTER 15

"OK. What songs have you picked out for your audition?" Enzo sank down onto the worn velvet upholstered chair in his finished basement.

I appraised the area, taking in all the stuff that decorated the place. Enzo's house was large, not quite like Cole's, but more like an actually lived-in space. His mom had even whipped up a dozen of chocolate chip cookies for us and brought them down before letting us know she had to run some errands.

"Earth to Rosalie," Enzo called out.

I snapped my attention from the bar and pool table and focused on him. He'd grabbed one of the guitars from its spot and had it propped up on his lap like he was going to play.

"Uh, I haven't picked one."

"Sunshine, you have what? Only a few weeks left to learn and get ready for this? What the hell have you been doing? Don't tell me it's been partying because I'd have seen you out and about."

I bit my bottom lip, not wanting to tell him I'd written a song for the audition but had gotten stuck on putting together the music for it. My focus had wandered in the past few weeks.

"Don't do that."

"Do what?" I crinkled my brows at him, releasing my lip.

"It drives me wild when you pull that lip between your teeth. It's hot as fuck."

Heat flooded my face at his words.

"Don't do that either." He chuckled, placing his guitar in its stand and getting to his feet. "That sweet, innocent look is even worse. It's what got you into trouble in the first place."

He moved to sit on the leather couch and patted his leg. "Come here."

I climbed to my feet and approached him nervously. I'd never been alone with Enzo before. Like the others, his reputation proceeded him. The memory of his crotch in my face in the locker room flooded my mind. While I hadn't gotten to actually see it, the thought he most definitely lived up to his *Italian Stallion* nickname jumped out at me.

Ethan was probably the only one without womanizer etched into his forehead.

"Sit on my lap."

I sat on his thighs, feeling completely awkward, butterflies hammering in my tummy. His warm hand rested on my lower back.

"Don't be scared," he murmured, rubbing my thigh with his other hand. "I'm not going to hurt you."

I swallowed, nodding.

"Talk to me. What do you want to do for your audition? I can play pretty much anything. My parents are big music buffs, so I've learned a thing or two."

"Why are you doing this?"

"Doing what?" He frowned at me, stopping the rubbing of my jean-clad thigh.

"Acting like you care." I stared at him, trying to gauge what he was thinking. He had a hell of a poker face though.

"Who says I'm acting? Is this your way of telling me I should try out for the play too?" His dark eyes twinkled with humor. I relaxed slightly.

"I just don't get what's happening. You guys acted like you were going to be so rotten to me."

"Have any of us been bad?"

I shrugged. "No. Not really. I mean, Cole is pretty dark, and Fox is an asshole, but you and Ethan have been tolerable."

Enzo chuckled as he went back to rubbing my thigh.

"Here's the thing, Sunshine. Fox is angry by nature. Cole is a fucking weirdo. Me and Ethan? We're the easy-going ones. But we're all best friends and balance one another out."

"Are you saying I shouldn't be afraid?"

"No." He shook his head. "I'm saying you can trust us to act accordingly."

"That doesn't seem like a good thing."

"Trust me, baby girl. It definitely is." He moved his hand from my thigh and pulled me closer to him. "I want to taste you."

I let out a soft whimper, our faces inches apart.

I didn't expect his next move. His lips met mine in a deep kiss, pushing through my barriers before I had time to recognize what was happening. I didn't kiss him back, confusion flooding through me.

"Kiss me, Sunshine," he whispered, kissing the corner of my lips. He shifted me on his lap, his growing erection apparent in his jeans. I swallowed hard, my breathing shaky as his grip on my thigh tightened.

"I don't know what's happening—"

"Anything you want. Just let go, and you can have it all."

"Are you recording me?"

He chuckled softly, placing another kiss on the edge of my lips. "If I am, it's for my eyes only."

A thrill of excitement raced through my body.

"I'm not like the others. I'll flat out tell you I want to be buried inside you."

"Jesus," I rasped as his lips moved to my neck.

"It's god, baby. Don't forget it."

CHAPTER 16

"Am I interrupting?" Cole's irritated voice huffed out as he entered the basement. Enzo's warm lips left my skin, leaving me feeling a lot more than hot and bothered. Hate was what I should've been practicing with the guys, but instead, I was all but panting to kiss Enzo back. I licked my lips, still tasting him on me. Enzo gave me a knowing smile, not looking the slightest bit perturbed at Cole barging in.

"You are," Enzo returned. "But I don't mind sharing."

My stomach twisted into a knot of excitement. Something was seriously wrong with my head. I wasn't this person. Or at least I hadn't been until they'd paid attention to me.

Cole cocked his head at us before moving to sit beside us on the couch. My heart thudded unevenly when he wrapped his arms around my midsection and tugged me onto his lap.

"Sharing, huh?" His blue eyes darkened as he drank me in. "What do you think, Rosebud? Feel like having some fun?"

I caught Enzo's look, not sure if this was a joke. Everything on his face assured me it wasn't.

"I-I'm not, I mean, I-I've never—"

"What?" Cole murmured, brushing his nose against my jaw and breathing in. "Been thoroughly fucked by two guys?"

I trembled on his lap, my heart nearly in my throat at his words.

"I've had a really bad day, Rosebud. Fucking you might make getting out of bed worth it."

I swallowed down my whimper as I squeezed my thighs together. *What the hell was happening to me?*

I hated them. I wanted them. I needed them. The emotions were conflicting, all of them leading to the same damn place I was trying to stay clear of: Giving in.

"It's OK to want, Sunshine. Our secret."

"You fuck boys need to knock it off," Fox growled, coming into the room with Ethan in tow.

I nearly jumped off Cole's lap, but he was quick to tighten his hold, keeping me in place.

"Aw, what's wrong, Fox? Bad day too?" Cole asked.

Enzo snickered beside him. Neither seemed bothered by the intrusion. *Me?* My face had to be flaming red. I was sure of it.

"Rosalie was just about to make mine better. I'm sure she'd help you out too if you asked nicely—"

"Fuck off," Fox snapped, flopping down into the green chair Enzo had vacated earlier.

Ethan sank down onto the matching leather sofa, offering me his kind smile. I ducked my head, trying to hide my embarrassment at what had nearly happened.

Not happened. I'd never...

I shut the argument up in my head, knowing damn well which side was going to win despite everything going on.

"Rosalie, get off Cole's lap and go sit next to Ethan." Fox glared at me.

I made to move, but Cole held me in place.

"What the hell is your problem?"

"Do I really need to tell you?"

Enzo laughed as Cole and Fox stared one another down.

"Fox, man. You know how to fix it. So why don't you—"

"Rosalie, I'm not fucking kidding. *Move.*" Fox silenced Cole with a glare. Cole released me, sighing as he rubbed his face in apparent frustration. Ethan slid over for me.

"I can actually leave." I cleared my throat as I sat on the edge of the sofa, my hands clasped as I stared at Fox. Being the apparent leader of the group, I knew it was him I needed to address. "I have some streaming to catch up on—"

"You're staying," Fox grunted.

I sighed and sat all the way back in my seat, knowing better than to argue with the grouch. Ethan got to his feet, went to the fridge, pulled out sodas, and handed them off to everyone before joining me back on the couch.

"What's the plan for Friday night?" Enzo asked, cracking open his drink. "Party at Cole's after the game or we waiting until Saturday night?"

"I was thinking we'd hit up Rocky's and hang out. Been a minute since we've been there." Cole sat forward and placed his drink on the coffee table. "We can hit my place after. My parents are gone to some conference in San Diego for the weekend."

"Nice." Fox nodded.

"You bringing Juliet?" It was Ethan who spoke up. I looked to Fox interestedly.

"I'm sure she'll show up. You know how she is."

"You guys still fighting?" Enzo asked.

"Yeah." Fox shifted in his seat, avoiding my eyes.

So there was trouble in paradise. I couldn't imagine a relationship with Juliet being easy, considering she was a grade-A bitch. The only reason I could figure Fox kept doing it was because of social status. He was the star quarterback. She was the cheer captain. That was just how high school politics worked. Of course, not even that would've kept me shackled to the bitch. I'd have chewed my own leg off to escape her claws.

"Did you tell her Rosalie is going to be a permanent fixture in our lives?" Cole took a drink and raised an eyebrow at Fox.

"Yeah. She didn't like it, which only fueled her fire for argument. She's still pissed over me letting Rosalie stay at our table at lunch."

"You know," I spoke up, clearing my throat. "All of this can be fixed by you deleting the video and letting me go. I'll be happy to stay out of your lives."

"Aw, Sunshine, don't be that way. We're only getting warmed up with you. No need to leave us high and dry." Enzo shook his head at me.

"You're not getting off that easily," Fox grumbled.

"I don't think she's easy to get off, dude. I think I should get to see how long it takes. For science." Enzo laughed, winking at me.

My face heated at his crude words, yet there was a tingle in my core, recalling how only a few minutes prior I'd ached for him and Cole.

"You know the rules," Fox snapped, the nearly-there calmness he'd had leaving again.

"Right. No one touches her until you—"

Cole was silenced by a pillow Fox chucked at him, nailing him in the face. He was quick to throw it back before getting to his feet.

I let out a gasp as he tugged me up and planted his mouth on mine. I tensed, but Cole grasped me tight, demanding I let go. Unable to fight it—or not wanting to—I let go and parted my lips for him. He dipped his tongue in, sampling me, before releasing me and looking over his shoulder at Fox, a smirk on his lips as Fox glowered back.

"You're really missing out. I'm not going to let a bit of her go to waste though. If you were smart, you wouldn't either." Cole pushed me back down into my seat. My breath whooshed out of me as I landed.

Instead of seeing the glare on Fox's face I expected, there was hunger as he stared back at me. Or at least I thought it was. He was quick to reel it in, the scowl replacing it.

"Whatever. I'm not into dumpster diving."

Cole let out a laugh as he went back to his seat. Ethan patted me on the thigh as Enzo shook his head. And Fox?

He shot me a glance, a pained expression in his eyes that he quickly wiped away as our gazes met.

"That's fine," I said, my voice strong. "I'm not into sloppy seconds."

The guys chortled at my response, Cole reaching over to give me a fist bump. A tiny smile tipped Fox's lips up as he shook his head, a glint in his eye that I recognized from when we were kids.

He was having fun.

CHAPTER 17

"I drove Rosalie here. You should take her home since you guys are neighbors." Enzo looked between me and Fox.

I'd been sitting around for hours watching them play video games and pool. Ethan pulled out his calculus halfway into it, and I'd helped him with his assignment, feeling good that he seemed to be getting what I was explaining to him. Even he looked excited if I had to gauge his feelings. Or maybe it was relief.

"Get your shit, Rosalie."

"I got my shit, Fox. Thanks." I got to my feet and grabbed my bag, waiting for him to further direct me.

"We'll work on your audition tomorrow. We can pick up where we left off." Enzo winked at me as he and Cole fist bumped.

A rush of excitement rocketed through me, and I ducked my head, not wanting them to know what they were doing to me. They laughed, making me think they knew exactly what they were doing.

Without saying anything more to me, Fox turned and walked toward the exit, which happened to be the walk-out door to the basement.

"Better catch up to him before he leaves you. If you stay here, we will definitely be picking up where we left off," Cole growled, his eyes dark as they roved over my body. I hesitated for a moment which made him and Enzo laugh.

"Bad girl, Rosebud," Cole admonished, that dark sparkle in his eyes I was growing accustomed to flashing at me.

"Rosalie! Now!" Fox shouted as he pushed the door open.

I rolled my eyes, but rushed after him, making sure to wave at Ethan on the way out who seemed to be finishing up his calculus with ease now.

The warm night air was a welcome relief as we entered the outdoors. I was able to clear my head for a moment. Fox moved to the passenger side of his Jeep and opened the door for me.

I gave him a surprised look which he returned with his steely one. Knowing better than to confront him on it, I climbed inside and put my seatbelt on. A moment later, he was behind the wheel, the engine rumbling beneath us.

The silence in the car was deafening as Fox drove us home. Not feeling like arguing with him, I stared out my window for what felt like forever, my mind fixated on what the hell was happening to me.

"How has everything been?"

I peeked over at Fox whose eyes were still on the road. "Good, I guess."

He snorted, shaking his head. "I guess I'd say so considering what I walked in on."

"What the hell do you even care for?" I shot back, balling my hands into fists. "You guys wanted me to do your bidding. You were the one instructing me on how to give Enzo a blowjob! If losing my virginity to one of you assholes is the goal, then what are you so mad about?"

A muscle worked along his jaw. "That's not how this works, Rosie."

"Oh yeah? How about you tell me how it works then, Mr. Tormentor? Explain it to me."

He shook his head again, not saying a word.

Sighing, I rolled my eyes at him. "That's what I thought. You don't even know how it works."

Before he could snap back, his phone went off.

"What?" he snarled into it. His face hardened as he listened to the caller. "I said no, Juliet. I'm tired of having this same conversation with you." He grew quiet.

Deciding the passing dark scenery beat listening to his conversation, I turned my attention back to the window. She was clearly upset and yelling at him. I couldn't make out her words though. Then again, I didn't give a shit.

Fox's thundering yell had me jumping in my seat and then clinging to the handle on the door as he weaved off the road into the gravel and slammed the Jeep into park. My head jerked forward, a gasp of fright escaping me as my seatbelt caught.

Fox got out of the Jeep, slamming the door behind him, his phone still pressed to his ear. My pulse thundered in my ears as I tried to reel in my nerves. He paced in front of the car, one hand holding his phone to his ear, the other running through his hair in frustration. A moment later, he stuffed the phone into his pocket, his back to me. I watched as he hauled in a deep breath and stared at the sky.

My heart went out to him for just a moment before I snapped it back. Fox didn't give a shit about me, so I shouldn't care about whatever the hell was going on with him. There was this tiny pull in my heart though when he hung his head before getting back into the car.

I braved a peek at him as he maneuvered back onto the road. We'd driven a mile or so when he finally spoke.

"I'm sorry I scared you."

I wasn't sure if I'd heard him correctly. "What?"

"I said I'm sorry." He glanced over at me. "Are you OK? I saw the seatbelt caught you." Something flashed in his blue eyes that I wasn't even sure he was capable of. Worry and concern clouded his gorgeous face.

"Yeah. I'll live."

He nodded as we fell into silence again for a few minutes until words tumbled from my mouth I couldn't help.

"Are you OK?"

"No," he answered, not looking at me.

I bit my bottom lip, contemplating my next question. "Do you want to talk about it?"

He was quiet, his Adam's apple bobbing. Just when I thought he was truly going to ignore me, he spoke. "Juliet hates you."

"I know."

He nodded before speaking again. "I hate you."

"Gee, don't sugarcoat it or anything," I snapped, folding my arms over my chest.

He whipped the Jeep into his driveway and put it in the park. I moved to grab the door handle and get the hell out of there, but he was quick to grab my arm, stopping me.

"Let me out, Fox."

"No," he whispered, his gaze flitting over my face.

I tried tugging my arm from his grasp, but he tightened his hold on me. "Fox, stop," I hissed, wincing as his hold became stronger. I glanced fearfully out at my house. All the lights were off which meant either my parents were out with the Mackenzies, their friends from down the street, or they were in bed. Either one didn't help me.

Fear coursed through me as Fox released my arm only to grasp my face with both hands.

"They all love you," he murmured.

I had no idea what he was talking about.

"Fox, let me go," I whispered as he continued to study my face. "You're hurting me." That wasn't a complete lie. His actions had been hurting me for years. And he was definitely terrifying me.

He shook his head. "I've been trying to, but I can't."

I tensed as he rested his forehead against mine. I didn't move as he fumbled with my rubber band before pulling my hair from its ponytail. It fell around us, and he breathed out a shaky breath as his fingers tangled through the curls.

"What are you doing?" My voice shook.

"I don't know anymore." He moved his forehead off mine then planted a fierce kiss to the center of it, his fingers still in my hair. "I just don't know."

CHAPTER 18

After Fox's strange display in his Jeep, he released me, leaving me stunned, before coming around to my door and opening it for me.

"Go home, Rosie," he murmured as I stepped into the night air. "Before I do something I regret." His gaze leveled on me.

I stared up at him, seeing no emotion on his face.

His hand moved out and cradled my cheek before he gently brushed my bottom lip with his thumb, his eyes locked on the movement.

"You have until the count of three, Rosie, before I hurt you."

"It's too late," I whispered. Then I swallowed down the scared whimper in my throat, unsure what he meant by hurt me, but not wanting to find out. I pulled myself from him and scampered to my house. When I chanced a look back before stepping into my foyer, he stood there, watching me in the dark.

I hurried inside, locking the door behind me, my heart hammering so hard I wasn't sure it would ever slow down.

I BARELY SLEPT, Fox's face in all my dreams. When morning finally rolled around, I went outside to find he'd left already. Getting into my car and driving to school relaxed me. I parked in the back lot and walked into the school. The guys were gathered where they always did, all of them looking cheerful. With the exception of Fox, of course. He was still brooding.

Ethan scribbled in a black notebook, Cole reading over his shoulder, a grin plastered on his face. I had the feeling it was the same notebook I'd seen with the guys before, but them sharing a notebook seemed odd. I was probably overthinking the entire thing.

"Sunshine!" Enzo called out, a grin spreading onto his lips when he saw me. "Come here, baby girl."

Despite my attempt to not feel anything for the guys, my heart couldn't help but thrum excitedly in my chest as I stepped onto the sidewalk and made my way over to them, all their eyes locked on me.

"You look good today," Cole commented, his gaze sweeping over me as he stepped away from Ethan who snapped the notebook closed and stuffed it into his bag. "I could gobble you up."

I blushed at his words.

"Did you sleep well?" Ethan asked, concern on his face as he took me in.

I gave him a wobbly smile, glancing at Fox who stood still as a statue, his eyes fixed on me.

"Not really," I admitted.

"Got you worked up too much last night, huh?" Cole winked at me, making me flush.

Enzo reached out and gave my ponytail a playful tug.

"You were supposed to pick me up this morning," Juliet's angry voice cut in before I could answer as she stormed over.

Fox tore his eyes away from me and stared at her like he didn't have a care in the world. "Must have slipped my mind."

That set her off. "What the hell is the matter with you?" Juliet snarled, getting in Fox's face even more.

I backed away awkwardly as his gaze roved over to me. She followed it, her glare hardening.

"You've got to be fucking kidding me," she hissed, advancing on me.

Enzo wrapped his arm around my midsection and pulled me to him.

"I'd step the fuck back if I were you," Cole growled, moving to stand in front of me and Enzo, effectively blocking Juliet.

Juliet halted in her tracks, her eyes narrowing.

"Is she fucking both of you now?" Her voice was like ice as her gaze swiveled to Fox's. "Or is it the three of you?"

"Juliet, you're making a fool out of yourself," Fox finally spoke, his voice soft and impassive.

"You're the one fucking freakshow—"

"You know I'm not," Fox snapped back at her.

"Come on, Sunshine. Let's let the lovers quarrel," Enzo said, giving me a squeeze.

Fox shot a glare in our direction which made Cole chuckle.

"Good luck, Fox. Oh, and Juliet?" Cole called out as we moved away from them. She tore her stare from Fox's and focused on Cole. "Fox isn't fucking Rosalie. Not *yet*, at least."

Juliet's face reddened as Fox locked his eyes on mine. A shiver raced through me as a hunger flashed through those baby blues. He didn't bother correcting Cole who only laughed in his dark way while falling in step with me, Enzo, and Ethan.

"You really enjoy screwing everything up, don't you?" I hissed at Cole as we walked away from Fox and Juliet who were now having it out on the lawn. I managed to push the idea of Fox and me out of my mind.

Cole shrugged. "I'm just waiting for Fox to make his move. Sometimes he needs a little push."

"I don't know what the hell you're talking about but don't drag me into your drama. I already have a hard enough time with Juliet. I'd appreciate if you wouldn't make it worse."

"She's right. Juliet is a bitch," Ethan piped up.

I shot him a grateful look for sticking with me. He smiled back sweetly, giving me a wink.

"I'm with Ethan. Fox should've ditched Juliet ages ago. This is the kick he needs to do it," Enzo chimed in.

"Not at my expense," I argued, the guys flanking me on the walk to my locker. Students stared as we passed by, the nerd escorted by three of the school's hottest and most powerful guys.

"Your expense?" Cole laughed. "Baby, you're going to thank us when this is all over."

"I'll only be thanking you if the video disappears."

"Hey, uh, Rosalie?" Jamie called out, stopping before she reached us.

I turned my attention on her, a pang in my chest. We'd barely spoken since the guys started hanging around, or rather, forcing themselves into my life.

"Hey."

"Uh." Her gaze darted between the three guys. When none of them made a move to leave, she swallowed and focused on me. "I was wondering if you wanted to catch up after school. Things have been hectic lately." Her gaze swept among the guys.

I knew what she was saying. Things had gone to shit since the guys' arrival into my life.

Before I answered, I looked to the guys.

"You should go," Ethan offered. "You really helped me out last night with that calculus. I think I might be getting it."

"Yeah, what I want has to wait anyway," Cole mused, his eyes sliding over my body, making me blush.

"We can meet up after you catch up with..." Enzo looked at Jamie. "What's your name again?"

Jamie flushed. "Jamie."

"Right, Jamie. Sorry, doll. I'm terrible with names." Enzo let out a good-natured laugh. "You cool with that?" Enzo cocked his head at me.

"Yeah. Yeah, that sounds good." I let out a breath of relief at the small amount of freedom given to me.

"Awesome. I'll see you at lunch?" Jamie questioned.

I hated having to do it, but I looked at the guys once more for their answer.

Cole smirked at me. I rolled my eyes at him and nodded to Jamie. "Yeah, see you at lunch."

Jamie cast one last confused look among us all before leaving us alone.

"You guys are ruining my life," I muttered, opening my locker.

"That's the point," Cole said.

"No, it's not. Don't listen to him." Ethan elbowed Cole who grinned widely.

"How much longer do I have to do this? Like, I want my life back. Now I'm a freakshow who has you guys' attention. People are saying shit—"

"Sunshine, it's all good shit from what I've heard," Enzo broke in.

"The hell it is!" I yelped, staring at him in disbelief. "I'm supposedly sleeping with you and Cole—"

"And you don't want to? Because last night suggested something else entirely." Cole smirked knowingly at me. "So what's really the problem?"

"You know what the problem is." I turned on him, furious. "You know I don't want any of this."

"Again with your damn lies, Sunshine. Ease up on yourself. It's perfectly fine to want us to run a train on you." Enzo chuckled, tugging my ponytail.

I flushed furiously at his words, feeling like dirt in the process, even though everything inside of me was begging to admit his words held truth.

"Guys," Ethan sighed. "Knock it off. She's clearly uncomfortable."

"Are you kidding me, Ethan? You want to be her first?" Cole's grin widened as he teased Ethan.

"Be better than you shit heads. At least, I wouldn't scare her to death."

"No, you'd probably spout sonnets to her and make her dinner," Enzo joked.

"Can we not talk about any of you screwing me? I'd like to not add orgy to my list of offenses here at this school."

Cole grinned again. "Is that what it would be?"

"Shut up," I muttered, shoving away from them. I was grateful they didn't follow, their laughter enough to make me shake my head, pushing down the excitement in my chest at the prospect of their words and promising myself I'd never let it happen.

CHAPTER 19

I stared at the mess of shaving cream and toilet paper on my locker at the end of the day. People snickered as they passed by. I didn't need two guesses to know who'd done it. Sighing, I opened my door to be bombarded with packing peanuts. Laughter erupted around me as I stood up to my knees in the styrofoam mess.

"Bitch," I hissed, kicking my foot out.

"Could be worse."

I snapped my attention around to find Ian standing behind me.

"Ian."

"Rosalie," his voice was cold. "You're really making a name for yourself around here. You can fuck the football team but not someone who gave a damn."

"What are you talking about?" I demanded.

He scoffed. "Don't play fucking stupid with me. We both know what you've been doing with the horsemen when no one is around."

"I haven't done shit with them," I snapped back, swallowing down the lie. OK, so maybe I'd kissed a couple of them and had weird feelings, but that wasn't enough to accuse me of screwing them all, or as Enzo had so eloquently put it, letting them run a train on me.

"Then why the fuck did I get cornered by Evans, De Luca, and Scott?"

"Maybe because you're an asshole?"

Ian punched the locker next to my head, his face contorted in anger. I flinched as he leaned into me.

"*Wrong*, Rosalie," he hissed at me. "You told your boys about what I said."

I shook my head, fear coursing through me. Ian had changed. No longer was he the playful friend I'd once had. In his place was an angry, jealous monster. He might even be more hell-bent on making me miserable than the guys were.

"Don't fucking lie to me." He'd backed me against the locker beside my own. "Do you know what they said to me as they beat me?"

I shook my head, my mouth dry.

"That you belong to them, and if I said a word about you to anyone, they'd kill me."

I shivered beneath his words. "You drugged me. You're lucky that's all that happened to you."

"So don't stand there and tell me you aren't fucking them. I want what's *mine*, Rosalie. I mean it. And if I don't get it, I'll have to take drastic measures. Starting with Jamie."

He pushed away from me, giving me a look that said all I needed to know. He was serious.

"Tell them about this and find out what happens."

He turned and stalked away, leaving me standing there, shaking.

Ian hadn't gone away. He'd only morphed into a bigger problem.

"Look who it is," Juliet simpered in the locker room. I eyed her apprehensively as she sashayed over to me. "If it isn't the little home-wrecker herself."

"I haven't done anything."

Juliet snorted as she stopped in front of me. "You were with Fox last night."

I shook my head, not in the mood to deal with her shit even more now since I had Ian to worry about.

"I wasn't *with* Fox last night. I was *with* Enzo, and Fox and the rest of the guys showed up at his place. And if you want to know what went down, they played video games and pool while I helped Ethan with his homework."

Juliet narrowed her eyes at me. "Fox said he gave you a ride home."

I rolled my eyes. "Fox is my neighbor. It only made sense. If it helps, he's an asshole."

Juliet took a dangerous step toward me, closing the small space between us. "If I hear you even came close to touching what's mine, I *will* wreck you."

"I'm sure you will. But right now, I have bigger things to worry about, so take your insecurity elsewhere." I pushed past her, my heart wild in my chest from the confrontation.

Luckily, she didn't try to stop me. Even at the end of class, she didn't look twice at me, opting to dress quickly and leave with her friends. That didn't mean they didn't whisper and shoot me dirty looks, but hey, as long as I wasn't being pushed around, they could do whatever they wanted.

"Sunshine!" Enzo called out, jogging down the hall toward me. People scurried out of his way. "Hey."

"What?"

"What time are you thinking about stopping by tonight?"

"Um, don't you decide that?"

He grinned. "Not tonight. It's up to you."

I cocked an eyebrow at him. "I thought you guys were in charge—"

"Oh, baby girl, we are, but it's nice to give you a little room to move your cute little elbows in. We want you to enjoy this as much as we do."

"That's not the impression I got," I muttered.

He grinned wider at me.

"And what exactly is *this*?" I studied his face for a moment, but he didn't give anything away. "I mean, it started off a few weeks ago as you guys acting like you were going to make me miserable—"

"And we're not," he cut in.

I nodded, biting my bottom lip.

"Mm, baby. Don't do that," Enzo warned, his eyes darkening.

I released my lip immediately.

"You're not, or at least, it's gotten better. But with what happened b-between me a-and you and Cole last night—"

"Did you like it?" His eyes swept over me. "You didn't kiss me back, but I didn't get the vibe you hated it."

I swallowed and stared up at his looming form.

"It's OK to like it, baby. We liked it or we wouldn't have done it."

"I'm just confused."

"I know." He sighed, running his fingers through his dark hair. "Fucking Fox."

"What does he have to do with it?"

"Everything." Enzo stepped closer. "This is about more than a video, Sunshine. It's about you. Me. Everyone. The video is just the bargaining chip to get what we want."

"But what *do* you want?"

"You know what we want. We told you."

Me. They wanted me.

He nodded, knowing damn well I knew what they wanted. *But why?* Enzo answered my unspoken question.

"Because we can, baby. Because we can."

CHAPTER 20

"It feels like forever since we've gotten to hang out," Jamie exclaimed as we slid into a booth at Rocky's, the local teen hangout later that evening.

"For sure." My phone buzzed, and I picked it up to see a message from Cole.

Cole: Enzo said you're going to his place. I'll see you there.

My heart thrashed in my chest.

"Rosalie, you OK?" Jamie called out.

"Uh, yeah. Yeah."

"You look like you're going to pass out." Jamie gave me a concerned look. "Did you get a bad message?"

"No. Um, it's just Cole."

"Oh." She sat back in her seat. "What's going on with you guys? One minute you hate them, and the next Cole is kissing you in the hall, Enzo is walking with you like you're a couple, and Ethan is sitting with us. Are the rumors true?"

I knew the rumors. That I was getting it on with them. When it started, the idea seemed far-fetched. *Now?* I wasn't sure what I'd do if it came down to it.

"What happened at that party?"

"Nothing." I gave her a forced smile. "I kissed Cole. A few people saw it."

"OK, but he's still around. Are you guys a couple?"

"No." I shook my head. "We're just friends."

Jamie rolled her eyes. "Whatever. I guess you don't want to tell me."

"There's nothing to tell," I answered helplessly. "It's just stupid shit they get off on doing."

"Rosalie, these guys are fire hot and get around with lots of girls, but *something* is up. I'm so worried about you. You hated them. They hated you right back. Now you're kissing on one of them and-and god knows what else with the others." She gave me a look filled with desperation. I frowned, her words making me feel dirty. "Just, if they're *making* you do this, tell me. Tell someone. We could help you—"

"Jamie, I'm fine," I murmured. "I'm just having a little bit of fun."

"Answer this. Have you screwed any of them?"

I shook my head, my curls bouncing with the movement. "No. I-I've kissed Cole and Enzo. It was a heat of the moment thing. A mistake. Nothing else. I'm fine."

Jamie's lips parted in shock at my admission, but she quickly righted her face before plowing on. "They have a rep. I want you to be safe. The Rosalie I know wouldn't just make out with a guy. He'd need to sweep her off her feet first."

I swallowed thickly. "But that never got me anywhere. I-I'm fine. Really, Jamie."

"Fine," she sighed. "But you know I'm here for you, right?"

I nodded, swallowing the lump in my throat. I hated that I had to keep all of this from her. "I know."

My phone buzzed again with another text from Cole.

Cole: I want to finish what we started.

With shaking hands, I sent off a reply.

Rosalie: I can't.

Cole: Rosebud, don't play me like that. We're both adults here. I'll see you tonight.

I blew out a breath and gave Jamie a shaky smile. Everything in her expression told me she was worried for me. Hell, *I* was worried for me. The feelings surfacing weren't of hate. *That* terrified me.

"Ian's been acting weird." Jamie frowned.

"Yeah?"

"Yeah. I don't know what his problem is. He hardly talks to me anymore. Do you think he's seeing someone?"

I shook my head. "No. Maybe he's just busy."

"Has he talked to you?"

"No." I hated the lie on my tongue but forced out a smile. "The guys sort of intimidate people."

Jamie nodded, looking stricken.

I had to change the subject. "Are you going to work backstage for the musical?"

"I think so," she nodded, relaxing. "I talked to Mr. Peters and asked him if maybe I could help out with producing as well. I think it would be a blast."

"I think you'd be great at it," I offered.

"Thanks." She gave me a quick smile. "Have you told your parents you're auditioning?"

I grimaced. "No. You know how my dad is. He wants me at Pendleton. He thinks my music and acting are a waste of time and energy."

"You have to tell them when you get the part, Rosalie."

I smiled wistfully. "*If*. If I get it. I think I'm going to just try for a chorus part. I don't even know if I should go for it at this point. If my dad finds out, he'll be pissed I'm taking time away from studying to do it. Hell, I've never even sung for my parents. You're the only one who's heard me aside from Mr. Peters freshman year when I auditioned. I mean, what if I do suck—"

"Rosalie." Jamie fixed her stern gaze on me. "You're a grown ass woman now. An adult. Do what you want. It's your life. You could literally get into the college of your dreams with this musical. I know Pendleton isn't your dream. I'm not stupid, Sis." She fixed me with her no-nonsense look. "Mayfair could see it and give you a full ride. They have the best music program on this side of the country. I just don't understand why you don't try for it. You're good. No. *Freaking incredible.* Don't doubt yourself. We've been friends so long. You're my favorite starving artist. Do this *one* thing for yourself. You owe it to yourself."

I nodded, swallowing the lump in my throat. "If I get into Mayfair and can't get a full ride, Dad won't pay for it. He already told me. I *have* to go to Pendleton. I won't be able to afford college on my own if I don't."

Jamie let out a sigh of frustration and shook her head. "You need to believe in yourself a little bit more, Rosalie. It drives me nuts that you don't. I happen to know Mayfair scouts are coming. Word has it, Juliet is aiming to try out too."

"What?" I blanched at the information. "Why the hell would she try out? She's never done one of our theater productions in her life!" The information set my blood to boiling.

Jamie shook her head. "It's Juliet. It's a spotlight. If she can get in it, she will. You know that."

"Bitch probably can't even sing," I muttered, folding my arms over my chest.

Jamie grinned. "Maybe she can't. It'll be hilarious to watch the audition though. Think positive."

"You're right." At least, I hoped Jamie was right.

We sank into normal conversation after that, laughing like nothing shitty was going on in my life. When it was time for me to leave, I hugged Jamie goodbye.

"Be safe, Rosalie. I'm worried about you."

"I know," I murmured, pulling away. "I'll be OK."

She gave me a wry smile and nodded. "If you're not, I'm going to kick some ass."

I grinned at her. "I know you will."

She smiled back and bid me farewell before I climbed into my car and backed out of the parking lot. My heart was in my throat as I drove to Enzo's, wondering what was going to happen. I almost decided to not go but thought better of it. The last thing I needed was them upset with me.

My anxiety over the audition grew. I knew if I got the part, I'd have to tell my parents. It would be in the local papers. They'd find out about it whether I wanted them to or not.

"You're late," Enzo commented, pulling his front door open. He was dressed in basketball shorts and a tank top, his muscles on display. I quickly averted my eyes from him when he caught me staring. "Come on in, you little minx."

I followed him inside and down to his basement.

"Where are your parents?"

"Out. They won't be home until tomorrow. Why? Something on your mind?"

"No," I denied, my anxiety kicking up a notch.

Enzo winked at me as we entered the basement. "Don't worry, Sunshine. We're just going to work on your audition. For now, anyway."

I didn't say anything as I sat on his couch. He pulled the guitar onto his lap and gave me an expectant look.

"Did you bring the song you were working on?"

I nodded mutely, handing him the music sheets from my bag. He rifled through them quickly, muttering to himself before grabbing a pen and scratching more notes on the page. I watched in awe as he worked. I had no idea he wrote music. The idea should've came to me sooner considering he had a recording booth tucked away in the corner of the basement behind all his musical equipment.

"You know Fox plays guitar and drums, right?"

"I knew he drummed. I can hear him sometimes."

Enzo nodded thoughtfully. "He picked up the guitar a few years ago. We could probably start a band if we wanted to. Even Cole plays bass, and Ethan is a piano whore by order of his parents."

"I had no idea."

Enzo chuckled, placing the sheet music down and adjusting his guitar on his lap. "We'd have started a band already, but you know how that goes. We never seem to have the time."

"I bet. Tormenting people takes a lot of energy."

Enzo chuckled, shaking his head as he strummed the first chord to my song. "Sing for me, songbird. Let's hear those pipes."

"I've never sung for anyone before—"

"And yet you want to be in the musical? Come on, babe. Time to get you out of that protective cocoon you're wrapped in." He strummed the chord again. "I finished the music for you. Just sing for me."

I reached out and looked through what he'd done, impressed.

"Not bad, huh?"

"Not bad at all," I murmured. "I'll do it. But if you laugh at me, I'll break your guitar."

"Cross my heart. I won't laugh," he answered solemnly, strumming his guitar again.

I waited for the intro for a moment before opening my mouth and singing the first line. Enzo stopped strumming and stared open-mouthed at me.

"What? You said you wouldn't laugh," I mumbled, feeling my face heat.

"And I'm not. What the hell was that?"

"Singing?" I fidgeted with a sheet of music, staring back at Enzo worriedly. *What if I did suck and Jamie had only been nice because we were friends?*

"Jesus, Sunshine. You've got an amazing set of pipes! Why the hell haven't you done anything with them?"

I shrugged, my face growing hotter at his compliment. I let out the breath I'd been holding, relief flooding through me.

He shook his head and strummed again. "OK. Don't stop. All the way through."

I nodded, launching into the first line again as he played along. I thought it would be hard to get through it, but we flowed together easily, our sounds perfectly in tune. We ran through the song what felt like a million times, Enzo tweaking it in places, trying it out, then tweaking it another way if he didn't like it. Despite how playful Enzo was, he took music seriously. By the end of our practice, we had a polished song on our hands.

"Amazing." Enzo put his guitar down, grinning. "You're one hell of a woman, Sunshine."

I ducked my head at the compliment which only caused his grin to widen.

"Come here."

I got nervously to my feet and moved to where he was sitting on his chair.

"I want you to straddle me."

"What?" I squeaked out.

"You heard me. And then you're going to kiss me because you refused to do it last time. Do you understand?"

I nodded mutely and moved to him, shutting off the voice in my head that screamed for me to just go home and take a cold shower. He stared up at me, waiting for me to do what he'd instructed. With a shaking breath, I sank down on him, my legs on either side of his muscular thighs, our centers aligned.

"So fucking hot," he rasped, tilting my chin up so we were eye-to-eye. "Now I want you to kiss me."

I stared at him for a moment, seeing no teasing in his dark eyes. I closed my own, waiting for his lips to meet mine. When it didn't happen, I opened my eyes to find him staring at me still.

"I-I'm ready."

"So am I. Just waiting for you to make your move."

"Oh," I answered dumbly. I wiggled on his lap, and he let out a groan.

"Fuck, don't do that or I'll take you right here on the fucking floor, Sunshine."

Tingles rocketed to my core at his words. Pulling in a short breath, I leaned forward, not bothering to fight my conscience on the matter. I knew I should stop. It didn't matter if I was supposed to say yes to every request. No wasn't in my mind or on my tongue. I wanted it despite every damn thing the matter with it.

My lips met his in a soft touch. The tingles hit their target, causing me to move against him. Enzo didn't waste time in cupping my ass and hauling me as close as possible, his hardness grinding against my center.

Enzo kissed playfully, teasing and nipping at my lips as his hands moved up beneath my t-shirt, skirting the edge of my bra.

He broke the kiss off, leaving me breathless, only to move his lips south, kissing along my jaw and down my neck. I lolled my head to the side, my breathing coming in small gasps as pleasure flooded through me. I wasn't this girl. But damn, did I like her.

A second set of hands came from behind and cradled my face. I opened my eyes to see Cole smiling down on me. He had to have come in while we were lost in one another. If it bothered Enzo, he made no qualms about it as his lips met my collarbone. Cole tilted my head back, planting his lips on mine in a slow, deep kiss that made my toes curl. I rocked against Enzo as I whimpered against Cole's lips.

"Such a bad girl," Cole growled in my ear.

I shivered at his words. A moment later, Enzo had my shirt off, leaving me straddling him in my lacy, pink bra.

"Fuck, you're delicious," Enzo appraised as he kissed his way back to my lips. Cole let out a dark chuckle that made the wanting growing in my core intensify.

Cole removed my rubber band, letting my curls free fall around me. He backed away as Enzo continued his onslaught of kisses on my body.

"What are you doing?" I rasped as Cole trained his phone on me.

"Recording you."

"Why? Stop." I scrambled to break away from Enzo, but he held me to him.

"Don't worry, Sunshine. This one is just for us. I promise."

"No," I whimpered. My vision grew blurry as tears filled my eyes. "Don't record this. Please."

"Rosebud, you have to trust me on this." Cole leaned in and kissed my lips in a manner uncharacteristically gentle for him. "Relax. I promise I'll delete it. Just do what you're doing. I've been recording since I walked into the room ten minutes ago."

I swallowed the lump in my throat as Enzo cupped one of my

breasts through my bra. Squeezing my eyes closed, I let him touch me, trying to push the idea of the camera out of my head as Enzo tugged my bra straps off my shoulders.

"Easy, Enzo," Cole instructed. "You know the rules."

"I want to fuck the rules and her," Enzo grunted as he shifted his hips beneath me, his erection hitting all the right places through his basketball shorts.

I let out a soft moan at the pressure building within me.

Desperate to tumble over the peak of euphoria, I ground myself against Enzo's hardness, my breathing short and raspy.

"Fuck," Enzo hissed. "Cole."

I wasn't sure why he was calling out to Cole, but it didn't take long to find out. Cole tugged me off Enzo's lap, causing me to stumble on my feet.

"Wha—?"

Cole tossed the phone to Enzo, who was breathing hard, before lifting me up. My legs instinctively wrapped around his waist as he brought us to the couch and placed me on it on my back, his hard dick positioned against my aching center.

Cole rocked against me, the heavy material of our jeans rubbing against my clit.

"Cole," I moaned against his lips as his forehead pressed to mine, his hips rocking with mine in a perfect rhythm.

"Tell me you want it," Cole growled, picking up his pace.

My eyes practically rolled back in my head. "I-I want it," I managed to say breathlessly. "Please."

Cole slowed down his movements, making me groan in protest.

"Easy, baby. I want it too." Cole placed a kiss on my lips. "But we can't."

"What?" I sputtered out as his movements stopped.

He chuckled and looked up to Enzo who was sitting across from us, phone still pointed in our direction.

"You hear that, Fox? She wants it."

Fox? What the hell did he have to do with any of it?

Cole moved off me and tugged me up onto his lap.

"When this happens for real, Rosebud, you're going to thank us that we stopped in this moment because we'll blow your fucking mind with the real thing." Cole's soft voice in my ear sent a shockwave of anticipation through my body. I sagged against him, my body still wired from nearly orgasming. One more hip grind from Cole, and I'd have soaked my panties.

"Send the video," Cole instructed.

I whipped my head in Enzo's direction, horrified. "No!" I called out, tumbling to the floor as I struggled to get to Enzo before he sent the video to wherever it was going.

Cole snatched me up, holding me back as Enzo thumbed out a quick text.

"Enzo! Please! Don't send that!"

He ignored me and pressed a final button before looking up at me, a serene smile on his face.

"Easy, Sunshine. It's going to Fox."

CHAPTER 21

After the night at Enzo's, I curled up in bed, my mind troubled. They'd sent the video to Fox. I hadn't heard anything from him, so I assumed no news was good news. However, Fox was more dangerous when he was silent.

I rolled over in bed, unable to sleep. My phone buzzing on my nightstand had me sitting up and reaching for it, wondering if Cole and Enzo were going to taunt me with the video like they were doing with the other one.

Fox: Can I call you?

I stared down at my phone in stupefied silence. *Fox wanted to call me? And he was asking for permission?*

Fox: I can't sleep.

With shaky hands, I texted him back.

Rosalie: Call me.

I held my breath, waiting for his phone call. A moment later, my phone buzzed in my hand, his name on the screen. Hauling in a deep breath, I answered.

"Hello?"

"Rosalie," Fox's deep voice greeted me.

"Hey." I stared down at my blanket, unsure what to say to him.

"I wanted to talk to you about Enzo."

I swallowed thickly. "OK."

"He told me you guys worked on a song for your audition."

I breathed out slowly, my anxiety dying down. "Oh. Yeah. He helped me to finish writing it today."

Fox grew quiet for a moment before he cleared his throat. "I'll play guitar for you for your audition if you want."

I pulled the phone away from my ear and stared down at it dumbfounded. I wasn't sure if I'd heard him correctly.

"What?" I asked when I put the phone back to my ear.

"I'll play guitar for you," he repeated.

"Oh. Um, OK. I guess if you want."

"I do."

There was an awkward silence.

"I can get the music to you—"

"I already have it."

"OK. That works."

We were quiet for a moment before he cleared his throat. "How are classes going?"

I frowned. *Was he drunk?* He never spoke to me, at least not in such a nice capacity.

"They're OK. Physics sucks."

"I bet. That's why I don't take it."

"Well, you probably wouldn't be able to handle it anyway," I retorted, biting my lip after the words came out.

Fox laughed a deep, genuine laugh at my words. "You're probably right."

I smiled, relaxing. "I'm surprised you called me."

"Me too." He grew quiet once more. "The guys really like you."

"Surprisingly, I like them too. Most of the time, anyway."

Fox chuckled. "Yeah, they can be pains in the ass sometimes."

"I can think of a few instances."

Fox cleared his throat. We both knew I was referring to the blackmailing.

"Any issues with Ian?"

I didn't answer right away. *What was I supposed to say?* Anything I did say would end up with Ian's face smashed in again and him spilling our secret to Jamie in retaliation.

"No." I swallowed down my anxiety. "Everything's OK."

"Good."

"I know you hurt him."

Fox chuckled, this time chills coursed through me. "He deserved it. He used you. He *drugged* you, Rosie. He's a piece of shit."

"I could say the same thing about you guys. You used me."

"This is different."

"How?" I whispered, desperate for answers. Needing him— needing them—to be different.

"Rosalie, come to the window."

I blinked rapidly. He switched gears so fast.

"Now," he commanded softly.

Knowing better than to defy him, I got to my feet, shuffled to my window, and pushed the curtains back to find a shirtless Fox sitting in his window seat, staring out at me. I slid my window open as he did the same and peered back at him.

"What are you doing?" I called out.

"I don't fucking know anymore," he answered, a stricken expression on his face. "Going crazy, I think."

"I heard I'm a freak. I'm sure crazy is part of that. Maybe I can help?"

Even with the distance between us, I could see the pain reflecting in his eyes.

"I think you might make it worse."

"You won't know until you try," I offered, my heart going out to him.

He looked so sad as he stared back at me. "That's the problem. I'm terrified of trying."

"Why?"

"Because I've spent years avoiding everything about it. And now that I have everything in place, I'm not sure I can go through with it."

"I know we've been apart for a long time, Fox, but do you

remember when we'd go to the old tree fort in the woods behind our houses? Do you remember when we were telling ghost stories and I said I was scared to go to sleep? Do you remember what you told me?"

Fox let out a soft, sad chuckle, resting his head against his windowsill. "How could I forget. I told you I'd chase all the monsters away."

I nodded sadly, tears springing to my eyes.

"The same stands true for me. I'd do it for you. Even now."

"Oh, Rosie," he sighed, closing his eyes. When he opened them, I could make out the sheen of tears in them, a mirror of my own. My heart ached for whatever he was going through.

"I don't know what's going on, Fox, but I'm here if you want to talk."

He looked down at his hands.

"I should let you go."

"If you want. I was in bed anyway—"

"No. I mean, I should delete the video and set you free."

My heart kicked wildly in my chest at the prospect of freedom. *Did that mean the other guys would go too?* Panic set in at the realization that I was beginning to enjoy our moments together, even when they were being jerks.

"Are you going to?"

"I should." He picked a piece of fuzz on his pajama bottoms. "I need to sleep, Rosie. Thanks for the talk."

"You're welcome," I answered softly as he gave me another sad smile.

"I'll see you tomorrow. Sweet dreams."

"Night, Fox."

He closed the window and shut the curtains behind him, leaving me to sit there wondering what the hell was happening to my enemy. Or was he my friend?

CHAPTER 22

"Party this Friday, Rosalie?"

I looked up from my notes. Ethan stood over my table in the library.

"Don't you guys have a game on Friday?"

"We do. We're all going to Cole's after."

"Well," I licked my lips. "Do I *have* to go?"

Ethan pulled the chair out next to me and sat down.

"I'd really *like* you to go."

"The last party didn't work out so well for me. I think I'll pass."

"Don't make me use my power to get you to come hang out with me." Ethan tucked a piece of hair behind my ear.

"I just don't want there to be any problems, Ethan. I'm really trying to get through all this stuff with as little damage as possible."

He grew quiet for a moment. "I understand. But I haven't had a chance to hang out with you aside from the calculus stuff and with the guys. It would be nice to have you on *my* arm for a change."

I studied him for a moment. Ethan was definitely the sweet one of the group. He wasn't as loud as the others either. And he was right—I hadn't spent much time with him.

"OK. I'll go but only for a little bit."

He grinned at me. "We'll have a great time."

I smiled back at him and placed my pencil on my notebook. "Hey, can I ask you something?"

"Anything."

"Is there something going on with Fox? He seems weird lately."

"There's always something going on with Fox. You'll have to be more specific."

I launched into telling him the conversation I'd had with Fox. Ethan sighed and shook his head.

"Fox is just, I don't know…Fox. One minute he's laughing, and the next he's pissed off. It's gotten a lot worse since you came into the picture."

"And that's another thing," I pressed. "I came into the picture, but I don't know why."

The thought of using Ethan to get the video prodded at my mind. Ethan would definitely be the one I'd have to cling to. I knew Fox said he was thinking about deleting it. I also knew I was growing fond of the guys. But in my experience, the good in situations was short-lived, and it was a necessity to strike while I could before things went to a place they couldn't come back from. Ian was one of those places. He'd been lying low, but I knew he was waiting for something. I just didn't know what I was going to do when he made his move.

"I don't know, Rosalie. We get bored. We noticed you that day in the cafeteria. Hell, we'd noticed you before, but it was *that* day when you really captured our attention. When Cole mentioned it before everything went down with Juliet, Fox was against it. But then that shit happened, and he was the one to step up. It just sort of spiraled from there." He gave me a helpless shrug.

"Boredom isn't a reason to try to ruin someone's life."

"Has your life been ruined because of us?" Ethan's gaze swept over me, worry in them.

"Not entirely, but Fox said that was the plan."

Ethan nodded, looking over my shoulder, seemingly lost in thought. "Fox won't ruin you, Rosalie. He's a good guy. He asks us all the time how you're doing. He worries about you, even if you don't think he does. He lo..."

I shook my head. I wasn't so sure about that, nor was I willing to test the theory, despite wanting to believe deep down beneath all his anger, he was still the little boy I'd loved when we were kids.

THINGS SEEMED to be dying down at school with the guys. They'd released a lot of their control over me, but every now and then, one of them would snake their way over to remind me who was in charge. I was grateful I hadn't been forced to sit with them at their table, enjoying the fact Ethan had started sitting with me and Jamie at lunch. Today, Enzo had joined us too.

"Are you coming to the party tomorrow?" Ethan asked Jamie when there was a lull in our conversation.

"Um, I'm not sure. Am I allowed to?"

"I'm inviting you. And you're Rosalie's friend, so of course you can."

"OK." Jamie smiled widely, excitement in her eyes. "I can ask Ian—"

"We don't keep people out of parties, but we also don't encourage the assholes to come in," Enzo interrupted, sitting on my other side.

Jamie closed her mouth, but the look in her eyes told me she wanted to defend Ian.

"Well, I don't know if I can make it then. Ian asked me out, and we're supposed to meet at Rocky's for dinner before catching a movie."

"What?" I practically shouted. Enzo gave my thigh a quick squeeze to quiet me down.

"I should've told you sooner, Rosalie. I'm sorry." Jamie gave me a pleading look to forgive her. "I was about to give up on anything ever happening with him when he asked me out."

I forced a smile on my face. "Are you sure you want to go out with him?"

"What? You've been telling me for ages to just ask him."

"I know. But do you want a serious relationship? We're in our senior year and all—"

"Rosalie, you know how much I like him. What the hell is the matter with you? Why do you want me to tell him no?" Her gaze volleyed between me and the guys. "Not everyone can screw around with multiple guys. Some of us prefer the ones who are more committed." She got to her feet, her face red.

I opened and closed my mouth several times at her outburst.

"We can't all be you, Rosalie, with your perfect life and screwing the entire football team." She turned on her heel and stormed away.

"Jamie, wait!" I called out, attempting to go after her. Enzo grabbed my wrist and held me in my seat.

"Let her go. She needs to cool off."

I shook my head in disbelief.

"But *we* should probably talk," he continued.

"I'm really not in the mood, Enzo—"

"I want to know when you started fucking the entire football team and why I wasn't invited."

Ethan chuckled behind me.

"This isn't funny."

"Yes, it is. Relax, Sunshine. She's jealous. She'll get over it."

"She doesn't have anything to be jealous about! It's not like I sought you guys out to ruin my life—"

"Easy. I thought we were bringing you plenty of joy." Enzo waggled his brows at me. I flushed at his words. He and Cole had definitely been close to that. "Maybe you can give Ethan a chance."

"You're definitely making me sound like exactly what she said—"

"Ethan, tell Rosalie you want her."

I looked over at Ethan, hating Enzo had put him on the spot.

"You don't have to answer—"

"I want you."

I blinked several times at him, unsure if I heard him correctly.

"Our arrangement was that you belonged to *us*. And you've been mine since I first saw you, Rosalie," Ethan's voice was a whisper, his eyes locked on mine. "If you'll have me."

"I don't think I understand."

"Just go with the flow. And enjoy the ride." Enzo gave my thigh another squeeze. "You'll be taken care of. Promise."

I blew out a breath and looked across the cafeteria, trying to get my bearings about me. My gaze locked with Fox's. My stomach twisted into nervous knots beneath his heated gaze. Juliet looked between us, her mouth turning into a sneer, causing me to tear my eyes away from Fox. The last thing I needed was to deal with her more. But I couldn't help the pull to him, the longing to go talk to him like we did the night before.

Rather than starting more battles I couldn't win, I turned back to Ethan."Tell me what that means."

"I can show you," he answered, giving me his sweet smile.

I nodded at him, feeling brave. "I think I'd like that."

CHAPTER 23

"There's our girl!" Cole threw his arm over my shoulder and planted a kiss on my cheek. "What the hell took you so long to get here? Party's been going for an hour now."

"I wasn't sure if I should come," I answered, snuggling into the crook of his arm.

He took notice of my move and grinned down at me. "We can skip this party right now, Rosebud, and take it upstairs."

"And miss all the hard work you put into this?" I gestured around to all the people with their drinks as they danced and laughed. "I'd never forgive myself."

Cole squeezed me to him, shaking his head, and then led me to the kitchen where he was quick to get me a drink.

"Why didn't you come to the game?" Enzo asked, wrapping me in a hug. "I looked in the stands, hoping you'd be there, but I got nothing."

"You didn't tell me I had to go."

He shook his head in disappointment. "Sunshine, don't play those games with me. I think you know the dynamic here is changing. We'd love for you to show up and support us. Right, Ethan?"

Ethan stopped in front of me. "You know you're missed when you're not around, right?"

I shrugged, feeling bashful. I wasn't quite sure what to make of it all. The fact these beautiful creatures had a thing for me made my heart pitter-patter.

"Well, you are." It was Ethan's turn to hug me. When he released me, he was quick to keep his arm around my waist.

"Fox played great tonight," Cole cut in, handing me a drink. "You should've been there, Rosebud. You'd have been proud."

I sipped my drink and nodded. I'd heard Fox was incredible, but I'd never witnessed him firsthand.

"You should go talk to him," Enzo urged, nodding behind us to the living room. I followed his gesture and spotted Fox talking to Juliet. Or maybe *talking* wasn't the right word. It looked like they were fighting because she was waving her hands and pointing at him, and his face was red. I could tell from where I stood that he was beyond frustrated.

"I think I'll pass."

"Go," Cole instructed, pulling me from Ethan and shoving me forward. "Take this." He handed me another drink.

I looked behind me at the guys, wondering why they wanted me to go to Fox so badly. The only positive thing was Juliet had stormed away, so now, he was alone.

Sighing, I went over and stood awkwardly beside him, not sure what to even say. A moment later, he noticed me and straightened up.

"You look like you could use a drink." I held out the cup. He took it and slammed it back, his eyes locked on mine. I shuffled from foot to foot.

"Thanks."

"Welcome."

We were both quiet for a moment.

"I heard you guys won."

"Yeah. It'll guarantee we make playoffs."

"Oh, cool." I didn't follow it enough, but I was sure I recalled something about that. I guessed that was why the celebration seemed so rowdy compared to last time.

"Well, good talking to you—"

"Rosie, wait," Fox called out. I turned back to him, waiting for him to say more. He ran his fingers through his hair and looked away. "Never mind."

I spun away from him with a frown and went back to the guys.

"How'd it go?" Cole asked, looking at me over his cup of beer.

"Not terrible. We didn't really talk."

"Damnit," Enzo grunted, his dark eyes trained on Fox in the living room, who was now talking to some of the football guys.

"Why is it such a big deal? No offense, but having everything let go would be nice."

"What are you talking about?" Enzo looked between the guys.

"Fox told me he was thinking about deleting the video and letting me go last night. If he does, I'm free, and you guys can be my friends for real if you want, instead of just some... sick game where I have to do what you want to protect myself."

Cole slammed his beer down, his mouth twisted into a deep scowl.

"Come on, Rosalie." Ethan took me by the hand and gave me a gentle tug away from Cole who looked pissed.

"What's wrong with Cole?"

"It's obvious, isn't it?"

We stopped in the living room where people danced to the DJ. I looped my arms around Ethan's neck, enjoying the moment with him.

Confused, I squinted up at him.

Sighing heavily, Ethan said, "We're not doing all this because we *have* to in order to keep you in line. This isn't a game. At least, not for me. Not for the others either, I don't think. We think a lot of you." Sincerity filled his eyes.

"You guys really *do* like me?" I asked, going up on my tip-toes and speaking into Ethan's ear.

He nodded, his hands tightening on my waist.

"How in the world would it ever work?" My heart rate skyrocketed in my chest as he pulled me flush with him.

"Use your imagination, Rosalie. Believe me, I have."

Tingles rushed through my body at his words.

"You'd...*share* me?"

"Mm, I like the way you think." Ethan nuzzled his face into my neck. This was a whole other side of him. If I thought Enzo and Cole were intense, it couldn't compare to the surprise Ethan was. Each hot breath against my skin left me gasping for air.

"Do you have any idea how long I've waited for a moment with you?" he continued.

I shivered against him. "Tell me."

He let out a soft laugh. "Since the morning of April twenty-fifth. You dropped your trig book in the hallway and bent to pick it up. You were wearing that gray hoodie and had it pulled over your head. All I could see was your red braid hanging out. I bent down when you did and grabbed your book for you."

"Oh, my god. Ethan, that was last year." I'd forgotten about it. My anxiety had been at an all time high. Juliet had tripped me on my way out of the classroom. Her cackle rang in my ears. I hadn't been watching where I was going after and had bumped into him, sending my books cascading to the floor.

"Do you remember what I said to you?"

We swayed to the fast beat playing, lost in our own world.

I swallowed hard. "You said, 'Those eyes could get you into trouble.' I remember it because I thought it was a joke."

"Not a joke, silly girl. I meant it. You have the most beautiful green eyes." He pressed a kiss to my jaw. "I never thought I'd get a chance with you."

"What?" I pulled away and stared up at him. "You do realize who *you* are, right?"

He grinned down at me and shrugged. "We're not all as confident as we pretend to be."

"I heard you and Cole were with Mona—"

He pressed a finger to my lips to silence me. "Stop talking. I want to kiss you."

I clamped my lips together as I stared up at him, anticipation cording through my guts. He leaned down, his eyes closing. My breath stuttered in my chest.

"Ethan," Cole called out. Ethan stopped halfway to me and let out a groan of frustration before pulling away.

"We need to talk."

"Now?" Ethan looked at me with what could only be longing before looking back to Cole.

"Yes. *Now*. It's missing."

"What?" Ethan froze. I looked between the two curiously. "How?"

Cole narrowed his eyes at me and moved between me and Ethan. "Rosebud, why don't you go say hi to your friend. I saw her here."

"She's mad at me—"

"Then tell her to take her piece of shit boy toy out of my house. Deliver that message," Cole snapped.

I flinched away from him, wondering what the hell his problem was.

"Cole," Ethan warned.

A muscle popped along Cole's jaw as his eyes darkened. "Do it, Rosebud. You know the rules."

I flipped him off and turned on my heel and walked away, not in the mood for whatever the hell was the matter with him. He blew so hot and cold it drove me nuts. He'd never outright given me a cruel task to complete. That in itself pissed me off, but I knew I didn't have much of a choice.

Or maybe he'd upset me to the point that I'd like to push his buttons.

Instead of going to find Jamie, I went back to the kitchen, grabbed a bottled water, and leaned against the counter, watching sullenly as Enzo and Fox joined Cole and Ethan. I had to admit, they all looked distraught as they huddled together.

I wonder what the hell is missing.

"Rosalie, right?" a voice called out. I tore my gaze away from the guys and looked over at the girl talking to me.

Mona Edwards. The girl in the middle of the Cole and Ethan rumors.

"Mona." I gave her a quick smile, wondering what she wanted.

She cleared her throat, her own smile shaky. "Can I talk to you for a minute?"

I glanced back at the guys to find them still talking. Sighing, I nodded my head at Mona and followed her out to Cole's patio where it was a lot quieter.

"I'm surprised you know who I am," Mona said as I leaned against the patio railing and turned to her, waiting for whatever she had to tell me.

I shrugged. "I don't really, I guess."

She nodded. "True, but I'm sure you've heard the rumors."

I shifted awkwardly.

"They're true mostly. I *did* make out with Ethan and Cole. In fact, I had it really bad for both of them. I did things with them I shouldn't have done."

"Why are you telling me this?" I frowned, anxiety kicking in.

"Because I was you once, Rosalie. I don't want you to get hurt. They're not the guys you think they are."

I pushed off the patio and looked around. "What do you mean?"

"They're gorgeous and popular. But they don't fall for girls like us." Her voice held a sad, desperate tone as her brown eyes swept over me.

I swallowed hard and nodded. She wasn't wrong. Mona wasn't popular by a long shot, nor was I.

"It's a game to them," her words came out in a rush as she stepped closer. "They don't care about any of us."

I frowned at her and started to open my mouth to interject, but she shook her head at me.

"Look at their track record, Rosalie. Sure, you see them with the popular girls from time to time, but you see them messing around with girls like us more." She widened her eyes at me, pleading for me to understand where she was coming from.

I bit my bottom lip, rifling through my memories of the guys. I knew they had their share of girls like me. I'd been pushing the *why* out of my mind for a while.

"We're a way to pass the time. That includes you. They're going to hurt you. Everything they say is a lie. None of them care the way they say they do."

"Mona—"

She grasped my hand and squeezed it. "Do they have cute nicknames for you? Do they each kiss you and try for more? Are they protective and sweet? Do they know how to get you with their words *every* single time, even when you're angry with them? Do they have dirt on you?"

I frowned, my heart thudding unevenly in my chest.

Nausea twisted my insides. It had to be a coincidence.

"They're perfect, Rosalie, but they're *not* perfect for girls like us. They ruin girls like us. Just...stay safe, OK?" She released my hand and backed away. "Ask the other girls like us. It's happened to them too."

"I think it's different with me," I argued weakly.

She gave me a sympathetic look. "I thought the same thing too. I told you we're a game to them. Our emotions are the prize. I'm almost positive of it. I gave in. Don't let them hurt you like they did me. Recovering from their brand of heartbreak is like fighting a war where there are no winners. And please, Rosalie. Don't tell them I tipped you off."

She turned and left me standing there, her words ringing in my ears.

I hated the nagging little voice shouting in the back of mind that *maybe* Mona was right.

CHAPTER 24

I didn't return to the party. I got in my car and drove home, opting to crawl into bed and stream my favorite show. I couldn't shake Mona's words from my mind. The guys had the cute nicknames for me—Rosebud, Sunshine, Sweetheart, Rosie. They tried for more. Hell, they'd beaten up Ian for me. They were protective. They were… perfect… except for the video. The bargaining chip.

My phone buzzing pulled me from my morose thoughts.

Fox: Are you OK?

I chewed my cheek for a moment before shooting off a reply.

Rosalie: Yes.

A moment later my phone buzzed again with a call from Fox.

"Hello?" I answered softly after a moment of contemplation. The prospect of not answering tempted me. At the end, curiosity and sheer desire had me hitting the TALK button.

"Rosalie, where are you?" Fox demanded, the distant sounds of the party in the background making him hard to hear. He must have realized that because a moment later, it got quieter.

"I'm tired and decided to go home."

"What's wrong?" The concern in his voice made my heart skip.

"Fox, can I ask you something?"

"Yes," his voice was breathless, making my heart kick up its pace in my chest.

"If I asked you to tell me the truth about why you guys are *really* doing this, would you tell me?"

"Something's wrong. Tell me."

I fiddled with my blanket for a moment before blowing out a breath. "I just feel overwhelmed. I know you don't owe me any answers, considering what you're holding over my head—"

"Meet me tomorrow."

I stared down at my lap, dumbfounded.

"What? Why?" I squeaked out.

"I haven't spent any time with you. We probably should."

"Are you drunk?"

Fox let out a soft laugh. "Maybe. Doesn't matter. Tomorrow. My place, OK? My dad's going out of town to work on a construction job. And we still haven't practiced your song."

"OK," I murmured. "Tomorrow."

"Good," he answered. "Sweet dreams, Rosalie."

"Bye, Fox," I whispered in the phone before I heard the click of him hanging up. I looked to his darkened window, wondering what the hell I was going to do.

Fox's dad didn't leave until after five the following evening. When I heard the crunch of gravel signaling his departure, I hauled in a deep breath and made my way over to Fox's house.

I hadn't been in his house since the day his mom died.

"Fox, have you seen Mom?" Kurt asked, poking his head into Fox's bedroom.

We sat on the bed, munching on popcorn and watching a scary movie.

"She said she had to run to the store," Fox answered, tearing his focus from the TV to look at his dad.

His dad frowned. "That was a few hours ago now. She's not answering her phone."

Fox shrugged. "Maybe she doesn't have service."

Kurt shook his head and backed out of the room. "If she calls, will you let me know?"

"Sure, Dad," Fox said, turning back to the TV. Kurt left the room.

"It's weird your mom isn't home," I commented, reaching for a handful of popcorn.

Fox shrugged. "Mom always takes a long time when she shops. It's why I hate going."

I chuckled.

An hour later, we made our way downstairs to the kitchen. Amy still wasn't home. Kurt was on the phone to someone sounding frustrated.

I was just about to comment my worry when there was a knock on the front door. I watched Kurt go to it and pull it open.

"Fox," I whispered as two large cops filled the doorway. Fox's eyes widened. He wordlessly moved to stand behind his dad. I inched closer, my heart clenching.

"Mr. Evans?" one of the large officers asked in a gruff voice. "I'm Officer Bennett, and this is Officer Mills."

"Yes?" Kurt asked, his voice shaking.

"Sir, there's been an accident," Officer Bennett said. Kurt visibly paled, and I moved closer still, worry eating at my guts.

"My wife?" Kurt choked out.

"Maybe you should sit down," Officer Mills offered gently.

Kurt shook his head, his knuckles white as he clutched the door. "Is she OK?"

The officers exchanged looks before Officer Bennett cleared his throat.

"Mr. Evans, there was an accident. A drunk driver was going the wrong way on the highway. Your wife was traveling southbound when she was hit head on. I'm sorry."

"S-she's dead?" Kurt's voice cracked. Fox took a step forward, his face white as a ghost, his blue eyes wide.

"We're sorry. She passed on the scene," Officer Mills murmured, reaching out for Kurt as his knees buckled.

"Rosie," Fox choked out. "Rosie."

In an instant, my arms were around him as he collapsed to his knees, a low wail trembling on his lips as he clung to me.

"Rosie." He repeated my name over and over as tears streamed down his pale cheeks. "Rosie."

"I'm here." I wept, holding him tightly. "Fox, I'm here."

He openly sobbed as his dad tried tearing him away from me. Fox clung harder, shaking his head. Instead of pulling him off me, Kurt wrapped us both in a bone-crushing hug, sobbing.

"Don't leave me, Rosie," Fox choked out through his tears. "Don't leave me."

"I won't," I vowed, his tears soaking through my t-shirt. "I'm not going anywhere."

Going back tore open a whole host of old, painful memories. I shoved them aside, wanting to focus on having a decent day with Fox.

He answered before I even had a chance to knock.

"Hey." His blue eyes swept over me, taking in my black t-shirt and jean skirt.

I fixed a nervous smile on my face. "Hey. Am I too early?"

"No." He moved aside and gestured for me to come in.

I followed him into the foyer, noting everything had changed since the last time I'd been there, right down to the new hardwood floors.

He strode past me, and I scurried to follow him. I was surprised when he led me to his bedroom. Even that had changed. I guess I expected it. He wasn't a kid anymore. The Spider-Man posters and comic books were gone. His walls were bare now, and no longer the baby blue I remembered. Now, they were a deep navy blue. His large bed was made, the rest of his room ridiculously clean.

"Wow." I gave a low whistle as I looked around, taking in all his football trophies and medals.

"What?"

"I guess I didn't expect your room to be this clean."

He grunted a response and nodded to his bed.

"Have a seat."

I quirked an eyebrow at him but did as he said. He grabbed a guitar out of his closet and sank down on the overstuffed chair by his bed.

"Did you warm up before you got here, or do you need to?"

"I warmed up a bit, but I can't really when Dad is home," I answered awkwardly.

Fox crinkled his brows at me. "Why not?"

"My dad hates me singing or doing anything related to theater. It's pretty much a cardinal sin in our house."

Fox frowned at the information before letting out a sigh. He strummed the first chord to my song and looked at me. "Then I guess it's good you're over here sinning and not there, huh?"

"Guess so." I gave him a shaky smile.

He didn't return it. Instead, he continued to play through my song, his eyes never straying from me. I shifted uncomfortably on the edge of his bed, wondering what he was thinking. The conversation I'd had with Mona replayed in my mind. I shook my head, as if to clear it.

A knock on the front door had me staring wide-eyed at him, saying a silent prayer it wasn't Juliet.

"It's just Enzo," Fox mumbled. A moment later, I heard footfalls on the stairs.

"Hey, Sunshine," Enzo greeted me, coming into the room with his guitar slung over his shoulder. His gaze swept over me, a smile curling his lips up. "Always so fucking beautiful."

I blushed at the compliment, catching the hard look on Fox's face.

Enzo sat on the bed beside me and grinned wider.

"Looks like we're working today, huh?"

"Yeah," I answered, glancing at Fox.

He'd gone back to strumming my song on his guitar, his mouth turned down into a deep frown.

"What?" he asked, reaching the end of the song.

"Nothing. We should practice."

He leaned forward, his eyes locked on mine. "I know the guys have lengthened your leash, but I'm not them. *I* say when, not you."

"They also don't refer to me as their dog," I snapped back, hating how fast his moods changed.

Enzo shifted beside me before resting his hand on my thigh.

Fox narrowed his eyes at me. "I didn't call you a bitch."

"You sure insinuated it," I volleyed back.

"Wasn't my intention," he muttered.

It wasn't an apology, but it was better than nothing.

"We should get this song figured out," Enzo said after a moment of silence while Fox and I stared one another down. He finally tore his gaze away from me and nodded, going back to plucking the strings on his guitar.

"I was thinking we could switch up a few lines. Make it hit a little harder." He strummed and sang the new lines, his voice in perfect pitch.

"Wow. That's good," I murmured, nodding.

He gave me a quick smile while Enzo made the changes on paper.

"Now you sing," Fox instructed. "From the top."

I cleared my throat as he started playing again. When it was time to sing, I belted out the lyrics. Fox kept tempo with me, nodding his head, his eyes fixed on me the entire time. When the song ended, I stared back nervously at him, waiting for his verdict.

"Incredible, Rosie. I'm impressed."

"Really?" I breathed out, butterflies taking flight in my tummy.

He offered me a small smile. "Really."

"Just like I said," Enzo broke in.

I'd been so fixated on Fox I'd forgotten Enzo was with us. He gave my hand a squeeze. When I turned to him, he was quick to press a kiss on my lips.

His warm hand came to rest on my hip as he deepened the kiss. I parted my lips, giving him full access, my heart hammering so hard I could hear it roaring in my ears. With every soft caress of Enzo's tongue, I waited for Fox to call out for us to stop. When he didn't, I broke the kiss off and looked guiltily over at him, expecting to see his angry frown. Instead, I was greeted with him leaning forward in his seat, his eyes locked on me.

"Fox," Enzo called out.

A muscle worked along Fox's jaw before he rose and moved to sit beside me on his bed, sandwiching me between him and Enzo. My breath hitched when he reached out and cradled my face. So much turmoil rolled across his, it left me breathless.

He leaned in, his blue eyes locked on mine. I sat frozen as his lips brushed against mine in a soft, tentative kiss.

Fox blew out a shaky breath as he leaned his forehead against mine. Time passed by in thick sexual tension.

"Fuck it," he muttered, diving back into the moment and kissing me again with such force I had to prop against Enzo, who wasted no time in holding me in place as Fox's mouth worked against mine in a violent frenzy.

I kissed him back, my tongue dancing against his as his hands found their way beneath my shirt. He broke the kiss off long enough to ask, "Is this OK?"

When I nodded, he pulled my shirt off, then dove back in. I leaned into his kiss. Enzo unhooked my bra. Fox quickly pulled it off and tossed it somewhere in his room, letting my breasts spill out into his waiting hands.

Fox's lips started traveling south, peppering my neck with kisses, then my collarbone before his hot mouth found my breasts.

"Oh my god," I rasped in a hoarse whisper.

Enzo angled my head so he could take a turn kissing me, his tongue delving deep as Fox nipped and sucked on my breasts. The heat from both of them swept through me, increasing my heart rate. I moaned into Enzo's mouth as Fox sucked my hardened nipple into his mouth, his tongue swirling around it.

Fox pulled back, causing me to stutter over his distance.

"F-fox?" I breathed out, reaching for him. A muscle worked along his jaw again. "What's wrong?"

"I—" He stopped talking, his eyes sweeping over my naked torso. His Adam's apple bobbed in his throat as he averted his eyes.

"Fox, come on," Enzo encouraged, pressing a kiss to my temple as he squeezed my breast from behind me. "She's here. She wants it."

"Do you, Rosie?" Fox asked softly, his eyes locked on mine.

I nodded. "Yes."

Fox moved back to me and cupped my other breast. A storm gathered behind his eyes. Finally, he gave in and pressed his lips to mine. Enzo let out a breath behind me.

I released a soft moan as Fox moved lower, pushing my skirt up, his fingers skimming my panties.

"Lie back, Sunshine," Enzo instructed softly.

I did as he said, watching as Fox positioned himself between my legs, his eyes dark. I swallowed hard as Fox leaned down and pressed a gentle kiss to my abdomen before moving lower.

I tensed as his warm breath blew over my most intimate area, his hands hastily dispensing of my panties. My face heated as Fox stared down at me, his lips parted.

"You're so wet," he murmured, sliding his finger over my center.

"Bet she tastes delicious," Enzo said, the sound of his zipper in my ear.

"I'll let you know."

I let out a soft moan as Fox swept his tongue up my slit.

"Fuck, Sunshine, I love that noise," Enzo growled, taking my hand in his and guiding it to his hard length, now free from his jeans. I moved my hand up and down with his guidance, causing him to breathe in short gasps.

Fox's tongue delved between my folds, finding my sensitive bundle of nerves and whirling over it. I arched my back in response, which only caused him to tug me by my hips back down to his mouth, where he ate like a man starving, his fingers threatening my slick channel.

Enzo lifted my head as he moved forward.

"Suck my dick, Sunshine," he commanded softly.

Eagerly, I obliged, parting my lips for him and allowing him entry. He let out a soft hiss as I tried to take all of him into my mouth. I gagged as he hit the back of my throat.

"Need more practice," he chuckled softly, fisting my hair.

"She'll get it," Fox said from between my legs as he inserted a finger into me. "She's so fucking tight. Damn."

All their talk had me panting hard as I struggled once again to suck all of Enzo into my mouth. He thrust his hips, helping me out. I licked and sucked, wanting to impress him.

"So good, Sunshine," he moaned as his length thickened in my mouth. "Faster."

I obeyed, sucking him harder.

Fox picked up his pace, and before I could so much as moan, the tingles took over, my pulse roaring through my ears.

"That's it, baby. Almost," Enzo breathed, thrusting faster. With a groan, he spilled into my mouth.

I swallowed it down as he pulled out, my eyes rolling back in my head as the sensations soared to new heights.

"Fox," I called out as euphoria slammed into me, sending me careening over the edge of a place I never knew existed.

He growled his approval, his hands like vices on my thighs as he continued his onslaught.

When I was breathless and boneless, Fox finally pulled away, his lips glistening with his accomplishment and his eyes shining with something I'd never seen in them before.

"How was it?" Enzo called out, tucking himself back into his pants.

"Everything I'd dreamed," Fox murmured back, his eyes locked on mine. He held his hand out for me. I took it and sat up.

"What about you?" I asked nervously.

"You've given enough, Rosie." He placed a gentle kiss on my lips. "Let's get you home, OK?"

I nodded wordlessly, exhaustion taking over me.

Enzo moved forward and handed me my bra and shirt. I quickly put them on.

"I'm going to take off," Enzo called out. "I have to go see Cole."

"OK," Fox said easily from his spot next to me.

"Sunshine, you're amazing." Enzo pressed a deep kiss on my lips before whispering in my ear, "You belong to all of us truly now."

He pulled away and grinned at Fox who managed to smile back.

"Ethan's. Tomorrow."

"See you there," Fox said. They fist bumped. Then Enzo left, leaving me and Fox alone.

Fox cleared his throat. "I hope that was OK, Rosie. I didn't want to make you uncomfortable."

"I-It was amazing," I said. "Thank you."

He gave me a tentative smile. He opened his mouth to say something else, but his phone rang. A growl slipped past his lips as he looked at the screen. Stuffing it back into his pocket, he glanced over at me.

"I should get home," I said.

"OK." Fox stood, and I followed him downstairs and out the front door. Neither of us said anything until we reached my front door.

"Thanks for tonight," I said.

He smiled at me. "It's probably me who should be thanking you."

"Why?" I crinkled my brows in confusion. "Um, you didn't get to… *you know*."

He chuckled softly and leaned in, pressing a gentle kiss to my cheek. "You were more important, Rosie."

My face heated at his words. He reached out and squeezed my hand.

"I'll see you later."

"Bye, Fox," I said as he stepped off my front step. He gave me one last smile before turning and walking back to his place.

I watched him go, deciding in that moment that Fox was the one I could lose myself in, and I didn't mind in the slightest belonging to him and the guys.

CHAPTER 25

"**G**ood morning, Rosebud. Heard you had a good weekend," Cole greeted me as I stepped onto the sidewalk.

I cast a quick look to Enzo and Fox. I hadn't heard from any of the guys after my evening with Enzo and Fox. Enzo winked at me. Fox stared at me with the same impassive look he always wore.

"Yeah. It was OK."

Cole snorted, shaking his head. "Guess I'll need to have a go so we fix that *OK* status."

"If you think you can." I shrugged at him which earned a howl of laughter from Enzo. Even Fox cracked a small smile.

"Is that a challenge, Rosebud?"

"Take it how you want, Cole. I'm just saying you have a lot to live up to."

Ethan chuckled. I winked at him, feeling happy for the first time in a long time.

"Listen, I'll rock your world, baby. Just say when," Cole growled.

"*When*." I peeked at Fox to see his reaction. A tiny smile played on the edge of his lips. He seemed happier than I'd ever seen him before. That relaxed me.

I couldn't get my night with him and Enzo out of my head all weekend.

I kept replaying how it felt to have their mouths on mine. Their hands on my body. Even now, I could still picture us together. My mind traveled to thoughts on what it would be like for all four of them to be with me.

Enzo winked at me like he knew my mind had gone into the gutter.

"Fox!" Juliet called out as she stomped across the lawn. The smile on his face faltered, his eyes locked on mine. "Fox! Why haven't you taken my calls all weekend?"

"Yeah, Fox. Why haven't you?" Cole asked innocently.

"I had my head buried in other matters," Fox shot back at Cole. "You know, the thing you haven't gotten to do."

"Not for long," Cole hissed, narrowing his eyes at Fox. "Come on, Rosebud. We have some work to catch up on."

Cole took me by the arm and dragged me away from Fox who now had Juliet poking her finger in his chest. He looked bored and slightly irritated as he stared back at her. Enzo stood with them, grinning and probably not making matters better. Juliet rounded on him, pointing her finger at him.

"That won't end well," Ethan muttered, falling in step with me and Cole.

"Good. Juliet needs to fucking get lost. She can't take a hint," Cole grumbled as he snaked his arm around my waist. "Why he ever got latched to her is beyond me. I told him she was a fucking nut job."

"He was just trying to take his mind off… things," Ethan answered.

I took the bait. "What things?"

Ethan and Cole exchanged looks.

"Nothing for you to concern your pretty, little self with, Rosebud," Cole said, tweaking my nose. "Fox is dealing with them now."

I ground my teeth. I knew Fox was an enigma. But the dynamic had changed. I needed to know what was going on with him.

I was just about to launch into asking for more information when we rounded a corner in the hall. Ian had Jamie pressed against the wall, whispering in her ear. She smiled as he squeezed her waist.

"Asshole," I hissed, starting to step forward.

Ethan reached out and stopped me. "Leave it," he said softly.

"I say let her have him," Cole countered. "Apparently his accident with a ladder didn't teach him anything."

"I can't just let him do this to her," I growled, glaring in their direction.

Ian glanced up at us, a smile curling his lips. The prick had the audacity to wink at me.

"Rats like Ian always get what's coming to them, sweetheart," Ethan said. "In time—"

"I don't have a lot of time, Ethan," I sighed and looked at him. "He's going to hurt her if I don't do something."

"If she's fucking dumb enough to let him, then I say who cares," Cole said.

"It's not about her intelligence, Cole," I snapped. "He drugs girls. *I* would know."

Cole's eyes darkened as he looked from me to Ian, who'd gone back to Jamie. I knew Ian was only doing it because he wanted the leverage to get me to finish what we'd started. Or rather, what *he'd* started.

"I guess we'll have to pay him another visit."

"No." I shook my head at Cole. "I don't want you involved—"

I let out a squeak as Cole tugged me into his arms, his lips brushing against the shell of my ear as he spoke. "*No one* touches what belongs to us, Rosebud. We went easy on him last time. Maybe he needs a friendly reminder."

I shivered beneath his words. My eyes shuttered closed as Cole planted kisses along my jawline before he found my lips. He kissed me deeply, stealing my breath as his hands tightened on my waist.

"Jesus," I stuttered out as he released me.

He answered with a smirk. "Mine," he said again.

I glanced over at Ethan simply standing there. He was the only one I hadn't done anything with. Not even kiss. He seemed to read my mind because he offered me one of his sweet smiles.

"Meet me at the bleachers for lunch?"

I nodded as Cole chuckled then resumed walking us in the direction of my class.

"Careful of him, Rosebud. He'll try to sweep you off your feet with sonnets and flowers."

"I like sonnets and flowers," I answered, smiling at Ethan. We'd arrived at my class.

"I've gotta jet. Rosebud, me and you later, OK?" Cole said as he planted a kiss on my cheek.

"OK," I answered breathlessly.

"Bad girl," he chuckled in my ear before pulling away and sauntering down the hall like he didn't have a care in the world.

"I'm sorry," I said, turning to Ethan.

"For what?" He cocked his head at me, a tiny grin on his face.

"You and I never—"

He pressed a finger to my lips. "I'm going to stop you right there. Don't worry about it. Good things come to those who wait. I'll see you on the bleachers." He dropped his finger from my lips. I nodded wordlessly at him.

"Bye, Rosalie." He pressed a sweet kiss to my temple and left me standing with shaky legs. A few people cast me strange looks but screw them.

Everything was really starting to look up. To hell with what Mona said. This was different. It *had* to be.

If it wasn't, it would devastate me.

CHAPTER 26

When lunch rolled around, I made my way to the bleachers like my shoes were on fire, eager to see Ethan. I hadn't seen Fox all morning, but I wasn't surprised. I never tended to. Something about that bummed me out. We'd had a good time together recently. Maybe if we ran into each other, he'd at least talk to me more or something.

"Hey," Ethan greeted me, opening his arms wide as I approached.

"How did you get here so fast?" I asked, falling into his hold.

He gave me a long squeeze before pulling away. "I left class early. As far as Collins knows, I'm still in the bathroom."

"Rebel," I teased with a laugh as we moved to sit on the bleachers.

"I brought lunch," Ethan said, pulling a sub from his bag and offering me half. "Hope you like turkey."

"I do." I grinned, taking the sandwich from him and biting into it.

He did the same with his half, and we sat eating in silence for a moment.

"How have you been?" Ethan asked.

"Everything seems crazy right now," I admitted. "And after the weekend, I feel… different."

Ethan swallowed his bite of sandwich and nodded. "Heard it was a hell of a time."

"It really was."

"I'm sorry I missed it."

Feeling brave, I reached out and rested my hand high on his thigh.

"For what it's worth, so am I."

He smiled at me, his eyes twinkling. "We'll get our moment. No worries, sweetheart. Then the four of us can be together."

I let out a soft laugh. "I can't believe I'm doing this."

"It's strange, huh?"

"Yeah," I admitted softly. "But I like it."

"That makes me happy. You have no idea how long we've all wanted this."

"How did it even happen?" I asked. "That you guys decided you wanted to do something like *this*?"

Ethan shrugged. "I don't know. We were just hanging out one day, and Enzo started talking about it. It sounded fun. We decided it might be cool to try out. We did it a few times with some girls. Not all of us together. Just two of us. Couldn't progress past that. Seemed to scare women away, honestly."

I nodded. I could see that. Hell, it had scared me.

"We've been looking for our unicorn, I guess," he finished. "We had our eye on you for a long time. We just needed to get Fox on board with it."

I bit my bottom lip and asked the question that was burning up in my mind. "What's up with him? Why did you need to talk him into doing this with me?"

"Aside from your history together?" Ethan asked.

I nodded.

Sadness darkened Ethan's eyes. "He hated you."

It felt like a lead brick had fallen into my belly.

"Don't think what you're thinking," Ethan said softly, taking my hand in his. "He doesn't hate you *now*."

"But why would he ever hate me? We were best friends since we were in diapers. One minute we were everything to one another then nothing. It was like he died when his mom did."

Ethan sighed and looked out to the empty football field.

"He blames you for his mom's death."

His words were like a hammer to my skull. They rocked me, making me choke on my next breath.

"W-what? How? Why?"

"Sweetheart, it's not my place to say. I've already said too much."

"Oh, no you don't, Ethan Masters. You don't hit me with that and then go silent on me. If you know something, tell me. *Please*. Fox has been mean to me. Then over the weekend, something changed. He was sweet again. Then today, nothing. While he hasn't said anything awful to me, it's the silence that's bothering me. Especially a-after what we did."

Ethan's gaze swept over my face, his brows crinkled.

"He's torn between caring too much and not enough. I know it seems impossible to believe, but he *does* care about you."

I nodded, swallowing hard.

"He does, Rosalie. He just needs to deal with his own demons."

"I don't understand why he would blame me for Amy dying," I murmured. "We were at Fox's house. I-I remember that day like it was yesterday. It was a Friday night. Amy made dinner. *Lasagna*. My parents weren't home, so I ate dinner with Fox's family. We holed up in Fox's room and watched scary movies." I frowned as a memory surfaced.

"What is it?" Ethan pressed gently, tucking a strand of hair behind my ear.

"Amy came up to Fox's room when he went downstairs to grab us more soda. I-I talked to her. She asked me how school was going. It was just normal conversation. Then I told her about these earrings I saw and fell in love with, but my parents wouldn't let me get my ears pierced. They were the last pair left. Tiny silver flowers with a small red gem in the center. My birthday was coming, and I told her it was the only thing I wanted."

Ethan squeezed my hand as I swiped at more tears.

"She left after that. Told us she wanted to run some errands before the stores closed. She never came home," my voice cracked. "I loved Amy like a mom. She was wonderful. My heart shattered that night when the cops came to the house. I'll never forget it."

Ethan wrapped his arms around me as I wept. I'd spent years pushing the memory of that night away. The look on Fox's face. How he'd fallen to his knees and cried, wails of torment falling from his lips. I'd never seen him cry before. How Kurt tried to hold him. How I did. How he clung to me and begged me not to go.

And days later, he proclaimed his hatred of me.

"I didn't know his mom, but I know Fox. He needs you, Rosalie. Since you've been in our lives, he's happier, even if he doesn't look like he is. It's just a lot for him to deal with."

"I hope he's happier," I said in a shaky voice. "I don't want him to hate me."

"He doesn't. I know he doesn't. He's just confused right now. Give him time. He's come so far already."

I nodded sadly, unable to shake the questions in my mind. *How was Amy's death my fault? Why did he blame me?*

"Do you hate him?" Ethan asked softly.

"No. I… as much as I would've liked to, Fox is impossible to hate. Even when I try."

Ethan smiled at me and pressed a gentle kiss to the corner of my lips. "This is going to work. Believe me?"

"Yes," I whispered. Because the alternative would break my heart.

CHAPTER 27

"It's been a while," Ian said, falling in step beside me as I walked across the parking lot later that day at school.

I groaned inwardly as I continued to my car. I hadn't gotten a chance to speak to Fox. My anxiety was choking me with worry that maybe we weren't OK due to his scarceness. The guys had football practice, so I was alone with my thoughts, not all of them clean ones.

"Not long enough," I muttered, reaching for my door handle and turning to glare at him. "Stay away from Jamie. I saw you two in the hallway."

"Ah, so you know we're dating." He gave me a Cheshire smile. "There's only one way me staying away from her is going to happen. And that all rests on you."

"Why haven't you told her yet? Why are you dragging this out? It's pathetic," I spat out.

"You know why. I'm really hoping you come around, Rosalie."

"I'm not going to—"

"If you don't finish it, it'll be her virginity I take. We've both spent enough time with her to know how important this is to her. I'll fuck her brains out. I'll make promises I don't intend to keep. Then I'll leave her without an explanation."

"You're an asshole."

"Or maybe I'll tell her she fucks like a wet paper bag, and I can't bear to do it with her again."

"Jamie is your friend, Ian. What the hell is the matter with you? You know what this means to her—"

"I know, and that's why you need to fall in line, Rosalie. I wanted you first. If those fuck boys hadn't come in and ruined it, you'd be mine right now, not sucking them off every chance you get."

"There's something seriously wrong with you," I snarled at him, my hands balled into fists.

"No, I just know what I want." A wide smile spread over his face. Dread filled my belly. "That's *you*. I'd hoped you'd want me too. When you didn't, I decided to settle with easing your resistance with a little chemical help. Now, you know the score. I *will* have you. I don't care if you had all their dicks inside you. Mine will be the last."

"I was drunk, Ian. You put something in my drink. That wasn't love, lust or anything related. *It was criminal!* That night shouldn't have happened. I was upset, and you took advantage." I shifted to open my car door, but he slammed it closed on me, making me jump.

"It was *me* you came to."

"It was an accident," I answered. "I ran *into* you. It could've been anyone. But the only difference is, they wouldn't have drugged me and tried to fuck me."

He let out a bark of laughter and pushed me against my car. "I want what's mine. Finish what you fucking started, or I really will take it from you."

"I'm done having this argument with you." I ground my teeth, trying to compose myself. "You're mental."

"I'm taking her v-card. Then I'm going to tell her about us."

"Go to hell," I snarled at him. "If you touch her, I will end you."

I didn't wait for his rebuttal. I shoved him aside, got into my car, and peeled away, leaving him where he stood.

CHAPTER 28

"Come on, pick up, Jamie," I whispered into my phone later that night.

Nothing. Straight to voicemail.

"Jamie, it's me. Please talk to me. I miss you. I-I need to tell you something about Ian. Call me back."

I hung up the phone and sighed. Without thinking it through, I sent Fox a text.

Rosalie: Hey. Can we talk?

I stared at my phone for a full ten minutes before letting out a growl and dropping it onto my mattress. I was just about to say to hell with it and call it a night when there was a soft knock on my bedroom door. My heart jolted in my chest. My parents were out for the evening. There was no one in our house but me.

I got to my feet and crept to my door, snagging the only weapon I could find. A ruler.

"W-who is it?" I called out, clutching the ruler.

"It's me, Fox," Fox's voice called out.

I breathed out a sigh of relief and pulled open my bedroom door to find him standing in there in his basketball shorts and no shirt. My heart kicked to life in my chest at the sight of all his rippling muscles, those baby blue eyes, and dark, windswept hair.

"Were you going to measure me?" he asked, stepping into my room, a tiny smirk on his lips as he eyed the ruler I was still clutching.

"I thought you were an intruder," I muttered, tossing the ruler onto my desk.

"Do intruders usually knock on your bedroom door?"

I stuck my tongue out at him and flopped onto my bed, still acutely aware he was half-naked in my room.

He sat beside me.

"Are you OK?"

"I-yeah. No. I don't know," I mumbled.

"Talk to me," he said. "What's wrong?"

I couldn't tell him about Ian even though I really wanted to. Instead, I shook my head.

"Guess I was lonely. I was worried when I didn't see you at school or talk to you that maybe you were regretting what we did."

He shook his head and stared down at his hands.

"I'd never regret what we did. I made you feel good, right?"

"Yes," I whispered.

"You made me feel good too, Rosie."

"But I didn't even do anything—"

"Trust me, you did." He chuckled. We grew quiet for a moment before he continued, "It's just... I don't know. It's a lot for me to deal with. I'm trying though. Promise me you'll give me some time to work through it all?"

"I don't even know what you need to work through, Fox. You've never told me." I watched him to see if he had any sort of reaction. The only thing noticeable was his shoulders hunching forward slightly.

"I will someday. I just need to get to the place where I can. I'm almost there."

I nodded and squeezed his hand. He was trying. Just like Ethan had said. It was better than how things had been a few weeks ago. I could accept that. For now. "OK."

"You looked beautiful today. It's all I could think about."

I bit my bottom lip. "You've been thinking of me?"

"Yes." He reached out and twirled his finger around one of my long curls. "In fact, you're all I've been able to think about lately."

My heart raced at his words, so it took me a few beats to get my next words out of my mouth. "I've been thinking about you too, Fox. But, um, what about Juliet?"

He scoffed and moved to cradle my face. "No Juliet. Just you."

"I-I thought you two were dating."

"No," he answered softly.

"Is that why you guys were fighting this morning?"

He smirked. "You ask a lot of questions."

"She hates me, Fox. If you're with her, and you and I, um, *you know—*"

"She won't touch you, Rosie. I'll lose my shit if she even thinks about bothering you. I made you that promise before, and I'm keeping it."

"You didn't always keep it," I murmured.

His eyes darkened as his gaze flicked to my lips then back to my eyes.

"That was before," he answered, leaning in.

"Before what?"

"I kissed you." He planted a soft kiss on my lips, his mouth trailing hot kisses along my jaw before he whispered in my ear, "Before I tasted you."

A thrill of excitement raced through me as he let out a husky laugh.

"You like me, Rosie." It was a statement. A cocky one that embodied all the confident swagger Fox possessed.

"You like me right back, Fox," I said breathlessly as he moved his hand to the small of my back and pulled me close. He planted another kiss on my lips.

"I do," he answered. "And I'd show you just how much if I didn't have to go meet someone."

He liked *me. He admitted it.* It took all I had to play it cool.

"Where are you going?"

He pulled away and gave my hand a squeeze.

"We've lost something important. Just going to go get it back is all. Hopefully."

"Oh—"

"I'll tell you about it later, OK? I'm meeting the guys. Cole has this OCD thing about punctuality." He pressed another kiss to my lips before getting to his feet. I escorted him downstairs.

"Fox?"

"Hmm?" He pulled open the door and turned to me.

Is it true about the other girls? Am I just another conquest? I stopped myself before the words slipped from my mouth. I knew they'd been looking for what they'd lost for a while now. Something about the subject made my tummy twist into uncomfortable knots.

"Be careful tonight."

A quick smile turned his lips up. "I will, Rosie."

He reached out and thumbed my bottom lip, a storm brewing behind his blue eyes.

"I'm going to make it up to you."

"Make what up?"

"All the wrongs. I promise. I just need a little time." Worry crowded his handsome features. He looked so vulnerable as he stared back at me.

"OK. I'll wait a little longer."

He pressed a tender kiss to my lips. "I'll text you later, baby."

Baby. He called me baby.

"Can't wait," I managed to whisper in a hoarse voice.

He let out a low chuckle as he walked out my door, turning as he reached the bottom step and giving me that sweet smile he'd been hiding for so long.

But the most important thing was he looked back.

CHAPTER 29

Fox messaged me goodnight. So did the others. I smiled as I lay in bed, giddy beyond imagination at everything working out.

Then the crushing weight of Ian came tumbling down on me. I had to figure out what to do about him. It was clear he hurt girls. If he drugged me and tried to screw me, *his friend*, then who else was his victim?

He needed to pay. I just had to figure out how.

Then I thought about my music. How Enzo and Fox's eyes had lit up when I sang. How my dad would kill me if he found out I wanted to go to Mayfair.

I cringed and punched my pillow. I barely slept. When Fox came home well after two in the morning, I was up, sitting at my desk. His goodnight text had come nearly four hours earlier. I knew he wasn't home when he sent it because he said he was still with the guys.

But what the hell were they doing?

My mind kept going back to what Mona said. As much as I wanted to believe I meant *something* to them, I had to know what the deal with all of that was. Maybe it was like Ethan said. They just really wanted a girl to share and had simply been looking for a long time.

I hoped that's what it was.

When I got back into bed, it was after three in the morning. By six, I'd slept for maybe an hour. The day was going to suck.

Fox was already gone when I went out to my car in the morning, so I drove to school like I always did and parked in the back of the lot. The only one on the sidewalk when I got there was Ethan.

"Hey, sweetheart," he greeted me with a kiss on the cheek. "You look exhausted."

"I am," I mumbled. "Where are the others?"

"They had some business to take care of. They'll be here later."

"Why does that sound like it's business with their fists?"

Ethan chuckled. "Why do you think that?"

"Fox said something was missing and you guys had to go meet someone. What was it?"

Ethan tensed before giving me a quick squeeze. "Nothing you should worry about. It's being taken care of."

"It's not nothing if you're keeping it from me," I grumbled. "It's definitely something. If it's bad and I find out, I'll kick all your asses for lying to me."

Ethan relaxed and laughed. "It's fine. Or it *will* be. Promise."

"Better be," I muttered, draping my arm around his waist as we walked together. I'd never done that with anyone before. We looked official. Students whispered behind their hands as we passed by. Instead of ducking my head in embarrassment, I held it high.

"I like the brave look on you," Ethan commented as we stopped at my locker. "I can't wait until it's official."

"What's official?"

"Us. All of us. Together," he said, leaning in and whispering it in my ear. I shivered against him. "We're going to flaunt you around. You'll be our queen."

"I can't wait either. But what are we waiting for exactly?"

Ethan backed up and sighed. "Fox."

As if his name alone explained it all. But it was all the explanation I needed. Fox was in charge.

We walked to my class, passing Jamie along the way. Ian was

beside her, his hand on her waist as she dug around in her locker. He winked at me as we strolled by, causing Ethan to let out a quiet snarl.

"I hate him," I hissed once we got around the corner.

"You're not the only one. He's going to get what's coming to him. I promise you that."

"I hope so. I don't want him to hurt anyone else, especially Jamie."

Ethan nodded. "I know. We're working on what to do about him. We need to catch him in the act though, so we have proof. It's always just been a suspicion. That doesn't do shit without evidence, you know?"

I nodded morosely. He was right. We could accuse all day long, but it wouldn't mean shit if we didn't have the proof. And me drunk off my ass in bed with him wasn't exactly the kind of concrete proof we needed.

"I'll see you at lunch, sweetheart. Leave the worrying to us. We'll get this sorted." Ethan gave me a quick kiss on the cheek as was his sweet fashion and departed with a wink.

Sighing, and wondering why he didn't just full on kiss me, I went into my class. I managed to make it through the morning without a hitch, all the while wondering if Fox and the guys had made it back.

When lunch rolled around, I didn't bother going to the cafeteria, opting for the bleachers instead. I took my usual spot and stared out at the field, lost in all my negative thoughts concerning Ian, Jamie, and Mona.

I figured I could just talk to Mona again, but whenever I tried to make eye contact with her in the halls, she ducked and ran the opposite direction.

"What has you out here looking so sad?" Enzo's voice called out.

I looked over my shoulder to find the guys coming up behind me. My heart raced as I took in the sight of them. There was so much perfection smiling at me it was near painful.

"Hey," I said, rising to my feet and rushing to greet them. I threw my arms around Cole's neck, causing him to laugh in surprise. It was a strange sound coming from him since he was always so dark and serious. He wrapped his arms around me tightly.

"Miss me?" he asked.

"Guess I didn't realize how much," I said, squeezing him once more. He released me, and I went to Fox.

"Are you OK?" he asked, hugging me tightly.

"I am now. But being left alone with my thoughts can be dangerous."

"Stop hogging Sunshine," Enzo grumbled, taking me from Fox before he could answer. "Hey."

"Hey yourself," I said as he planted a kiss on my lips.

"You don't have to go to Ethan. You already saw him today," Enzo teased.

Ethan shoved Enzo aside amid laughter and squeezed my hand. "Figured you were out here. Didn't even bother looking in the cafeteria."

"We brought lunch," Cole piped up. He shouldered off his backpack and gestured for me to follow him to the bleachers. We all piled onto the seats, Enzo pulling me down onto his lap.

"What are we eating?" I asked as Cole rifled around in his bag for a moment.

"Sandwiches from Remo's Deli." Cole handed me a turkey one, and I took it happily, sinking my teeth in.

Enzo bit into my sandwich, taking a large hunk and chewed it, winking at my protest.

"Where were you guys?" I asked as Ethan offered me a drink. Eagerly, I sipped at the cool water.

"Worried?" Cole asked, smirking at me.

"Well, yeah."

"We just had some things to do," Fox said, shrugging. "Nothing important, Rosie."

"Is it about whatever you lost?"

"Yes. And you don't need to concern yourself with it," Enzo said.

"Well, I'm going to, so how about you guys tell me what's going on before I have to find out on my own?"

Cole chuckled, and even Fox smiled.

"Rosie, come here." Fox held his arm out for me.

I got to my feet and moved to him.

He pulled me down onto his lap and planted a kiss on my cheek. "I promise it's nothing for you to worry about. Didn't I tell you that I'd explain it to you later?"

I sighed and nodded.

"Are you pouting?"

"Maybe," I mumbled.

The guys laughed. Fox tilted my head up and planted a gentle kiss on my lips.

"Maybe there's something I can do take your mind off it," he purred in my ear.

I wiggled against him, causing him to groan softly.

"My parents aren't home. We can go to my place," Cole broke in, his eyes fixed on me.

"I-I can't," I said, pulling away from Fox. "I'd miss afternoon classes—"

"Don't be such a good girl, Rosebud. Let us dirty you up a bit. Promise we'll make it worth your time," Cole said, tugging me off Fox's lap and bringing me to his. "I want to taste you."

My face heated at his words, warmth pooling between my legs. He nodded knowingly.

"Come on," he breathed out, kissing my neck.

"I can't lose my scholarship, Cole. My dad would kill me."

"One day won't cause you to lose it," he scoffed. "Don't you want to have a little fun?"

"I do, but not at the expense of disappointing my parents. You guys have the video. If what my parents thought didn't matter, then your video wouldn't matter."

"You're only here because of the video?" Ethan asked softly.

I widened my eyes at him as the rest of the guys stared at me. "No." I shook my head. "I mean, at first, yeah. But now?" I looked helplessly at them. "I-I want to be."

"So that's it? All of us? You're ready for that?" Cole asked gruffly. "We don't have to entice you with our wicked ways or blackmail you with videos?"

I looked to Fox. He sat forward, his brows crinkled.

"No. I want this. All of you."

"Fuck yeah," Enzo called out. "Let's make this shit official."

"How?" I asked, nervous laughter bubbling out of me.

"We run that train on you." Enzo winked.

Cole grinned, and even Fox cracked a smile.

"How about her and Ethan go behind that shed?" Cole said, glancing at Ethan. "She can suck his dick."

"I'm not going to make her suck my dick behind a school building, asshole," Ethan shot out, glancing at me. "As much as I want her, I have some class."

Cole rolled his eyes. "Whatever. Then she can suck my dick."

"She's not going to suck *anyone's* dick. We have ten minutes until classes start again," Fox broke in. "She already said she wasn't skipping. I assume that also means she doesn't want to be late. You can at least appreciate that, can't you, Cole?" Fox lifted a brow at Cole.

"You suck, Evans. Fucking cock block."

Fox let out a laugh and shook his head at Cole who was pouting.

"If it helps, she hasn't sucked my dick yet either. Enzo's the only one lucky enough to have experienced her mouth."

"And it was magnificent," Enzo joined in, winking at me.

I flushed at the compliment. "But really how will *this* work? I mean... not in private... but in public, at school? I don't want..." I trailed off unsure how to say what was worrying me.

"You don't want people to think bad of you?" Ethan guessed.

"Talk shit about you, call you a slut?" Enzo chimed in.

My cheeks heated as I nodded. Cole growled at the word slut.

"If anyone dared talk shit about you, we'd take care of it. We'll protect you. We protect what's ours," Fox said.

"But for the time being, I think the easiest solution is for you to be mine in public," Cole said, winking at me.

"What the hell?" Fox glared at him.

"It makes the most sense. People have already seen the two of us behaving like a couple," Cole explained matter-of-factly.

Fox narrowed his eyes. "Fine. But that arrangement is only

temporary. In a few weeks, she can decide she likes me better and prefers to just be your friend. Then she'll be mine in public, and in private, she'll be all of ours." He smirked at Cole's grumbled acceptance.

"When do I get a turn for her to be mine?" Enzo griped.

"Let's not worry about all that right now. We'll figure it out," Ethan rushed to assure me.

"Yeah. When you're more comfortable, we can make things public," Enzo reassured me.

"We can make it official for just us this weekend," Fox continued, eyeing me. "What do you say, Rosie?"

I glanced around at the guys, who all stared back at me eagerly. I nodded. "OK."

"Hell yeah," Cole said as Enzo grinned at me.

"Let's head back," Fox said, getting to his feet. He took my hand in his and helped me down from the bleachers. When my feet hit the ground, he planted a kiss on my forehead before releasing me.

Cole wound his arm around my waist, and we made our way back to the school. When we reached a dark corner of the building, Cole tugged me to stop, the guys following.

"See you later, Sunshine," Enzo said, winking at me.

Ethan planted a quick kiss on my cheek before following Enzo into the building. Fox dragged me out of Cole's arms and leaned in, placing a deep kiss on my lips that curled my toes.

Cole grunted his approval behind us, before tugging me away to kiss me himself. Fox let out a soft, dark laugh as Cole's hands moved to cup my ass beneath my skirt.

He lifted me and hauled me to the wall, pressing me against it, his tongue dancing along mine.

"I fucking want you, Rosebud." He nipped at my lips, growling. "Come on, Fox."

I looked past Cole to see Fox with a hungry look in his eyes. Fox took a step forward and drew me into his arms, his lips crashing against mine. He cupped my breast as he hauled me deeper into the dark corner with Cole right behind him.

I let out a yelp as Cole lifted my skirt, his fingers skimming over my damp panties.

"What are you doing?" I breathed out between Fox's kisses.

"Having dessert," Cole growled, going to his knees and lifting my sundress over his head. I let out a soft moan as he moved my panties aside and slid his tongue over my slit.

"Spread your legs wider," Fox's soft command had me nearly melting as I widened my stance for Cole. Fox's lips found mine again as Cole's tongue lapped at my wet center. He sucked my clit into his mouth, causing my eyes to roll back as Fox's hand found its way beneath the top of my dress. He squeezed my breast, pinching my hard peaks as I trembled from Cole's onslaught.

"Give it to him, Rosie," Fox demanded, punctuating his command with hot kisses. "You'll be late if you don't."

"Oh god," I whimpered as Cole inserted a finger into my tight channel, his mouth never breaking away from my warmth. His tongue and fingers worked faster as the tingles grew. I trembled. My fingers gripped Cole's hair and yanked him closer while my tongue danced with Fox's.

The sparks grew into a hot tension, the heat burning deep in my center before bursting into wildfire and swallowing me whole. I moaned softly against the intense pleasure, my inner walls clenching around Cole's finger as he slowed his tongue, taking a languid lick and swallowing my pleasure.

"Good girl," Fox said breathlessly as Cole emerged from beneath my skirt, his lips and chin glistening with my orgasm.

With my fingers, I reached out and touched Cole's moist lips, wiping his mouth and chin clean. Fox grabbed my hand before I could dig into my bag for a tissue and sucked my damp fingers into his mouth, his eyes locked on mine.

Cole let out a soft laugh as my lips parted.

"Don't want to waste a drop of you, Rosie," Fox said, giving my finger one more suck before releasing me.

"*Holy hotness,*" I whispered.

Fox smirked at me as Cole adjusted my dress, making sure I was completely covered.

"We best get to class. We're going to be late." Cole dragged me out of Fox's hold and wound his arm around my waist.

Fox laughed softly. "Enjoy it, Cole, because once we make this official, we're going to fight over who gets to hold her."

Cole laughed. "Can't wait, brother."

A thrill shot through me. *Truth be told, neither could I.*

CHAPTER 30

The rest of the week passed by quickly. I was still down in the dumps about Ian and Jamie. I hadn't had much of a chance to talk with her about Ian. She'd been busy spending all her free time with him and still wasn't returning my calls. But at least I had musical try-outs to look forward to. Yet when I stopped to think about them, even they left me with a knotted ball of anxiety.

As much as I wanted a repeat of my time with Cole and Fox. Or Enzo and Fox, I knew I had to wait until the weekend. Something else which added to the tension rising in me. They'd been busy with football practice since they were playoff bound. Fox was up for some state football award. It was the buzz of the entire school. It would earn him a position on Mayfair's football team in the fall.

Mayfair. *My* dream college. The college with the incredible music program. The college Cole had already been accepted to, and Fox would probably end up at with a paid football scholarship. Even Enzo and Ethan had applied there and were awaiting acceptance letters. They wanted to stay together, no matter what.

And then there was me. Sick to my stomach knowing I'd be halfway across the state at Pendleton. Alone.

More anxiety.

But things were going good with the guys. *Too good.*

"What's your deal?" Melissa hissed at me as I tied my shoes on the bench in the girls' locker room on Friday afternoon.

"I don't have one." I finished with my shoe and made to stand up, but Juliet shoved me back down.

Tara moved behind me, blocking any escape route I may have had. Juliet had been scarce in recent days, the rumors of her and Fox's breakup echoing throughout campus. I'd hoped it had taken her down a peg or two. Now as she stood glaring down at me, I knew her absence was only her ramping up to her super form.

"You must have one." Juliet narrowed her eyes at me. "Everyone's talking about how you're the guys' new queen bee. I imagine it's easy to get their attention when you're a fucking slut. It doesn't matter what they say or do for you. You'll always be trash. Gleaning from their social status won't change any of it."

My cheeks heated at her words but not from embarrassment. Anger coursed through me as I balled my hands into fists. I'd taken so much from her already. While I hadn't wanted what I had with the guys in the beginning, now I missed them when they weren't near. Her standing there and making it sound like I was trash made me sick. Fox promised this wouldn't happen again. He *swore* it. My day had gone from really bad to terrible.

I moved to push past them, but Tara and Melissa caught me by both arms and slammed me against the lockers, holding me in place. Juliet lifted a brow at me, malice in her eyes.

"Leave me alone," I growled, struggling against the girls' hold.

Melissa dug her nails deep into my skin, making me cry out. I stilled since moving was making her claw harder.

"Here's what I know. You're *not* one of us. It doesn't matter if Cole, Enzo, or Ethan fucked you. It doesn't even matter if Fox has. You're just another whore to anyone who matters." Juliet rifled through her bag and pulled out a black marker.

I licked my lips, worried my worst nightmares were about to come true.

"I know about you, Fox, and Cole. I saw *everything*. You should be a little more careful about where you're spreading your legs, *Rosebud*. Word of advice, sweetie. Fox is *mine*. And I fight for what's mine." Her eyes darkened as she glared down at me. "Just because he's giving you pity, doesn't mean he's the good guy. Why do you think I'm here?"

"What?" I asked, my voice shaking.

"Aw, honey." She *tsked*, jutting her bottom lip out. "You didn't think it was *real*, did you? Fox sent me today to deal with you. The game is up, and I get to give you your prize. You're just one of *many* they've done this to."

Dread washed over me at her words. *No.* No, it couldn't be true.

"Hold her."

Melissa and Tara tightened their grips on me as I came to life, desperate to flee. We toppled in a pile onto the hard floor, me landing on the bottom and Tara twisting my arm painfully. I gasped as Melissa fisted my hair and tugged my head back.

Juliet kneeled in front of me as tears rolled down my cheeks. She cocked her head, contemplating her next move. Then she leaned in, the marker tip touching my forehead.

I tried to buck out from beneath the girls' hold, but Tara twisted my arm harder to the point I thought it would break.

Fat, ugly tears rolled from my eyes as Juliet scrawled on my forehead, her words on repeat in my head. *Fox sent her. Fox sent her. Fox sent her. No! Why... he wouldn't... would he?*

Sitting back, she smirked in satisfaction.

"It's so you don't forget. I'm sure the guys would agree." She gave a nod to the girls who released me, letting me fall onto my back sobbing. I had no idea what she'd written on my forehead. All I knew was that it had to be bad.

"Stay away from Fox. If I catch you near him again, it'll be worse. Got it?" She didn't wait for an answer.

With a cackle, they all left the locker room, leaving me on the floor. I had to get out of there. I climbed to my feet and went to the sink, hoping to scrub it off my face. My heart stuttered as I stared at the word on my forehead in big, ugly, black letters.

Freakshow.

Sobbing, I turned on the faucet and scrubbed furiously at my head, whimpering as it barely faded.

"Shit," I hissed, scrubbing until my skin was sore and red, the black still bold. "*Shit!*"

I couldn't miss classes. I stared at my red, swollen eyes, tears still trickling out. I couldn't tell anyone about Juliet and her posse. It would only make matters worse. I had to push through. Not that telling anyone would erase the ugly letters on my forehead anyway. And if Fox and the guys *did* have something to do with this… my guts twisted at the prospect.

I couldn't let them win. I didn't want to believe it of them, but Mona's words still rang in my ears. How this was a game to them. How they didn't really care. I swallowed down another sob, forcing myself to focus.

Through the mirror, I spotted the lost and found bin. I went to it, sorting through old shirts, shoes, and random odds and ends until I found a black beanie.

"Yes!" I released my hair from its ponytail and let the wild waves cascade around me. Then I tugged the beanie low over my head, hiding the ugly scrawl. I studied myself in the mirror. I had a study hall and a physics lecture left. I could get through it. Then I'd go home for the weekend and lock my doors, ignoring the world.

Getting through study hall wasn't hard. Mr. Ballard, the teacher, didn't care about my beanie. I sat in the back, my head down, working on homework. When the bell rang, I was on my feet, racing out of the room, my head ducked low.

While I didn't want to see the guys, I at least thought one of them would walk me to class like they'd been doing. But nothing. I never even spotted them in the hall. It only solidified that they'd something to do with Juliet's attack. My heart ached at the thought.

When I reached my physics class, I sank down in my seat, keeping to the idea if I couldn't see people, they couldn't see me.

"Miss Bishop," Mr. Hines called out. I stiffened in my seat as I stared at him. "Is there a reason you're in my class with something on your head?"

"Um." I glanced around, my cheeks heating as all eyes were on me. *So much for the no one seeing me concept.* "I'm cold?"

"You know the rules. Hats off."

I stared down at my notebook, knowing exactly what would happen if I took it off.

"Miss Bishop, the hat? Now, please."

With shaking hands, I pulled the beanie off. Snickers shot out around me as people saw what was scrawled on my forehead.

"Freakshow!" Cameron Deacons, one of the guys on the football team, cackled loudly, setting off peals of outright laughter from the other students. Mr. Hines stood, staring stupidly at me, his mouth agape at a loss for words.

"Juliet was right. Now *Freakshow* is even advertising!" Jenna Elkins, one of the cheerleaders, snorted, pointing at me to more raucous laughter.

I didn't bother grabbing my books. I raced from the room like a streak of lightning, wanting to get the hell away from everything about the place.

"Rosalie?" Fox called out to me. His timing was perfect as he came out of a classroom with a bathroom pass in his hand. I shoved him away and raced down the hall as fast as my feet would take me. "Rosalie!"

Sunshine blanketed my face as I slammed open the door. I let out a sob as I got into my car and flew out of the parking lot. I pulled into my driveway in record time.

My parents weren't home, having left again for another of my dad's trips. When I got inside, I ran straight to my room and threw myself into bed, squeezing my eyes closed and counting, the only thing I could think to do to try to calm myself. Eventually, it led to me finally falling asleep.

CHAPTER 31

hen I finally woke, hours had passed, and it had grown dark out. Thunder rumbled in the distance. I shivered and decided I wanted something sweet and warm, so I made my way downstairs and dug around in the kitchen until I found everything I needed to make a mug of hot cocoa. I let out a groan when my doorbell rang. Considering I was on the outs with everyone, there shouldn't have been anyone at my door at nine at night.

Sighing, I jerked it open to find Fox staring back at me.

"Go away," I said in an even voice.

"Christ, Rosalie, your face—"

"Oh, this?" I let out a bitter laugh as his brows crinkled. "Tell your girlfriend thanks. Now that you've had your look, run along and laugh about it." I made to close the door, but he held his hand out and stopped me.

"What the hell? Let me help you."

"You can help me by going to hell, Fox." I tried closing the door again, but he wasn't having it. He pushed me aside and stepped into the foyer.

"I told you to get the fuck out," I snarled at him. All the anger I'd been harboring came bubbling out. "I'll call the cops."

245

"You can call an army. I'm not leaving here until I help you." He didn't wait for my answer. He strode past me like he really wanted to help. I stared dumbly at him for a moment before letting out a grunt of frustration. *Whatever*. I'd go up to my room and lock the door. He could sit downstairs by himself.

I ambled into the kitchen, but he wasn't there.

What the hell? Where did he go?

Figuring I didn't really give a damn, I went back to making my hot cocoa, telling myself I probably would call the cops if I couldn't get him out of my house in the next ten minutes.

"Sit." He came back in the room carrying rubbing alcohol and a washcloth. I eyed the items nervously and shook my head.

"I don't take orders from you. I want you out of here—"

"I'm not playing around, Rosalie. Sit your ass down before I put you down." The way his blue eyes flashed told me he wasn't playing.

I already knew how very serious he could be. Rather than fight more with anyone, I sat at the kitchen island, eyeing him nervously. He shuffled beside me and uncapped the alcohol as he faced me.

"Tell me what happened."

"You already know—"

"*No, I don't.* If I did, this would be a different conversation. Who did this to you?"

"I told you already. Juliet and her plastic patrol."

A muscle in Fox's jaw tightened as he dabbed the alcohol on my forehead. "When?"

"After gym. In the locker room."

"Did she do it alone?"

"No," I mumbled, telling him about Melissa and Tara. He dabbed more on my forehead, scrubbing slightly.

"Did she say why?"

"Does she *need* a reason to be a bitch?" I countered. "But if you want to know the reason, she said *you* sent her. That it was part of the game you guys were playing. Somehow, I'd lost, so she got to have a little fun."

"Fucking bitch," he growled. "I had nothing to do with this, Rosie. I swear to you. I'd never do this to you. *Never.*"

I grew quiet as he continued his work. My throat ached as I tried to push away my feelings.

"She said I was trash. A whore. She said she knows about me, you, and Cole. She saw us earlier this week at school. She said that I needed to stay away from you. This was my warning."

Fox nodded tightly, his eyes darkening as he continued dabbing alcohol on my forehead.

"She won't bother you again, Rosalie."

I snorted and looked away from him.

He was quick to grab my face and turn me back. "I'll make sure of it."

I scoffed. "Right, just like you already promised. *Twice!*" I threw my hands up and got up from my seat, all my emotions pouring out of me. "If you'd have just let me be that day in the cafeteria with her, none of this would be happening right now! It's all your fault!"

"You know damn well when someone wants what they want, they *will* find a way to get it," Fox snapped back, getting to his feet. Thunder rumbled louder outside. The lights flickered in my kitchen as the wind picked up. I could make out lightning streaking across the sky from the patio doors behind Fox. This was going to get nasty in more ways than one.

"I wouldn't know shit about that," I snapped. "I've never gotten what I've wanted."

"Didn't you want *us*? Didn't you want *me*?" he demanded. "Because the girl I've spent time with these past few weeks, sure acted like she did!"

I glowered at him. "I was *forced* into it, in case you forgot! You were mean to me. Just awful. Then you bossed me around. And then to gain leverage to make me do your bidding, you filmed me almost being *raped* and blackmailed me to keep you from showing the video. And now that you made me feel more for *you*, more for all of you, you decided to have one more fucking laugh at my expense by siccing your psycho girlfriend on me."

A muscle popped along his jaw, and he shook his head in disbelief. "I thought we were beyond that. I thought you knew we never intended to actually use the video. We just wanted... *I* just wanted..." He chuckled wryly, rage and sorrow warring on his face. "I'm sorry. But haven't you ever wanted something enough to actually fight for it? Have you ever fought for anything in your life? No, wait. I can answer that for you. *No, you haven't.* You don't even fight for your dreams, Rosalie! I know damn well you don't want to go to Pendleton. I saw how happy you were when you were singing in my bedroom. You're settling so you don't have to fight—"

"Get the hell out of my house, Fox. I'm not fucking kidding. Don't come in here acting like a white knight after everything, thinking you can play these mind games with me. I'm not letting you in anymore! Whatever sick game you're playing with me is done! So get the *fuck* out and don't come back!"

He stared me down, a vein pulsating in his forehead. His mouth opened to say more, but I wasn't finished yet.

"You don't fight for what you want either. Our failed friendship is a shining example! I hate you, Fox. I hate you so fucking much it hurts!" I pounded my palm against my heart. "You've done nothing but ruin my life. But that's what you wanted, wasn't it? To leave me in ruins? It's what you vowed. To make me pay for whatever the fuck you think I did to you. I was a *kid*, Fox. A fucking child. I didn't have shit to do with your mom dying. I know you blame me for it! It wasn't my fault! The only thing I ever did was love you. I loved you even when you hated me. But now, that shit is over. *This is over.* Get out. And don't fucking come back."

He pushed passed me and went out the front door, slamming it so hard the windows rattled. Torrents of rain came down, and the storm intensified outside.

But it had nothing on my heart. I fell back onto the stool, sobbing. I caught my reflection in my mom's China cabinet and let out another sob.

Fox had gotten the words off my forehead.

CHAPTER 32

I sat sobbing on the stool five minutes later when the faint sound of the doorbell rang through the air. Before I could stand, a pounding on my door sounded out. The storm outside was so intense, the power had gone out only minutes before. I hurriedly wiped at my eyes and went to the door and yanked it open.

A whoosh of air escaped my lungs as a soaking wet Fox came rushing back inside. He captured my face in his hands, his lips crashing against mine. I let out a whimper as his tongue delved into my mouth, his desperation at my acceptance of him screaming frantically as he cradled my face.

"I didn't do what she says I did," he choked out, his gaze searching mine. "I'd never do that to you, Rosie. I fucking swear on my life I wouldn't. Please. Believe that."

The way his eyes locked on mine, wavering in desperation, made me nod, accepting that he didn't have a hand in it. I guess I'd known it. Or at least thought it. Hurt over being embarrassed had been what bubbled all the emotions inside me. I tossed aside all reason. He came back. That's what I focused on. He let out a breath, and his lips collided with mine again.

Every current of electricity flowing through me told me despite everything, this kiss was the key to mending bridges we'd set fire to and watched burn. I parted my lips for him, letting the pain at truly missing him in my life take over. Years of anger and desperation came out through that kiss as he held my face in his hands, his tongue dancing against mine.

When he finally pulled away, he rested his forehead against mine.

"Please don't hate me, Rosie," his voice shook with his words. I stared up at him, tears rolling down my cheeks as he tangled his fingers in my hair. "I fucked everything up. I should've told you how I felt a long time ago. I should've showed you so much more than what I did. I should've kissed you in the cafeteria that day instead of yelled at you. And I should've made love to you instead of what I've been doing. I'm so fucking sorry." He kissed the tears gently away, whispering his apologies over and over as he ran his fingers through my curls. "Tell me you believe me, Rosie."

"I believe you," I whispered back, seeing the truth in his eyes and hating myself for not believing him in the first place.

When his lips found mine again, I fell back into him just as easily as I had moments before. He lifted me into his arms and carried me upstairs to my room and laid me down on my bed, his lips never breaking from mine.

I let out a soft moan as his fingers moved beneath my shirt, his hand finding its way to my breast. He shifted back, hands trembling as he lifted my shirt.

My breath hitched as he stared down at me in my black bra. He didn't move. He didn't speak. Fox wanted to see me. His eyes drank in every inch of me, his lips parted. It was like he was trying to memorize every bit of me he could. I sat up and tentatively ran my hands along the taut muscles beneath his wet shirt. His eyes were hooded as he peered down at me, still speechless. Feeling brave, I pushed his shirt up, bringing it over his head so we were both shirtless.

My fingers fumbled with the button on his jeans as he silently watched me. The only sounds in my room were the storm outside and our heavy breathing.

Once I had his button and zipper undone, I swallowed hard and peeked up at him. His hands landed on my waist as he tugged me to him, his lips finding mine. A moment later, he shoved my pants down my thighs and laid me back on the bed, his own pants gone.

I didn't know what the hell we were doing. In that moment, nothing but the two of us, together, mattered. Positioning himself firmly between my legs, he gazed down at me. So many emotions flitted over his face it made my heart clench.

"I'm sorry, Rosie. For everything," he rasped. He pressed a kiss to the edge of my lips. "I hurt you. I don't *want* to hurt you."

"Make it up to me," I answered breathlessly, shifting my hips beneath him.

"I want to." His thick erection pressed against my damp panties. "I have a lot to apologize for."

"We have all night."

A tiny smirk cut across his sad face before his lips met mine once more. His hands found my breasts again, this time making sure to remove my bra. Before long, we were naked, our hot bodies pressed firmly against one another's.

Fox trailed his lips down my neck, to my collarbone, making a path to my breasts, where he licked and sucked each pebbled bud with such fervor, the tingles in my center grew hot, and my toes curled. I was certain I was going to explode beneath him as he nipped at a nipple, drawing it into his hot mouth.

"Fox," I moaned.

He murmured my name in return, moving lower on my body, his mouth leaving a trail of fire from every kiss he planted on my skin. When he reached the apex of my thighs, his blue eyes locked on mine.

I parted my legs, giving him permission. It was all he needed. He pressed a kiss to my most intimate area before darting his tongue out against my slit, languidly running up it. I arched my back beneath his hot tongue, my heart pounding against my chest. With a strong grip, he latched onto my hips and tugged my center firmly to his mouth, his tongue disappearing inside of me.

"Oh god," I choked out as his tongue whirled and swirled around my tight bundle of nerves. On instinct, my fingers dove into his hair, pulling his face closer to my wet center, my hips rocking in time with his licks and sucks. Fox buried his face in me, eating like a man starving.

I tensed as he inserted a finger into my tight channel, never breaking his rhythmic assault on my clit. The feelings were so intense I neared my breaking point. He must have sensed it because his movements sped up, his tongue working over my quivering button until I crashed down around him, his name on repeat on my lips.

I laid, feeling boneless, as he scooted back up to me, his mouth glistening from my orgasm. He licked his lips, staring down at me, still not satisfied.

"Can I return the favor?" I managed to whisper up at him.

"You don't need to, Rosie," he whispered back, nuzzling my neck, his warm breath sending goosebumps through me.

"I want to." Boldly, I reached down and grasped his thick cock, my heart stuttering in my chest at how large it was.

He closed his eyes as I stroked him up and down. He moved onto his back, and I quickly found myself between his legs, his massive length in my hand.

His breath came in small gasps as he watched me lick his shaft. Those blue eyes rolled back in his head as he relaxed against the pillow. I kissed the tip, licking up the drop of salty sweetness.

"Fuck, Rosie," he moaned as I sucked him deep into my mouth, swirling my tongue over the head of his dick.

I bobbed up and down on him, licking and sucking. His fingers tangled in my hair, pulling my head down until I had all of him down my throat. I relished in the feel of him filling my mouth, throbbing against my tongue.

I let out a yelp as he tugged me off him and rolled me onto my back.

"I don't want to make a mess in that pretty mouth," he murmured, pressing a kiss to my lips. "I'd much rather make it somewhere else."

My heart fluttered in my chest as he situated himself between my legs. Holding my breath, I stared up at the impossibly beautiful man looming over me.

"Do you want this?" he asked softly. "I won't do it if you don't, Rosie."

"I want this," I answered back hoarsely. "I want *you*."

"If it hurts, tell me, and I'll stop. I-I don't want to hurt you."

I nodded mutely as he took his dick in his hand and rubbed it against my entrance, his eyes locked on mine.

"Are you on the pill?"

I nodded again, and he let out a slow breath.

"Don't look away from me, baby" he whispered, pushing forward.

I winced, my breath hitching as he entered me.

"Look at me," he instructed gently as he pushed in further.

I tensed beneath the pressure as he inched slowly inside of me. A tear squeezed out of the corner of my eye, and he was quick to kiss it away. A moment later, he buried himself completely inside of me, our bodies fully connected.

"You're incredible," he whispered, shifting as he moved out of me slowly before pushing back in. "So fucking incredible."

I whimpered, but he was quick to kiss it away. His movements sped up until I was meeting his thrusts with my own, the ache of his intrusion having receded and waves of pleasure replacing it.

The swell of tingles swirled deep in my center, making me moan out his name.

"Give it to me, Rosie," he commanded, moving faster as he pounded in and out of me.

A moment later, I crashed down around him, my walls clenching around his dick. He let out a moan, spilling himself inside of me, before finally coming to a breathless halt, both our bodies covered in a sheen of sweat.

He lifted himself up onto his elbows and stared down at me, so much wonder and adoration on his face it left me breathless.

"There's no going back, Rosie. Never. You belong to me. To us."

CHAPTER 33

I woke up early, sunlight barely shining through the window. Fox's naked body was curled around mine. My heart hammered in my chest as I remembered what we'd done. I didn't think about anything Mona had said. I didn't think about Juliet's ugly words. I didn't think about Ian. I only thought about Fox and how I felt about him. How I'd always felt about him.

Needing a glass of water, I gently untangled myself from him, pulled on my robe, and made to go to my bathroom. I nearly stepped on something by my bed and stopped to examine it.

Fox's phone.

I bent down and picked it up, my heart in my throat. Everything that could ruin me was inside it. If ever there was a chance to save my own ass, this was the moment. While my trust in Fox was growing, I knew the video was the key to my downfall. I glanced over at him snoring peacefully in my bed and swiped his screen. Carefully, I went through his gallery and found the video right away and opened up the options.

Delete?

"What are you doing?"

I jumped as Fox's arms wound their way around my waist. Lost for words, I stood holding his phone, knowing he caught me.

"You can delete it, you know." His lips skimmed against my jaw.

Instinctively, I angled my neck so he could traverse the sensitive skin. He moved his hands up to cup my breasts over my robe, his breath hot on my neck.

"You know you want to."

"I do," I rasped as he gave my breasts a firm squeeze.

"Then do it already so I can bury myself in you again."

Hell, yes. I hit the button and watched the video disappear.

"Mm. Bad girl." He nuzzled his face against me once more before turning me around to face him. His lips crashed against mine. My legs wound their way around his waist as he hauled me into his arms. Goosebumps flooded my skin as he lay me on my back in bed.

"I love how I make this happen." His fingers brushed along my thigh where the goosebumps adorned my skin. His hand moved from my leg to the knot on my robe. He undid it, opening the fabric so my breasts spilled out. He rolled me over, so I was on top of him. Strong hands captured my breasts. His eyes locked on mine.

"I meant what I said last night, Rosie." He thumbed gently over my nipples.

"What was that?" I asked, breathlessly.

"That you belong to me. *To us.*" He leaned in and sucked a hard nipple into his mouth, causing me to moan his name. In one fluid movement, he had me beside him, his fingers making quick work of finding my center and dipping inside.

Feeling brave and empowered, I reached out and stroked his length, relishing in how hard it got for me.

We were breathing heavily as we pleasured one another, his fingers moving in time with my hand on his manhood. His kisses were deep. Ferocious. Brutal in such a way that made me want more.

"Fox," I gasped as he kissed along my neck.

"Rosie," he growled, nipping at me.

A sputter of protest left my lips as he removed his fingers, but he quickly silenced me by leveling his body over mine, in perfect position to make anticipation crawl through my core. I winced as he pushed forward, his dick begging for entrance. I parted my legs further for him, my breath held as he slid fully inside with a groan.

"Fuck, you feel so good, baby," he whispered as he placed punctuated kisses on my lips, his hips shifting against mine. "Tell me you want it."

"I want it," I gasped as he moved out before thrusting back inside with a smooth motion. "Fox, please."

"Please what, baby?" His voice was breathless as he moved slowly in and out, torturing the pleasure from my body.

"Fuck me. Please. Faster."

The boldness of my words unleashed a wild beast in him because he slid out and slammed back into me. I dug my nails in his back as he growled, pistoning in and out of me, the heat from our linked bodies making us both pant and sweat.

I arched my back, his arms wrapped around me, as I tumbled over the edge of delicious euphoria, his name on my lips. He followed a moment later, breathless. Then he slowed his movements, moving gently inside me for a few more blissful seconds. We laid together, him over me, his forehead pressed to mine.

"Incredible. So fucking incredible."

Butterflies tickled low in my belly at his endearment, and I placed a tender kiss on his lips. He responded in earnest, gifting me a kiss that made my toes curl and my center ache.

"I'll be right back," he murmured against my lips.

I watched as he went to the bathroom and returned a moment later with a damp washcloth. Gently, he swiped the cloth between my legs, cleaning me up. With a mischievous grin, he planted a kiss on the apex of my thighs before tossing the rag into the hamper.

"I, uh, should go."

"What?" I frowned at him as he pulled his boxers and jeans on. He'd gone from being Mr. Sweetheart to acting weird.

"Sorry." He leaned down and planted a kiss on my lips. "I'm supposed to help Dad with the gutters this morning."

"Oh… OK."

"Don't worry. We'll talk later, OK?" He pulled his t-shirt over his head. "I'll make you dinner. Your favorite. Mac-n-cheese with hot dogs. Ketchup on the side."

I chuckled, feeling giddy inside. "Fox, we aren't eight anymore. That meal is gross."

He grinned at me. I hadn't seen him look that happy in years. My heart lit up at his joy.

"Fine. Hold the hot dog. *My* hot dog." He winked at me, causing me to snort. This Fox was nothing like the Fox I'd experienced the past few years and not even the Fox I'd interacted with the past few weeks. This Fox was playful and sweet. *Why the hell had he been hiding him for so long? He was even happier now than he was over the past week.*

"Deal." I grinned back at him, angling my head up so he could kiss me again. He did so without hesitation.

"Fuck, I don't want to go," he growled.

"So don't."

"My old man will have my ass if I'm not there. He's been bitching about these gutters since July. I'll make it up to you. We'll talk. Tonight."

"Talk?"

He nodded, his face serious as he pulled away from me. "I think we should, Rosie. I have a lot I need to say to you."

I bit my bottom lip. "Is it bad?"

"Not really. Just things I need to say. I promised to tell you about what was going on with everything. What we lost and were looking for. Figured tonight might be a good time to clear the air. Besides, we're making it official, right?"

A smile worked its way onto my lips as I nodded. "Yes."

"OK. I'll see you tonight then."

He pulled away and went to my door. "If you open your curtain, you can watch me. Maybe I'll take my shirt off for you."

I laughed as he shot me a wink before leaving me alone in my room. For the first time, I felt like maybe we were finally on the right track.

It was a start anyway.

Fox worked on the gutters and in the yard all day. I watched him from my bedroom window, totally in awe of how beautiful he was, even when he frowned, which seemed to be far too often.

When night fell, I waited until Fox's dad, Kurt, pulled out of the driveway. Hastily, I fluffed my loose hanging hair and dabbed lip gloss on my lips. Opening my closet, I pulled on a blue sundress. Then I raced downstairs, torn between feeling nervous and excited.

I hadn't even knocked when Fox yanked the door open with a massive grin on his face and tugged me inside. His lips locked on mine immediately, making me giggle.

"Do you have any idea what you're doing to me?" he growled, moving his mouth to kiss across my jawline.

"Mm, no, but if it's along the same lines as what you're doing to me, then I think I may have a good idea."

He laughed and pulled away from me, taking my hand in his. We went into his kitchen where he offered me a seat at the kitchen island. I took it and watched as he spooned out a runny mixture of cheese and macaroni into a bowl for me.

"It's more like mac and cheese soup," he laughed sheepishly. "Cooking isn't really my thing."

I grinned and dug my fork into my cheesy noodle soup and took a bite.

"This isn't bad," I offered through a mouthful.

Fox beamed at me and dug into his own bowl.

We ate in playful silence, him reaching out to squeeze my hand or play footsie with me every few minutes. When I'd swallowed my last forkful, he grabbed my bowl and rose from his seat.

Something I'd been pushing out of my head since last night finally came tumbling out of my mouth. "Fox? What about Juliet?"

Fox stilled at the sink for a moment before placing the bowls in it and turning back to me. His eyes locked on mine.

"I broke up with her a bit ago… before anything happened with us. She's been bitter. Angry. I'm sorry, Rosie. I should've eased your mind when you asked me before. I just… I don't know. I get so caught up in you that I don't think straight. I don't want to waste time talking about someone like Juliet. Someone who doesn't matter to me."

He strode back to me and took my hand in his, drawing me to my feet. Wordlessly, he led me to the living room where he tugged me down onto his lap on the couch.

"She hurt you," he murmured, squeezing me to him.

"She's always done that. You've always been fine with it—"

"I was never *fine with it*," he ground out. "I hated it, but I hated my feelings more, so I didn't do anything about it."

"What changed?" I whispered.

Sincerity covered his face. "Everything, Rosie, absolutely everything. There's so much I have to tell you. Things I'm afraid to tell you because of what they could mean."

"Just tell me, Fox. I want to know."

He grew quiet as I studied him.

"I'm sorry for all the things I've said and done to you over the years." His gaze stayed trained on my face. "It's hard for me to admit everything. I'm trying, Rosie. I am."

I studied him for a moment longer before speaking. "We haven't spoken in years, Fox. Why?"

He gave my thigh a squeeze, a faraway look in his eyes.

"My mom loved you like a daughter. She'd have done anything for you."

I nodded, swallowing hard. I knew that about her. She'd been a wonderful person.

"I loved her too," I whispered.

He let out a soft laugh. "I know you did. She always wanted a daughter. She and dad tried for years to have another baby after me. I guess it wasn't in the stars for them. A lot of things weren't."

My heart clenched. He'd grown quiet and sullen. I was losing him to his sadness and grief.

I reached out and tilted his chin up. Bravely, I placed a soft kiss on his lips. He kissed me back, everything about his touch and kiss gentle and caring.

"Do you remember when you first kissed me?" I whispered against his lips.

"Yes."

"You were my first kiss."

"I know," he murmured. "You were mine. I intended on being your first everything. And I still want to be with you for each new thing you try."

I blushed at his words. He was doing a great job so far.

"You giving yourself to me last night was amazing," he continued softly. "I've wanted you for so long." He kissed the corner of my lips sweetly.

"Really?"

"Mhmm." He nuzzled into my neck, hauling in a deep breath and giving me a gentle squeeze. "God, you're amazing. I'm such a fuckup, Rosie."

He stilled against me.

"You're not, Fox. We all do things we regret." I ran my fingers through his messy hair.

"I have so many regrets. I won't ever be able to make them right."

"Then learn from them," I offered gently. "Be a better person."

"Rosie, I'm really trying." He pressed another kiss to my lips. "It starts with you."

In a flash, he had me on my back, looming over me, his hands delving beneath my skirt.

"Fox," I choked out. "What about your dad?"

"Not here," was his muffled reply as he kissed between my breasts.

"He could come home though." I angled my neck for him so he could kiss me more.

"Then he's going to see me buried inside you."

I slapped at him amid his soft laughter. "We're supposed to go to Cole's house."

He stilled against me before getting to his feet, hauling me with him. A slight frown of disappointment tugged his lips for a moment before he replaced it with a smirk.

"You're right. We're making this official."

He led me out the front door and had me seatbelted in his Jeep in moments.

"You seem so eager," I teased.

He leaned over and kissed me. "Baby, you have no idea."

I let out a laugh as he put the Jeep into reverse and pulled out of his driveway, his hand in mine.

"I HEARD ABOUT WHAT HAPPENED," Ethan said, the moment we stepped into Cole's living room. He pulled me into a tight embrace. "You know we'd never do that to you. Neither would Fox."

"I'm glad Fox got it off your forehead," Cole said, eyeing me. "I was ready to pay Juliet a visit and show her how it feels."

"I'm still ready to," Enzo scoffed, giving me a hug next.

"I'll take care of it," Fox said.

"You better or I'll do it. Trust me, I won't be gentle." Cole's face had grown dark, sending a shiver through me. If anyone was going to do something bad, it would be Cole. He and Fox would be a force to be reckoned with if they were pissed and teamed up. Ian was a good example of that. And I was certain that was only a taste of their darkness.

"I ordered pizza," Enzo broke in, glancing at Cole. Sometimes he needed to be brought back to our world from wherever his dark thoughts led him.

"I could go for some pizza," I said, reaching for Cole. The tension melted away as I touched him. I went to him and kissed him lightly. "Relax," I murmured.

He responded by hugging me tightly and blowing out a deep breath. "I'm sorry," he apologized so low only I could hear him. "But when it comes to you, I lose my fucking mind, Rosebud."

I kissed him again, making sure he knew exactly what his words meant. He let out a growl and nipped my bottom lip before releasing me.

The doorbell rang then. Fox turned and answered it, taking the boxes of pizza from the delivery driver and bringing them to the coffee table in the living room. We all settled on the couches. Ethan got me a piece of pizza after Cole retrieved the plates from the kitchen. We ate in silence for a bit.

"So, what's the deal?" Enzo asked after his third slice, looking from me to Fox. "Do you still want to do this with all of us?"

"She said she's in," Fox said, smiling at me. "She's ours."

I nodded, a shy smile on my face. *Theirs.* I liked the sound of that.

"You popped her cherry?" Cole asked, winking at me. I flushed hot at his words.

"Best I've ever had." Fox grinned at me. "Seriously. She's amazing."

Cole's gaze swept over me, a look of longing in them.

"We running that train, Sunshine?" Enzo laughed.

"I want to, but um, I'm kinda sore after Fox," I admitted bashfully. "Can we sort of do it slowly? I don't want to rush it."

"Good lord, she's another Ethan," Cole groaned.

Ethan threw his balled-up napkin at Cole, bouncing it off his head. Cole chucked it back, grinning.

I got to my feet, feeling braver than I'd ever felt before, and went to

Ethan. He stared up at me, his lips hitched in a curious smile. I sank down onto his lap.

"Hey, beautiful," he murmured, surveying me.

I breathed in deeply and pressed my lips to his. He came to life beneath me, his tongue sweeping against mine as his arms encircled me. His lips were soft, molding to mine. He was gentle but demanding. Insistent.

He deepened the kiss, his fingers tangled in my hair. I shifted on his lap, so I was straddling him, our centers align. He pulled me closer, his hard length hitting me in all the right places as I rocked against him. I let out a soft moan which had him grinding harder on my center.

"Ethan," I rasped as the heat hit low in my belly, the impending euphoria making goosebumps pop along my skin.

He kissed me again, continuing his movements. We both were breathing heavily when the bliss took hold, sending me toppling over the cliff of pleasure. A soft moan erupted from my lips.

He let out a soft chuckle as our movements slowed, my body trembling from our heavy make-out session. I collapsed against his hard chest, feeling sated. He ran his fingers through my hair as he cradled me in his arms.

"That was the hottest thing I've ever seen," Enzo murmured.

"And here I thought you two would be the shy ones," Cole mused. "Guess I was fucking wrong on that account."

I locked eyes on Fox, who stared back at me with parted lips, lust in his eyes. A flurry of heat swept through me at his hooded gaze.

"I can't wait until you're rested, Rosie," Fox growled. "We're going to have a lot of fun together."

I blew a kiss at Fox and then cuddled closer to Ethan. "I can't wait either."

CHAPTER 35

ox never told me what he wanted to talk to me about. I didn't want to push it since we all had so much fun at Cole's. After Ethan and I's show, we'd gone to Cole's basement where the guys tried to teach me how to play pool. We ended the evening with me kissing each of the guys goodnight before Fox took me home.

As always, things were hectic the rest of the weekend. I worked more on learning my lines for the musical audition. I opted to commit a monologue from Shakespeare's *A Midsummer Night's Dream* to memory.

The guys had football practice on Sunday. Cole reminded me to take a warm bath to soothe my aches. He acted like he was teasing, but I knew he meant business.

And Fox… My text messages beeped around ten Sunday evening.

Fox: Hey, baby. Missed you today.

I snapped back a reply, the butterflies coming to life in my tummy.

Rosalie: I missed you too. All of you.

Fox: I have something for you.

I waited a few moments for his next text. My mouth went dry when I saw what it was. A link to the application for Mayfair.

Fox: I know you're going to Pendleton, but I also know Mayfair

needs you. *We* **need you. Cole and I are going. I know Ethan and Enzo will get in. Please consider applying.**

I blew out a breath, my heart in my throat. I wanted to go so badly. It was my dream. Knowing two of my guys were already on their way there only made the yearning deeper.

Rosie: I want to, Fox, but my dad will freak. I can't afford to pay for college on my own.

Fox: At least apply, baby. If you get in, we'll figure something out.

I bit my bottom lip for a moment before answering.

Rosie: Promise?

Fox: Yes. Always.

I smiled to myself.

Rosie: OK.

He sent me a kissy emoji that had me grinning as I fired up my laptop and went to the Mayfair site. My cursor hovered over APPLY.

"Screw it," I muttered, clicking the link.

"GOOD MORNING," Fox greeted me Monday morning as I stepped out my front door. He reached out and snagged my backpack off my shoulder.

"Good morning to you." I giggled as he gave me a quick kiss before leading me to his Jeep.

"So, I guess I'm riding with you today?"

He let out a laugh and opened the passenger door. "How'd you know?"

"Girlfriend intuition," I ventured nervously.

He tensed, his eyes fixed on me. "What did you say?"

"Girlfriend?"

He hauled me close to him and planted his lips on mine in a deep kiss. "I love the sound of that."

I blew out a nervous breath and smiled. "Officially official?"

"Absolutely." He grinned at me. "But I thought you already knew that."

I shrugged. "I had a hunch."

He laughed and closed me in the Jeep and went to his side and got in.

"Did you apply to Mayfair?"

I nodded. "Yeah, I did."

He reached out and twined his fingers through mine before bringing our hands to his lips where he pressed a kiss to my skin.

"You'll get in. If I have to work two jobs to pay for your tuition, you're going. All of us being there without you next fall won't work."

"How do you even know we'll all last that long? You and Cole piss me off sometimes," I joked.

"Boyfriend intuition." Fox winked at me, causing me to grin wider.

The rest of the ride to school was spent in playful banter that just felt *right*. Everything had changed between us in a good way. All of Mona's words from the party weeks ago faded in my mind. Even Ian's threats were left hazy. I knew I had to deal with them soon though. The feeling I may have waited too long weighed heavily on me. *If he hurt Jamie. . .*

Guilt ate at me. I'd been selfish, ignoring the Ian problem. I deserved for Jamie to hate me. I should have been there for her sooner. *What if he already hurt her? What if. . .*

"What's wrong?" Fox called out as he parked the Jeep in his spot in the parking lot.

"Huh?"

"You're a million miles away."

"Oh," I let out a nervous laugh. "I don't know. I was thinking about Jamie."

Fox frowned, his eyes raking over my face. "She'll come around. I'll talk to her if you want me to."

"No." I shook my head, a tight smile on my face. "It's something I need to do."

Fox kissed my hand again. "If you need me though—"

"I know."

The answer seemed good enough for him because he got out and came to my side. Strong hands gripped me to help me out. We walked side by side, our pinkies linked, until we reached the sidewalk. Ethan strode toward me, a confident smile on his face. He glanced around the parking lot, which was mostly empty of students, before he wound his arm around my waist.

"Dibs," he called out, smirking at Cole who scowled back at him.

"Not fair. I was texting Colt."

Ethan shrugged. "You snooze, you lose, brother."

I hazarded a peek at our surroundings. No one was paying attention to us, so I stood on my tiptoes and pressed a soft kiss to the corner of his mouth.

"Dick," Cole shot back. "She's supposed to be my girlfriend, remember?"

"Only in public, and just for a little while. But there's no law that says I can't escort my beautiful, good friend to her locker, is there?"

"Easy now, boys. There's plenty of Sunshine to go around," Enzo chimed in, casting me a smile. "Right?"

"Yes," I answered.

Cole's eyes darkened as they raked over me in my low-slung, skinny jeans and black scoop-neck.

"I can't wait to put that theory to the test," he growled. Heat flooded my body at his words.

He grew quiet for a moment before speaking again. "Are you feeling better?" he asked tenderly.

"Only one way to find out," I teased.

Cole took a step toward me, but Ethan pulled me away.

"Sorry, Cole. I'll be taking my girl now."

"Asshole," Cole called out as Fox and Enzo laughed.

When we were away from them, Ethan spoke again, "I had fun Saturday with you. You surprised me." He squeezed my hip before dropping his hand as we entered the building.

I mourned the loss of his touch. I wished people wouldn't be so judgmental. And if it wasn't for worrying about breaking my parents' hearts, I'd say screw it and plant a kiss on each of my guys for the whole student body to see. Maybe one day.

Ethan's hip bumped mine, bringing me back to the present.

"I surprised me too," I admitted. "But I wanted it, so I took it."

"You have no idea how hot it was."

We stopped at my locker, and I grabbed my books from inside. "I think I have *some* idea."

Ethan's smile widened as he let out an easy laugh.

"Hey, wait up," Enzo called out as we merged with hall traffic.

We paused, waiting for him.

He didn't hesitate in planting a kiss on my forehead, not even caring if half the student population saw him do it while Ethan held me.

"People are going to start talking," I said, glancing around at the students who were already whispering or giving us odd looks.

"Sunshine, where have you been? They've been talking for weeks now." He snaked his arm around my waist, separating me from Ethan who didn't fight the intrusion. Enzo pulled me into a hug. "I don't care if they talk. I'll kick their asses. But I know you're worried about your parents, so I'm sorry. I just can't seem to help myself when you're around. You make me lose my head. Both of them." He leaned back so he could see my face and waggled his eyebrows at me suggestively, making heat creep across my cheeks.

I knew what he meant. They made me lose my head too. All of them. A big part of me wanted to dig my fingers in his hair and tug his face down to mine. I wanted to claim the kiss I craved but had to deny because I didn't want to be labeled a slut. Because I never wanted to hurt my parents.

Leaning down, he growled in my ear, "I owe you a *real* kiss when we're in private later." He spun me to his side and left his arm draped over my shoulders.

I didn't answer because we rounded a corner to find Ian and Jamie together. I tried to avert my eyes, but not fast enough to miss the surprise on Jamie's face at Enzo's arm around me or the look of anger that clouded Ian's face.

"Hey, Jamie," Enzo called out. "Looking good."

"Fuck you, De Luca," Ian snarled as Jamie's face flamed red.

Enzo let out a soft, dangerous laugh.

"And fuck your whore too."

It happened so fast, I barely had time to register it. One moment Enzo was walking with me and Ethan, and the next he was fighting Ian. They exchanged blows, Enzo dodging most of them as Ian fumbled around trying to gain an upper hand.

Jamie cried out as Enzo swung on Ian, knocking him into the locker, a cut over his eye appearing.

Ethan moved me aside and dove into the fray, separating the two.

"What the fuck is going on?" Cole growled, stepping past me with Fox in tow.

"Ian. You little fucking leach, what did we tell you?" Fox snarled.

Ian wiped at his bloody nose and glared at the guys.

"I think he needs a reminder," Cole said, taking another dangerous step forward. Ian's eyes wavered as he glanced between the guys. A circle had formed around them as students watched.

"Or maybe *you* do," Ian snapped. "I'm not afraid of you."

Fox's dark laugh made chills course through me. "Try me."

"Stop," Jamie called out in a shaky voice. She made her way to the center of the circle and blocked what she could of Ian from the guys. "You guys are bullies. Ian told me how you beat him up."

"You mean his unfortunate *ladder* incident?" Cole asked innocently.

"Did he tell you what he did to make the ladder crash into his face?" Ethan said.

My heart thrashed wildly in my chest. I dodged forward and gripped Fox's arm, his muscles tight beneath my hold.

"Please," I whispered urgently to him. "Don't."

"You will get what's coming to you, Hall. You fucked up," Enzo snarled, backing away and reclaiming his spot at my side.

Ian stared the guys down, but I could see his tremors.

Enzo urged me back.

"It's over. Back the fuck up," Cole called out to the crowd. People began scurrying away.

"Jamie." I made to step forward as she and Ian turned to go. She stopped and stared back at me.

"Don't talk to me, Rosalie. Ian's right. You've become their whore. You're no better than they are."

My mouth went dry and tears filled my eyes at her words. She turned and followed Ian.

"Don't listen to her," Ethan said, giving my hand a squeeze.

"I'd floor her ass too if she wasn't a chick," Cole huffed, glaring after her. "No one talks to my girl like that."

"It's OK," I choked out, sagging against Enzo. "S-she's just mad."

"She's just a fucking idiot," Fox snapped. "You can't help people like her, Rosalie. You need to let it go. We could have outed him right here."

"I don't want anyone to know," I whispered, pulling away from Enzo and staring up into Fox's blue eyes. "What if no one believes me? Then I really will be what they say in their eyes."

"You will *never* be what they say," Fox hissed, cradling my face in his hands. "Do you understand me?"

I swallowed hard. "It's more complicated than that."

"Well, I'll uncomplicate it," he grunted, releasing me. "I promise you that, Rosie."

Something about the way he said it, or maybe it was the dark look in his eyes, made me believe him.

CHAPTER 36

With the guys' grueling football schedule and practices, we didn't see each other much outside of school in the following days. Their coach kept them exhausted with training and studying their upcoming opponents since they had a shot at the state championship.

By Thursday, I was missing their deep kisses and playful touches in hidden parts of the school. Hoping to catch Fox before he went to practice, I rounded the corner and came to halt. Fox and Juliet were in a deep discussion. Fox told me they'd broken up a while ago, so anger raced through me at the sight of them together.

I backed up and peeked around the corner. He stared down at her with no emotion on his face. I ground my teeth as she rested her hand on his chest. I was just about to go out and claw her eyes out, or his, when he pushed her hand away and shook his head at her. I wish I could hear what they were saying to one another. Whatever it was, Juliet was pissed, stomping her foot at him. He shrugged at her and backed away.

She stared after him as he turned and walked away. I watched as she called out to him. He didn't stop. He didn't look back.

I moved back around the corner, breathing out.

It's nothing. He clearly put the stops to whatever she wanted.

~

I STAYED after school that night, singing in the auditorium in the hopes of listening to the acoustics and getting a feel for things. When I was done, I made my way to the football field.

"Rosie?" Fox called out as he walked off the field, his hair wet with sweat.

"Hey, Sunshine!" Enzo greeted me with a grin, his dark eyes shining as they raked over me.

Cole's face lit up, and Ethan broke into a jog to get to me. My heart warmed to see them so excited.

"Hey," I said, giving them a nervous smile.

"What are you doing? Is everything OK?" Fox asked, his worried gaze sweeping over me.

"Yeah. I, uh, was practicing my audition in the auditorium and thought I'd come see you guys."

"Nice." Cole grinned, kissing me quickly.

"And what else?" Enzo narrowed his eyes at me as Ethan kissed my cheek.

I twisted my fingers nervously and looked to Fox.

"I saw you with Juliet in the hall," I blurted out.

The surprised look on Cole's face as he darted his gaze to Fox let me know he didn't have a clue what was going on. Even Enzo and Ethan looked surprised.

"What the hell is that about?" Cole demanded. "I thought that shit was over."

"It is," Fox growled, taking my hands in his. "It was nothing. She wants to get back together. I told her no way."

"Great," Enzo grunted. "Now she'll get pissed because she didn't get her way."

Ethan sighed and shook his head.

"I won't let her bother you, Rosie." Fox squeezed my hands.

"So she knows about me? Officially?"

"How could she not?" he murmured, tucking a strand of hair behind my ear. "Aside from seeing me with you and especially with Cole that day, she'd be stupid not to get it. I promise you, you have *nothing* to worry about. I swear on my life."

"She better not," Cole broke in. "Don't fuck up our shit with that bitch, Fox."

"I'm not," Fox snapped at him. "Trust me."

Cole grunted and looked away, a muscle popping along his jaw.

"Seriously, Rosie. *Nothing*." He leaned in and kissed me before resting his moist forehead against mine.

"You're so. . ."

"What?" he murmured. "What am I?"

"Gross," I finished, pulling away from him and wiping my forehead.

His face broke into a grin, and the guys laughed. When he reached out and tugged me to his body, I didn't resist, but something deep in my belly sent a warning.

And as much as I hated it was there, I knew I had to recognize it. Juliet was a threat. Enemies never disappeared. They only got worse. Ian was a prime example.

CHAPTER 37

I decided to go to the game on Friday night. I sat in the stands, watching as Fox threw touchdown pass after touchdown pass. Cole scored the majority of the goals while Enzo blocked. Ethan was the kicker.

It was nice learning these things about the guys. Before, all I knew was that Fox was quarterback and they all played. I had no idea how good they were. Or how damn good they looked in their blue and white uniforms. Especially with those tight pants.

Cole scored one final touchdown with a few seconds on the clock. It was a complete shutout, the guys winning 33-0.

The crowd cheered and rallied around them. They'd knocked out another team in the playoffs. I tried to get to the guys, but it was impossible as people swarmed them. Sighing, I gave up and walked to my car, hoping to catch them when they came to the parking lot. Cole had decided not to throw a party, promising we'd all hang out together instead tonight. Just us.

I let out a gasp as a hand grasped my arm and whipped me around.

"Ian," I breathed out. My pulse thundered in my ears as he glared down at me. He sported a black eye where Enzo had punched him.

"Hey, Rosalie," he growled.

I let out a squeak as he roughly hauled me to a dark corner of the building and slammed me against the brick wall. My head banged off the bricks, blurring my vision.

"Stop," I hissed, struggling as he held my arms with one hand. "Ian—"

He clamped his other hand over my mouth.

"Stop fucking moving or I swear I'll fuck you right here."

I stilled at his words, tears threatening to spill from my eyes.

"Listen closely. I'm done fucking around. The little stunt with Enzo was cute, but I want what's due to me. You *will* give it to me. Do you understand me?"

I shook my head and let out a whimper behind his hand as he pushed my head harder into the bricks.

"I know you think the guys want you, but they don't. Friend to friend, I'm here to tell you they keep a notebook with the name of every girl they've all fucked written inside it. Your name's listed in there. It's all a game to them, Rosalie. You've been blinded by them. I'm giving you a way out. Be with me."

He removed his hand from my mouth and stared at me.

"You're lying."

"No, I'm not. Mona even told you. Juliet is in on it. You're a fucking joke, and you didn't even realize it. That's what's so pathetic about all this. We can get them back, Rosalie. Join up with me. They deserve to pay."

I shook my head at him, hating that his words had a ringing of truth to them.

"You really don't believe me?" He let out a bark of laughter and reached into his back pocket.

I tensed, debating on running, but Ian was fast. I wouldn't stand a chance.

He pushed a black notebook into my hands. The same notebook I'd seen the guys with.

"Take it with you. Read it. Call me when you're done. Maybe give it to them. They've been looking for it. I already read it."

He backed away as I clutched the notebook to my chest. He turned and left me standing in the dark.

I looked down to the notebook, sickness and a sense of dread washing over me.

CHAPTER 39

ole: Where are you?

Fox: Rosie, we're waiting. I stopped at your house on the way to Cole's, but no one is home. Call me.

Enzo: Sunshine, you're an hour late. Where are you?

Ethan: I'm worried. We all are. Please call or text when you get this. You were supposed to be here almost two hours ago.

Fox: We just went to your house. You aren't answering your phone. Rosie, you're scaring me.

I shut the screen off and stared out at the dark lake in front of me. After leaving the school, I'd driven to the beach and walked to the edge of the water and sat with the notebook in my hands. The memory of Fox's story of the lake monster surfaced in my mind from one of our last treehouse adventures. I scoffed, shaking it away.

I hadn't worked up the courage just yet to check inside the thick notebook, terrified of what I'd find.

But I had to. It was getting late, and I was tired. Not that I planned on going home. I knew Fox and the guys were probably at his house, waiting for my return. It wasn't like I could call Jamie for a place to crash.

Sighing, I turned on my phone's flashlight, and with shaking hands, flipped open the notebook.

Lists of names greeted me. Page after page. Pictures of girls were attached next to the names. Scrawled on the lines were descriptions of things the guys had done with each girl. My stomach rolled as I took in the commentary on all of it from how big their boobs were to how good they were at sex or blowjobs. There were even incriminating photos of the girls. Some only had one. It looked like the guys passed the book back and forth between them, adding comments as they went along. Every single guy wrote in it. By now, I recognized all their handwritings.

Each page I flipped left a growing sickness and a rush of disgust gnawing at my guts.

When I got to Mona's page, I paused. Cole scrawled about her shyness. Ethan wrote she was sweet but not much else. Fox said she turned him down. Enzo said he wasn't interested but would fuck her if they all wanted to. She earned a two-star rating from them.

My stomach twisted into knots as I flipped to one of the last pages and saw a picture of myself. I was sitting alone at the lunch table, a book in my hand, my long red braid over my shoulder.

Rosalie Bishop

Big boobs. Tight body. Beautiful. Cole's writing spelled out his thoughts on me.

I swallowed down the bile in my throat as I continued to read. Fox vetoed me. Cole demanded me. Enzo said he was game. Ethan said I was smart, and he needed the help in calculus.

Farther down the page, someone had drawn some obscene artwork of my body. Then there was commentary from the day Cole and Ethan talked to me on the bleachers.

Ethan's messy scrawl noted: *Shy. Didn't seem opposed to the idea. Gorgeous body. Beautiful face. Scares easy.*

There was a note from Fox about the cafeteria.

I'll do it just to get back at her. That's it. I fuck her first. You guys can have the leftovers.

Then they'd written about Cole's party.

Enzo wrote: *Hall possibly drugged her. We rescued her. She owes us for it. We have the video proof of her and him. She doesn't want her friend to find out about it. We can use the video to get her to agree to us.*

My heart cracked as I read what Cole wrote next. *Fox gets to fuck her first because he wants revenge since she's for the reason his mom died. The plan is to make her fall in love and fuck her before leaving her in ruins. Record the encounters so she knows what it's like to be broken.*

Ethan responded with: *I'm not comfortable with that.*

Enzo wrote next: *Ethan, you aren't comfortable with anything. Shut up. You want that pussy as much as we do.*

Then an entry from Fox: *I'm sure that pussy is just as sloppy as the rest of her seems to be.*

And one more from Cole: *Sloppy or not, I've never fucked a redhead. Think the curtains match the drapes?*

I snapped the book closed, unable to continue reading. Breathing hard, I allowed the tears to stream down my cheeks. *It had all been a lie. Just like Mona said it was.*

Every instance had been documented within those pages. Me with Enzo and Cole. Me with Enzo and Fox. The conversations. The kisses. The touches. The sweet things. Everything I'd been through with them was in those pages, or at least I assumed it was given what I'd already seen. It made me too sick to keep turning the pages.

It took me hours to get myself together. When I finally walked to my car, I locked the doors and lay in my backseat, a fresh wave of sorrow hitting me.

Fox: Baby, it's 3 in the morning. Please answer me. I'm worried sick.

I stared at the screen through blurry eyes as Fox's name popped up on the caller ID. I didn't move, frozen as I peered at his name.

Ethan: Rosalie, this isn't like you to disappear. Please. Just let us know you're OK. We're at Fox's.

Cole: Rosebud, if we did something wrong, just tell us. We're at Fox's, waiting.

Enzo: I've driven all over town looking for you. What happened? We heard you went to the game.

I turned my phone off and closed my eyes, waiting for sleep to claim me. Tomorrow, I'd have to deal with everything. The thought did nothing to calm me.

CHAPTER 40

$\mathcal{I}$t was nearly three in the afternoon when I finally went home. My parents were gone for the weekend, so they hadn't missed me last night since I'd spoken to them before going to the game.

I clutched the notebook in my hand and got out of my car, not bothering to go to my house first. I marched to Fox's and knocked on the door. When he didn't answer, I opened it, knowing someone had to be there since there was a car I didn't recognize parked in his driveway.

Angrily, I marched up to his bedroom, ready to tell him to go to hell. Voices coming from within made me freeze. I waited outside the nearly closed door, breathing hard as Juliet's voice filtered through the crack.

"I want this, Fox. I know you do too."

"Why are you like this, Juliet? Why now? I tried to get you to do this for months, but you always said no. It's not like you're a fucking virgin," Fox shot back.

I swallowed hard, trying to control my breathing as I listened. *If they broke up, why the hell was she in his bedroom?*

Then it hit me like a fist to the face. He'd been lying the entire time. I had the notebook to prove it. If he'd lied to me about his feelings, then this shouldn't come as a big shocker.

"Why are *you* being like this?" she countered. "You wanted to have sex with me for ages, Fox. I'm giving you permission, and you're being a jerk about it. I even agreed to the guys since you're into group activities."

Fox let out a soft chuckle.

"You know how I feel, Juliet. And you know how they feel."

"And *you* know what I told you. If you don't want to, I can always tell—"

"Shut up," he snarled.

I flinched and moved to the wall beside the door as Fox's footsteps thudded. They stopped a moment later.

"I told you to leave Rosalie alone. I fucking meant it, Juliet. You will not even *look* in her direction."

"You've had me on her for a long time, Fox. I did what you wanted. Now give me what I want, baby," she purred back. "You know how to make it go away."

Fox was quiet. All I could hear in that silence was the roar of my pulse in my ears.

"And if I do this, you'll stop your shit?"

Juliet giggled. "Yes. As long as you hold up your end of the deal."

More silence met my ears before Fox spoke again, "Come here," he whispered in a shaky voice.

I nearly gagged when I heard the unmistakable sounds of kissing and heavy breathing followed by the dull thump of someone losing their clothes and the sounds of a zipper coming undone.

I stood outside his door as the ugly sounds flooded my ears. The creaking of the bed. The soft moans of Juliet. Fox's heavy breathing.

Finally, I found my courage and stepped forward. I wasn't going to play their games anymore. I flung the door open. It banged against the wall, and Fox sat up abruptly beneath the covers, no shirt on. It didn't take a genius to figure out Juliet was missing her clothes beneath the covers.

"Rosie," Fox choked out, struggling to untangle himself from his sheets.

I glared at him as he rushed to me, his boxers still on at least.

"It's not what you think."

"It doesn't matter," I managed to say, my voice stronger than I anticipated. I shoved the notebook into his bare chest. "I'm only bringing back that *thing* you've been looking for." I looked past Fox to see Juliet smirking at me from her spot in his bed. I shook my head and glanced back at Fox, whose face was a mask of devastation.

"Rosie, *don't*. Please. Let me explain." He reached for me as I backed away.

"No need, Fox. Your book answered *a lot* of questions. And this?" I nodded to Juliet. "Proved the rest."

"Rosie, it's not like that! Stop!" He reached for me again, but I lifted my hand and smacked him across his face. He stood, stunned, gaping at me, my red handprint on his cheek.

"Your plan was to ruin me. But you didn't. You only made me stronger. If it's games you want to play, then let's play, Fox," I hissed, breathing hard as I glared at him. "Try to keep up."

I backed out of his room, taking in the terror on his face as he stared back at me.

"Rosie," he choked out, tears slipping down his cheeks. "No."

I kept moving, my eyes locked on his, and didn't turn around until I was well out of his room.

And then I ran.

I didn't look back. There was nothing left to see anyway.

To Be Continued in. . .

In Silence: A Black Falls High Novel
Available Now on Amazon!

Thank you for reading In Ruins! Please consider leaving your review. Be sure to flip forward for a sneak peek at In Silence.

ABOUT THE AUTHOR

Known mostly for being strange, USA Today bestselling author K.G. Reuss knows what it takes to wear the crown of town weirdo. A cemetery creeper and ghost enthusiast, K.G. spends most of her time toeing the line between imagination and forced adulthood.

After a stint in college in Iowa, K.G. moved back to her home in Michigan to work in emergency medicine. She's currently raising three small ghouls and is married to a vampire overlord (not really but maybe he could be someday).

K.G. is the author of The Everlasting Chronicles series, Emissary of the Devil series, The Chronicles of Winterset series, The Middle Road (with co-author CM Lally) Black Falls High series and Kings of Bolten, The Boys of Chapel Crest, with a ridiculous amount of other series set to be released.

Sign up for her newsletter to stay updated on all the things happening in her freakishly ghoulish world. You'll also receive episode one of her new short story series, The Blood Legacy Saga, a paranormal romance. https://storyoriginapp.com/giveaways/1bfeb040-d679-11e9-8fe5-2fd907134791

Can't get enough? Visit her website at www.kgreuss.com or join her street team at www.facebook.com/groups/streetteamkgreuss

Stay ghoul, fellow weirdos.

IN SILENCE

PROLOGUE

Fox

I fisted her hair, jerking her head back.

"Fox," she rasped, reaching out for me. "Please-"

"Don't touch me," I snarled, gripping her hair harder. She let out a whimper as she stared up at me with wild, lust-filled eyes. "You want me to fuck you?"

"Y-yes," she whimpered again. I released her and tossed her roughly to the floor. The thought of burying myself inside her made me sick to my stomach. She was a fucking coffin for my dead soul. All I could think about was Rosalie. She hadn't spoken to me since shit went down with Juliet. She'd blocked my number. Threatened to call the cops on me if I kept pounding on her door. Wouldn't even look at me. And the guys? It took them a week to speak to me.

I fucked up. Bad.

I glared down at Juliet as she struggled to sit up, her mascara smeared in ugly black blotches on her cheeks, her breasts barely in her red bra.

"You going to fuck her or what?" Cole asked lazily from his leather chair in his living room as he sipped at a glass of whiskey.

"You can," I grunted, turning and going to the bar in the corner and pouring myself a drink.

Cole scoffed and sat forward, his blue eyes locked on Juliet. Ever since Rosie had left us, we'd made sure to hold to the bargain we had with Juliet: Fuck her and make her our queen over anyone else and she would keep all the stolen videos she had of Rosie tucked away. She wouldn't release them and ruin Rosie's life. As a bonus, she wouldn't release our notebook to the world and hurt the other girls or ruin our lives. Pretty sure my full ride to Mayfair on a football scholarship would be ripped away from me. The disappointment at that alone would tear my old man to shreds.

I ground my teeth at the thought of all of it, especially Rosalie getting hurt. I'd been haunted by the look on her face since she walked away from me that day. Being blackmailed by Juliet seemed a fitting punishment for our atrocities. Who would've thought a bit of fun could ruin so many lives.

Looks like the tables have turned.

We were stuck between a rock and a hard place. We'd lost Rosie, but we could still preserve her innocence. We were helpless though, at least until we figured out what to do about Juliet. The feeling of not knowing what to do was well-deserved, considering we'd done it to Rosie only weeks ago.

Guess that backfired on us.

"Come here, you fucking bitch," Cole spat. Juliet crawled across his floor to him, her eyes hooded. None of the guys wanted her. But she had to be queen at everything. She knew about the notebook since the beginning. She knew we wanted Rosalie. It drove her nuts knowing that someone like Rosie won our hearts over her.

And this was the punishment.

Juliet stopped at Cole's feet as Enzo, who had been quiet the entire time, got to his feet. Ethan quietly drank in the corner, looking down at the floor.

"You want my dick so bad, fucking suck it," Cole snapped at her.

"Why are you such an asshole?" she huffed, going up to her knees and resting her hands on his thighs.

"You can't be that stupid," Cole snorted. "I could be buried in a tight pussy right now, instead all I have is you."

Juliet's cheeks flushed at Cole's crude words. This would be the first time we'd all be with her as per her demands. Hell, it would be my first time with her. She'd always held out on me while we dated, offering me weak blow jobs instead while I fingered her. Now I knew why. She wanted to be the one we worshipped. She'd been running her own game, the bitch.

I swallowed down my glass of whiskey and took a hit from the joint I lit, my eyes focused on Cole as he stared at Juliet, disgust on his face. My heart went out to my friends. I'd gotten us into this mess with her and in the process, had lost Rosie.

It hit us all hard. While I knew it fucked my world, it was Cole who lost his shit first.

"What the fuck is the matter with you? How could you fuck us like this?" Cole snarled, his eyes wild. He fisted his hair as he stared helplessly at me.

"I trusted her—"

"It's fucking Juliet, you dumb fuck!" Cole shouted, his face red, spit flying from his mouth as he stormed around his living room. Enzo looked on from his spot in a leather chair as Ethan rubbed his face, his head down.

"The only thing you can trust about that bitch is that she'll royally fuck you over! How the hell did Rosalie even get the fucking notebook?" He stopped his angry march long enough to glare at me.

"I don't know. Whoever took it knew how to use it."

"We need to find out and beat the shit out of whoever it was," Cole spat. He kicked at an end table before grabbing it and pitching it across the room. It burst into splinters against the wall.

"Relax, Cole," Enzo called out. "We need to figure this shit out, not destroy the damn house."

"Fuck the house and fuck you," Cole shouted back, his face going from red to purple.

"You're not the only one who lost her, you know. We'll fix it." Ethan finally looked up, his eyes bloodshot. My heart clenched. Ethan had legitimately given a damn for Rosie right from the start. He was a bleeding heart

like that. Always kind. Always trying to find the bright side and make things better.

"You can't fix everything, Ethan! Not even you can with your fucking emotions and tears."

"Fuck you, Cole," Ethan snarled. "At least I have a grip on my shit."

"For now," Enzo murmured, glancing at Ethan. "But what are you going to do if this is permanent and she won't talk to us? You're already starting to slip, man."

Ethan let out a sigh and looked away, a muscle thrumming along his jaw.

"That's what I thought." Cole let out a bark of deranged laughter, his blond hair a mess. He looked certifiably insane as his body shook.

"We need a plan," I said calmly. "We should try to talk to her."

"Oh, hey, you fucking genius, let's see how that works." Cole stopped laughing and pulled his phone out and hit send on Rosalie's name. We all waited as he put it on speaker, the ringing like death knocking with every pulse.

"You've reached Rosalie. I'm not here right now, so leave a message!"

Cole ran his hand over his face and hung up only to hit redial. He did this several times before eventually his calls went straight to voicemail. With an angry snarl, he heaved his phone across the room where it smashed to bits against the wall.

"It's over," Cole breathed out, glaring at me.

"We'll fix it," I assured him, my throat tight. "Like Ethan said, you're not the only one who lost her—"

"Yeah? What the fuck are you going to do to fix it, Fox? You were so fucking eager to let her go in the beginning. Maybe this is just part of your mental fucking bullshit—"

"Fuck you," I snarled, shoving him. He shoved me back. Enzo was on his feet, jumping between us.

"I've loved her for as long as I've known her." I glared at my friend, ready to beat his ass.

"Me too," Cole shot back, breathing hard. He walked away, fingers in his hair. We all watched him for a moment before he stormed back in, his face red. He let out a yell before his fist connected with the glass coffee table, shat-

tering it. Blood streamed in angry red rivers down his arm as he glared at me.

"Fucking fix it, Fox. I-I can't lose her."

I shook the memory out of my head. I hadn't anticipated any of this shit. I'd been careless, letting Juliet too close. Trusting her when I knew I shouldn't. I'd been fighting my feelings for Rosie for years. Ever since my mom died. Ever since the earrings Rosalie had wanted were given back to us with Mom's possessions. The earrings she'd made the special trip to get for Rosalie's birthday before Daniel Hall hit her and killed her in a drunk driving accident. Ian's dad. Cole's dad was the attorney who got Ian's dad locked up. He was up for parole in a few weeks and would be free to ruin someone else's life.

Life just wasn't fair sometimes.

I'd blamed Rosalie for years for my mom's death. I took another hit from the joint and closed my eyes, seeing Rosie's pretty face in my mind's eye. Flawless porcelain skin. Bright green eyes surrounded by thick, black lashes. Full, pink, pouty lips. Lips I couldn't get enough of. Those large breasts and that narrow waist that gave way to that sexy hip flair. I imagined twining my fingers through her thick red curls. How she would whisper my name, her nails in my back as I thrust inside her tight body.

"Give me some," Enzo grunted, taking the joint from me and inhaling deeply.

We were quiet for a moment. I tore my eyes away from Juliet who had her mouth around Cole's dick. His mouth was turned down into a frown as she bobbed up and down on him.

If we were grading her in the book, her dick sucking skills were barely a one.

"Ethan, you cool?" Enzo called out. Ethan didn't acknowledge him. He took another drink before pulling out a bottle of pills, spilling one into his waiting hand. He popped it into his mouth and washed it down with his whiskey. Ethan had anxiety and a whole host of other issues. It wasn't a widely known fact by others, but we knew it. If Ethan was drinking and popping pills, then something was seriously wrong because Ethan always tried to be the straight-laced one of all of us. He had his own issues he didn't like to talk about. Issues we were aware of but didn't press him on.

"Want some of this?" Enzo tried again, offering Ethan the joint. Ethan's green eyes flicked from Enzo's face to the joint before he shuffled to his feet and came to us, seizing what was offered and taking a hit.

"I'd rather you suck my dick than her," Ethan grunted, blowing out smoke, his eyes fixed on Cole and Juliet. Cole had taken his phone out and was looking through it as Juliet continued her attempt at a blow job.

"If it got us out of this fucking nightmare, I'd slob your knob right now," Enzo answered, sneering in Juliet's direction.

Juliet released Cole's dick with a loud popping noise. He lifted a brow at her from over his phone.

"I can hear you," Juliet called out, looking over at us, her mouth set in a pout that may have worked on me months ago but did nothing for me now. "Maybe you should suck Ethan's dick, Enzo."

Enzo paled. Ethan shifted where he stood. Juliet got to her feet and sashayed over to us, a wicked glint in her dark eyes.

"I actually like that idea. You two sucking each other off."

"Juliet," I growled. "We're not gay."

She let out a soft laugh. "Prove it. Choke on Enzo's dick. Maybe I'll let you all off the hook early. If you don't, then I'll just send this video you guys so graciously took of Rosalie, off to her daddy. I'm sure he would love to see what his daughter has been up to. Heard he's a real prick."

"You're going too far, Juliet," I murmured. "We'll fuck you, but we aren't going to fuck one another."

"We could kill you and be done with it," Ethan snarled, his green eyes filled with storm clouds. I stared at Ethan. In that moment, he looked like he could rival me and Cole for dark thoughts.

"You're fucked up, Juliet," Enzo snapped.

"What's wrong, *Lorenzo*, you too insecure to suck off Ethan?" Juliet reached out and rubbed Ethan's crotch. In a move that surprised me, Ethan shoved her hard. Ethan was the gentle one of us four. The caring one. The one Rosie dubbed sweet. To see him get handsy meant he was pissed.

Juliet stumbled back and landed on her ass with a thump. Cole watched interestedly from his chair, a smirk on his lips. We didn't intervene when Ethan moved forward and fisted her hair, angling her head to the side. Juliet let out a gasp, wincing beneath his hold.

"You disgust me," Ethan snarled, tugging her hair harder. Tears filled Juliet's eyes as she stared up at him. "The fact you're trying to force us to *fuck you* makes you the vilest piece of shit I've ever dealt with."

"But you did it to other girls. You did it to Rosalie-"

"We never once forced a girl to fuck us. None of them ever said no to us. Rosie did what she wanted when she wanted with who the fuck she wanted." Ethan released her hair and moved his hands to her throat where he squeezed. Her eyes widened, her cheeks reddening from the pressure. Enzo cast me a worried look. I took a step forward, not even sure if I wanted to stop Ethan if he choked her out. I cast a glance at Cole who wore his dark smile as he lazily drank his whiskey. At least he'd tucked his dick back into his jeans.

"And the difference between you and Rosalie is that we genuinely give a shit about her. You? I'd enjoy watching the light fade from your eyes as you choked on my dick."

"Ethan," she rasped, reaching out for him as he tightened his grip.

"You're lucky I fucking love her," Ethan whispered, his breathing heavy. "Or I'd have killed you already. Enjoy this while you can because once I figure out a solution, you're going to wish you didn't know me."

He released her and got to his feet as she sputtered, her eyes bloodshot from him choking her. He shot us an angry look before storming to the front door and slamming it closed behind him. The squealing of his tires let us know he'd left.

"Well, looks like you pissed Ethan off." Cole laughed, breaking the silence. "Still want to suck some cock or is your throat sore?"

"Fuck you, Cole," Juliet rasped, her voice hoarse. Ethan's handprints were still on her throat.

"Nah. Not tonight. You ruined the mood. Get dressed and get the fuck out." Cole got to his feet and grabbed her shirt before tossing it at her. "We'll try again another time."

With her face flaming red, she put her shirt back on and got to her feet.

"Fox?"

"Walk home," I said evenly.

"I'll release everything I have—"

"No, you won't," I said, stepping over to her and thumbing her bottom lip. "You know why?"

She leaned into my touch. "Why?"

"Because you're a pathetic bitch and need us. You like controlling us. Now get the fuck out like you were told." I dropped my hand from her face. She let out a throaty whimper that had me rolling my eyes. Her desire of us did nothing for me.

"Fox-"

I pressed my mouth to hers to silence her before shoving her away.

"Shut the fuck up and get the fuck out. Those are the only *fucks* you get today." I turned and walked away without looking back at her. A moment later, the front door opened and closed signaling her departure.

"We might have to kill her," Cole said softly, swirling his whiskey in his glass. "I'd rather fuck her dead body. Satisfaction in knowing she's gone and all."

Enzo chuckled. "Someone should call Ethan. I'm sure he has some ideas."

"I do too," was all I said before pouring another drink.

Get In Silence here:
https://books2read.com/insilence

ALSO BY K.G. REUSS

May We Rise

As We Fight

On The Edge

When We Fall

Double Dare You

Double Dare Me

Church: The Boys of Chapel Crest

Ashes: The Boys of Chapel Crest

Stitches: The Boys of Chapel Crest

Emissary of the Devil: Testimony of the Damned

Emissary of the Devil: Testimony of the Blessed

The Everlasting Chronicles: Dead Silence

The Everlasting Chronicles: Shadow Song

The Everlasting Chronicles: Grave Secrets

The Everlasting Chronicles: Soul Bound

The Chronicles of Winterset: Oracle

The Chronicles of Winterset: Tempest

Black Falls High: In Ruins

Black Falls High: In Silence

Black Falls High: In Chaos

Black Falls High: In Pieces, A Novella

Hard Pass

Kings of Bolten: Dirty Little Secrets

Kings of Bolten: Pretty Little Sins

Kings of Bolten: Deadly Little Promises

Kings of Bolten: Perfect Little Revenge

Kings of Bolten: Savage Little Queen

<u>Barely Breathing</u>

<u>The Middle Road</u>

<u>Seven Minutes in Heaven</u>